THE CRACKS IN THE ÆTHER

Borgo Press Fiction by ROBERT REGINALD:

THE NOVA EUROPA FANTASY SAGA

THE HIEROMONK'S TALE
1. *Melanthrix the Mage*
2. *Killingford*
3. *The Dark-Haired Man*

THE ARCHQUISITOR'S TALE
4. *The Righteous Regicide*
5. *The Virgin Queens*
6. *The Exiled Prince*

THE PROTOPRESBYTER'S TALE
7. *Brother Theo's God*
8. *Quæstiones*
9. *"Whither Goest Thou?"*

THE HYPATOMANCER'S TALE
10. *The Cracks in the Æther*
11. *The Pachyderms' Lament*
12. *The Fourth Elephant's Egg*

Other Fiction: *Academentia: A Future Dystopia* * *The Attempted Assassination of John F. Kennedy* * *Dead Librarians and Other Shades of Academe* * *The Elder of Days: Tales of the Elders* * *If J.F.K. Had Lived* * *Invasion!* (War of Two Worlds #1) * *The Judgment of the Gods and Other Verdicts of History* * *Knack' Attack* (Human-Knacker War #2) * *The Martians Strike Back!* (War of Two Worlds #3) * *The Nasty Gnomes* (Phantom Detective #2) * *Operation Crimson Storm* (War of Two Worlds #2) * *The Paperback Show Murders* * *The Phantom's Phantom* (Phantom Detective #1)

THE CRACKS IN THE ÆTHER

THE HYPATOMANCER'S TALE
BOOK ONE

BEING THE TENTH ROMANCE OF NOVA EUROPA

ROBERT REGINALD

THE BORGO PRESS

MMXI

THE CRACKS IN THE ÆTHER

Published by Wildside Press LLC

www.wildsidebooks.com

DEDICATION

To the memory of my dear friend,

Susan Werner
(December 3, 1966 – May 22, 2009)

Who would have loved it;

And for

Michael R. Collings,

Fellow traveler on the Via Litteraria.

CONTENTS

Chapter One: "Help Me!". 13

Chapter Two: "The Green—or the Puce?" 16

Chapter Three: "Should I Ask the *Second* Question?". . . .21

Chapter Four: "Queen L's" 26

Chapter Five: "'Twas a Vile, Vicious Thing". 33

Chapter Six: "I Only Doubt Her History and Her Sincerity" 38

Chapter Seven: "You Want to Do *What*?" 42

Chapter Eight: "The Otherworlds Are Not at All What You

   Imagine". 49

Chapter Nine: "Fishing for Ifrits?" 55

Chapter Ten: "The Price Will Be Very High" 61

Chapter Eleven: "Good Fleas Are So Hard to Find" 64

Chapter Twelve: "I've Seen You Before, My Friend" 68

Chapter Thirteen: "You Can Never Truly Escape". 72

Chapter Fourteen: "We'll Always Have Paris". 75

Chapter Fifteen: "Whilst I Live, I Hope". 80

Chapter Sixteen: "Tell Me 'Bout the Goat" 83

Chapter Seventeen: "So Mote It Be!". 86

Chapter Eighteen: "Give Me a Little Kissie" 89

Chapter Nineteen: "No Safe Way to Get There from Here" 95

Chapter Twenty: "Let's Have Squabs with Every Meal!" . .98

Chapter Twenty-One: "The Tenth Day of Blossoming" . . 104

Chapter Twenty-Two: "I Don't Hold No Stock with Them

Belchers" 108

Chapter Twenty-Three: "The Curious Case of the Magical

Magpie..." 112

Chapter Twenty-Four: "This One I Just Call Bird" 117

Chapter Twenty-Five: "Ignoramuses, All of Them!" 120

Chapter Twenty-Six: "Goddess, My Head Is Killing Me!" . 123

Chapter Twenty-Seven: "I Heard It from Silphus the

Snake" 128

Chapter Twenty-Eight: "At the Sign of the Legless Toad" . 135

Chapter Twenty-Nine: "We Put It Up Your Nose" 139

Chapter Thirty: "It Might Have Been the *Marrowbone*" . . 142

Chapter Thirty-One: "Judging by What Has *Not* Been

Said" 145

Chapter Thirty-Two: "Saint Misogyna!" 148

Chapter Thirty-Three: "Oh Great Gryphon-Dung!" 151

Chapter Thirty-Four: "The Pulling-Off of Wings" 156

Chapter Thirty-Five: "But They're *Your* Trash!" 160

Chapter Thirty-Six: "The Jewel, She Is Cursed" 166

Chapter Thirty-Seven: "Do You Have the Nose of

    Nagha'aïd?" 168

Chapter Thirty-Eight: "An Equal-Opportunity Whore" . . 172

Chapter Thirty-Nine: "Is She Trained to Use the Box?" . . 177

Chapter Forty: "A Little Short of Colddust" 182

Chapter Forty-One: "Who's What's-Her-Name?" 187

Chapter Forty-Two: "The Goods, the Bads, and the Uglies" 191

Chapter Forty-Three: "Be Glad You Have a Fur Coat". . . 197

Chapter Forty-Four: "What Can I Say? I Know These

    Things" 200

Chapter Forty-Five: "On Gnomette-Netting Duty" 207

Chapter Forty-Six: "Well, I'm Damned!" 211

Chapter Forty-Seven: "The Holy Grail of All Magical

    Tomes" 216

Chapter Forty-Eight: "It's Definitely Getting Colder" . . . 220

Chapter Forty-Nine: "The Commode, the Loo, the John,

    the Crapper". 226

Chapter Fifty: "They're Covered with Metal Objects". . . 232

Chapter Fifty-One: "I Made One Last Deal with the Devil,

    Ha, Ha!" 237

Epilogue: "Be Careful What You Wish For" 242

Afterword: "Cracking the Elephant's Egg". 244

About the Author 248

ANNO DOMINI 1622
ANNO JULIANI 1262

When Adam delved, and Eve span,
Who was then the gentleman?

CHAPTER ONE

"HELP ME!"

"Help me!"

Just two little words, almost a gnawing at the edge of my consciousness—but I was certain that I'd actually heard something.

I'd been scanning the northern perimeter of the sixty-ninth ley on the fortieth tier of the Quietus, looking for a route to the Otherworlds, when I'd brushed past a presence that shouldn't have been there.

I had to be careful. There were traps in the æthernet that could easily ensnare the unwary.

"Scooter!" I hissed.

The wherret hunched up next to me.

"Master?" it said.

"I need your help," I said, and the creature scratched my arm with one of its little paws, just enough to draw a line of blood.

It licked the cut, and then I felt its presence suddenly within me, both alien and comforting at one and the same time. It lent me some of its strength.

I probed the ætherwall once again, more gingerly this time, but couldn't find whatever it was—whatever it might have been.

Finally I broke the link.

"I know it was there," I said, slumping back in my chair; and then I explained what I'd felt.

"There are many entities roaming the void," the creature said. "Perhaps this was one of them, seeking a likely victim in an unpracticed acolyte."

"No!" I said. "It was a person, of that much I'm certain. I'm not a neomage, to be so easily fooled."

"Anyone can be fooled," it said. "You humans are simply more subtle in your lies."

"And you are the most subtle being I've ever known," I noted.

"I rest my case, Sir," the wherret said.

Then it coughed: "Ahem. While you were skrying, Master, a message arrived from the Queen. She desires the presence of her Scanner Prime."

"Does she indeed?" I said, not really paying much attention. "I suppose she wants me to read her fortune again. She doesn't seem to understand that what I tell her just represents possibilities, not realities."

"She desires verities," my companion said. "She wants to encompass her world with the certainty of fixed boundaries. Alas, that the universe fails to function in quite that reasonable a manner."

I waved my hand over the orb and uttered a word of command, shutting off its power.

"Very well." I sighed. "Let me go splash something on my face, put on a decent shirt and pantaloons, and then we'll transit to Paltyrrha."

I left the wherret to do what wherrets do in such intervals (all of which was fairly disgusting), and wandered back into the living area. The basin still had some water in it, and although it wasn't clean, I used it just the same, and then stared at myself in the mirror.

The face peering back at me was thin and long, framed by a mop of unruly brown curls. The sideburns on the cheeks were beginning to show a few ragged strands of gray—they looked like little worms trying to claw their way to the light. I shuddered. The shadows under my brown eyes hinted at too many late nights, with small lines highlighting them on either side. It was the visage of a man of five-and-thirty years, perhaps.

No, Morpheús, I told myself, *you're* not *a neomage.*

I wet my hands and ran them back through my tangled locks, trying to smooth them down. They wouldn't cooperate, of course.

Then I put on my second-best suit, and I was ready to go.

Scooter was waiting for me at my *viridaurum*, the man-sized mirror of green-gold metal. The wherret ran up my leg and perched at its usual spot on my right shoulder, where it could whisper sweet nillions in my ear.

Wherrets were animorphs, and could become many things in many different sizes, as they willed, but this was my companion's true shape (or so I believed at the time).

I reached out and through the æther and twisted the leys sideways, and we found ourselves standing in a similarly apportioned alcove in the Royal Palace in Paltyrrha. A gryphon was stationed just outside.

"Pathth?" it hissed at us, its forked tail twitching.

I held up my right hand, all five fingers stretched wide, the open palm facing the creature, and the beast touched my lifeline with the tip of its tongue.

"Morpheuth, Thcanner Primuth," it stated. "And Thcooter. You may enter."

The scaly one stepped aside, and we trod a familiar path down the winding, weary corridors of Tighrishály Palace.

CHAPTER TWO
"THE GREEN—OR THE PUCE?"

Her Puissant and Sublime Majesty had embarked upon a massive redecoration project shortly after her accession fifteen years earlier, and the overall result was somewhat less than the rendition of the parts. The grand old *tableaux* etched in stone had been covered over with ghastly, garish tapestries and paintings harkening back to a time and an art that had never actually existed. I found them, well, distasteful and disrespectful, but most of the minions at Court seemed to think otherwise. Perhaps I was just out-of-touch, or maybe this feeling of growing *ennui* with my situation derived from some other sphere entirely. Whatever the case, I did not relish the thought of another somnolent session with the Queen.

The Majordomo Baldvín announced us, and then we entered the "Little"—the Crimson—Throne Room.

Queen Evetéria I—long may she reign!—had seated her expansive rear on a padded chair at the left-hand wall, surrounded by long-suffering sycophants and simpering signorinas. Among them I spied the shiny white cowl of Bishop Palladios, her favorite spiritual advisor, bobbing up and down in the *mêlée* like some bloated maggot, sucking on the hopes and fears of his congregation.

"Morphy!" she screamed, as soon as she spotted me. "Oh, do come here, you silly little thing! I need your help!"

I waved my arms to the right and left, and the masses parted before me. I felt like a modern-day Moses.

The Queen had several swatches of cloth clutched in her crab-like claws.

"Do I go with the green—or the puce?"

She thrust them into my face.

I must confess that I thought neither sample suitable for anything but the garde-robe, but of course I couldn't say so, not with Scooter present—its sensibilities would have been severely tested.

"The green, Majesty," I said, dropping to one knee in acknowledgment of her rank.

"Oh, how absolutely sublime!" she said. "You're absolutely, absolutely right as rain, as always."

She grabbed the samples with one hand, and raised me up with the other, and I found myself looking her straight in the face.

Queen Evetéria was some five-and-fifty years of age, with a bulging bush of oily black hair (a wig, I knew), and a narrow, almost pinched face saddened with two spots of rouge. She had never been intended nor trained for the place of power she now occupied, but the unfortunate death of her younger brother, Prince Féliks, in battle against the Liets, and the subsequent passing of her father, King Ánatol, and his childless male heir, Prince Zakháry, before him, left her the only possible candidate for the throne. Thus she became just the second Regina Regnant of Kórynthia, after Her Late Majesty, Queen Grigorÿna I, who had reigned more than a century earlier.

She was not a mean person or an evil one, but she lacked the judgment and decisiveness needed to rule a country as large and diverse as ours. She spent her days in a royal fairytale she called Tighrishály, playing her games of "Praise the Queen" and "Renovate This Room"; and that, with a constant attendance upon the duties of the Church, encompassed all the days of her life.

She shooed away the Lady Balbina, and patted the seat next to her.

"Here, Morpheús. My Scanner Prime absolutely needs to

find some of that sooth for me in the æther, so pray *do* sit down and tell me true: is green the way to go?"

"Indeed, my Queen," I said, "It's not easy being green, but I know that someone with your sense of style can always find a way."

"Oh, I do agree, I *do*," she exclaimed, clapping her hands together, almost like a little girl. "Do you hear that, Balby?—it's *green!* It's going to be green!"

"Then green it shall surely be, Your Majesty," the lady said.

"I hereby order it done!" Evetéria said, putting her hands together once again.

Then she turned sideways to me: "Tell me, Morphy, *tell* me about my future. What's in store for me this next year?"

What, indeed? I thought to myself. *And what's in store for you, pray tell, oh soothsayer?*

I decided to play at chiromancy. I gently took the Queen's narrow hand in mine, and turned it palm skyward, slowly tracing the life lines etched therein.

"Hmmm," I said.

"What *is* it?" she asked, almost breathless with anticipation. I suddenly envisioned her as a girl of fifteen.

"Hmmm," I repeated.

"Tell me, tell me, oh *do* tell me," she said.

"This is unseemly, Your Majesty," Bishop Palladios suddenly interrupted. "The Church frowns on such pursuits."

The cleric was a fat, flashy, frumpy little toad of two-and-sixty years, who owed his meteoric rise in stature solely to the fact that he had been the Queen's chaplain before her unexpected succession to the throne.

"Oh, you're such a fussbudget at times, Pallády," Evetéria said. "Why don't you go pray for my soul or something?"

She waved the prelate away, and he had no choice but to obey. The Queen could be vacuous and vacillating, but I knew from my own observation that to cross the will of Her Imperiousness could invite sudden and brutal repercussion. Those of her creatures who dwelt in Court quickly became aware that her moods often wavered on the winds of whim.

"Now, Morphy, what do *you* see in my future?"

I saw plenty of things, including Her Majesty's undignified death some years hence—for such was the nature of my talent—but I could relate none of these things to Evetéria. They flashed through my mind like a stack of cards, images that slipt by quickly—*one, two, three!*—and then were gone, barely leaving a trace.

For it is the simple, sad truth that most people do not welcome the simple, sad truth, particularly as it relates to their own lives. Perhaps that is why a hypatomancer can only envision the future of others, and never, ever—of himself.

"A glorious destiny indeed, Majesty," I exclaimed, in a voice loud enough to be heard throughout the room. "Glorious and grand. You will be known to history as *La Demoiselle Décoratrice*, the greatest ruler of her kind, who created an entirely new standard of fashion in the East. No one will ever be able to match your fantabulously fantastic designs."

"Oh, oh, oh," was all she could say. "You're *so* good to me, Morphy."

She had no idea, which was perhaps just as well. I could feel the silent humor of the wherret beating upon my soul.

"Oh, oh, oh," the creature whispered in my ear. "You're *so* good to me, Morphy."

I had to bite my cheek to keep from laughing out loud.

"Is something wrong?" Evetéria asked, looking at me with deep concern in her eyes—well, as deep as her concern ever reached with anyone.

"A, um, a frog in my throat, Majesty," I said. I coughed several times. "Perhaps, if Your Majesty doesn't mind...."

"Of course, of course. You should retire at once. Oh, thank you, dear Scanner Prime. I shall increase your stipend to three thousands of pounds of salted herring a year."

Oh, joy! I thought to myself.

"Thank God for all the fish!" Scooter hissed.

I almost lost control at that moment, but I somehow managed

to keep my face straight-laced until I reached my quarters.

"Thank God for all the fish?" I said, starting to laugh.

"Well," my companion replied, "at least one of us gained something from the encounter. Salted herring—why, that's one of the very best things about Nova Europa."

"That might be a slightly biased perspective," I said.

I pulled the cord to order dinner.

I nearly choked when the servant delivered a platter piled high with eels.

CHAPTER THREE
"SHOULD I ASK THE *SECOND* QUESTION?"

The next morning, I was surprised to receive a summons to a meeting of the Council of State, to be held early that afternoon. As Scanner Prime, I was technically a member of the highest advisory body in the Kingdom, but was rarely asked to participate, since many of my official duties were necessarily kept sealed from public view by my binding oath of privacy. A hypatomancer cannot function without such safeguards—and everyone understands this.

"We need your soundings, Scanner Prime," the Queen said, when I'd seated myself at the open chair at the middle of the left side of the table. She was perched on her small throne at one end of the great slab of inlaid marble, while Chancellor Gronos sat at the other. The twenty-odd lords temporal and spiritual filled the remaining spots to either side.

"Whatever I can do, Majesty," I said.

"My government seems to feel that we must decide very soon on a designated successor. The main candidates are our second and third cousins, Zoltán Duke of Walküre, Zacharias Prince of Mährenia, Istiál Count of Kosnick, Víka Count of Westmark, and Karlyna Lady Elasma, who have, of course, been excluded from these proceedings. What sayest thou?"

All eyes turned to me, and I wanted to slither right out the door. This was a pretty state of affairs, indeed. Each of the five "Noblenesses," I knew, had partisans and detractors, some of them present at this table; and no matter what I said, someone here was bound to take offense. Yet, this is what I was being paid to do: to prognosticate.

Very well, then: I centered myself, closed my eyes, and let my consciousness barely scrape the ætherspace. Without protection—indeed, without my familiar's help—I could safely venture no further. I posed the question, and waited for the response to come.

I was almost slammed to the floor by the virulence of the images that flashed through my skull, twisting me this way and that with their violence and rage. I gasped out loud, completely overwhelmed by what I was experiencing, and abruptly cut myself free.

"What *is* it?" several of the attendees asked, clearly alarmed by my physical reaction.

I struggled to regain my breath, huffing and puffing.

"If...if you name a successor...now, Majesty," I managed to hiss out between long-drawn inhalations. "The result will be a terrible—a civil—war, almost immediately. The center cannot hold under such circumstances. You would die, and the Kingdom disintegrate within a few years."

"See, we told you!" the Queen bleated from the head of the table, pointing her finger at old Lord Gronos. "We told you this several times, we did, and you wouldn't listen to us, neither. So there! So *there!*"

The Chancellor blanched, but still had the courage to press the issue further.

"Master Scanner," he said, turning his shaggy sideburns towards me. "And what would the result be of doing nothing?"

I looked directly then at the Queen, because I dared not proceed without her official endorsement. She pouted for a moment, frowning at the man who'd had the audacity to challenge her judgment, but finally she nodded, ever so slightly, and I sighed. I didn't really want to undertake this reading, but I had no choice in the matter, of course.

So once again I edged out from underneath the blanket of my

natural protections, finely honed from many years of practice, and dared to essay the query a second time, but on this occasion hedged with the conditionalities of yea and nay. Even so, the result was almost the same, and I again was racked and almost ruined with the scenes of pillage and rapine that surged through my consciousness. I believe that I even passed beyond the void for a few seconds.

When I came to my senses, I again had their rapt attention.

I managed to choke out just two words, "The same," before their heated reactions filled the room with vitriol, giving me a short respite in which to regain my composure.

"But," I yelled out over the din, "For so long as her Majesty doth reign, peace shall prevail!"

At that the voices became silent, until one querulous soul, Metropolitan Polylogas, suddenly gasped out the obvious question, "And how long will that be?"—and then fell back in his chair, appalled when he realized what he'd said.

"Belay that!" the Queen shouted. "Thou shalt not respond, Master Morpheús, on the pain of death! And thou, foolish churchman"—she sent a pair of dagger-shaped glances down the row at the hapless prelate—"thou shalt leave us forthwith. Thou art dismissed from this Council permanently!"

"Yes, Majesty," the little, bald-headed man choked out, before backing his way towards the door.

"Gentlemen," she said, her face as stern and resolute as I'd ever seen it. "This matter shall remain closed, until we choose to bring it before this Council again. Is that well understood by all of you?"

When she'd received murmurs of acquiescence and nods of the head from around the table, she added: "This meeting is closed. You may all leave me—all save my Chancellor and my Scanner Prime. And you may *not* discuss what you heard outside of this room. Now go, all of you!"

And they all filed out, one by one, eyes rooted to the carpet.

"Come," she ordered Lord Gronos and me, when the rest had left, pointing to the two chairs flanking her.

"Your vision was true?" she asked me.

"My probing was sound, Your Majesty," I said, "and while I might be able to refine it further by adding various details, I do not believe the essentials will alter with any future reading. What will be, will be, just as I have said it."

"So mote it be," she intoned. "We believe you. What can we do to forestall the war that will come?"

"You cannot stop it from coming," I said, "Unless...."

"Unless *what*? What is it that you're not telling us, Morpheús?"

"If you had a true heir, Majesty, that might postpone the chaos for a time. But what I saw was a swirling of the æther so profound, so beyond my previous experience, that I do not believe it can be put off indefinitely. It was as if the cosmos itself had broken in twain, leaching chaos throughout this world. For I tell you true, my Queen, that if Kórynthia falls, so will the Empire; and if the Empire falls, well, none of us are safe."

"As you know," she said, looking almost thoughtful, "we are beyond the child-bearing years, and we have no other close relations yet living. What about...?" She turned to the head of her government. "Chancellor, could I legally adopt an heir-apparent?"

"Not without changing the law, Majesty," Lord Gronos said. "And I do not think that would be possible, given the present circumstance. You can forbid people talking—but people will talk nonetheless, as you well know."

"I should not have asked the question, should I, Grony?" She had retreated very nearly to girlhood again.

"In my opinion, no, Majesty," the Chancellor said. He sighed, long and loud. "But what is done, is done. It cannot be taken back. And perhaps it too is part of the scheme of things. I also feel this rush—this mad route—towards chaos, and I cannot seem to stop it, no matter what I do. Mayhap a younger man...."

"You are the only one we can trust to this position," she said, "precisely because you have no ambition beyond it. The rest...."

She saw the look on my face and laughed out loud. "This is beyond your usual experience with these things, isn't it,

Morphy? You poor innocent soul. You won't be innocent much longer, I fear. Should I then ask the *second* question, my Scanner Prime?"

I dropped my head and examined the swirling pattern of *tughras* on the table, the intertwined emblems of the House of Tighris. I thought a very long time before responding, but no one prodded me for a quick retort, which I much appreciated.

"No, Majesty," I finally said.

"Very well. This audience is ended. We thank you for your service, Scanner Prime. You may leave us," Queen Evetéria said.

I glanced up just once before I headed for the door. The Queen had aged a decade or more in just an hour. Or so it seemed to me, the official High Hypatomancer for the Kingdom of Kórynthia and the Heir of Paltyrrha.

CHAPTER FOUR
"QUEEN L'S"

My meeting with the Council had left me shaken right down to my bones. Never in my memory had a vision so immediately and harshly impacted my psyche, so that I found myself questioning everything that I regarded as "normal." For if what I'd seen was true—as I had to believe—my entire world was on the verge of disintegration, even destruction.

As a member of the Court, I couldn't escape being drawn towards one faction or another, willy-nilly—and if I tried to hold myself somehow above the fray, so to speak, that wouldn't protect me in the end. First I would be courted, and then, when I refused the overtures of one pretender over another, I would fall under immediate suspicion of collaboration with the "enemy," whomever that might be.

No, there was no safe ground here that I could see anywhere, and the end would come as soon as the aging Queen lost her sensibilities or died, thereby destabilizing the fragile balance at the heart of Paltyrrha. Even I could not see precisely how much time was left to her, but it could not be much more than a decade. I had to find some way to extricate myself from this conundrum, and survive to fight another day.

I also needed the counsel of someone wiser than myself.

I dispatched a message requesting an audience with the Chancellor, not certain of how or even whether he would respond. We had never been close: my previous contacts with him had been limited to my few Council appearances, various receptions and public functions, and one consultation on a personal matter—the whereabouts of a grandson who'd gone missing years earlier. I was hoping that our short, shared experience during that period of heartache would prompt him to make time in his hectic schedule for a consultation of my own.

I received his reply within the hour: "Queen L's. Tomorrow at the third hour."

I recognized the reference, of course—any denizen of Paltyrrha would. The statue of Queen Landizábel had been erected at the center of the maze in the Hanging Garden built by King Tarás I for his eighth and last wife. Even as a child, I'd heard the stories of how the White Lady still roamed the maze at night, looking for an honest man; and I'd actually met someone once who'd claimed to have seen her—but that's another story. And it was there, too, that Melanthrix the Mage had once plotted the overturning of the realm; and that Afanásy Ivánovich, his friend and foe, had envisioned and eventually accomplished the restoration of Kórynthia's glory. Many important events had swirled around the symbol of the Tighris *tughra* that formed the heart of the hedge-lined puzzle.

"What do you hope to gain, Master?" Scooter asked, as I nibbled on a light supper of fruit and cheese and bread. I'd already given the wherret an account of the afternoon's events.

"I wish I knew. I just haven't been paying enough attention to what's been going on in the Kingdom, and now my lack of political awareness is rapidly becoming a liability, personally and professionally. I need to understand what I have to do in order to survive what's coming."

"And what if you can't, Sir?"

"I just don't know."

And truly, gentlebeings, truly I didn't. I'd spent my life to this point working unceasingly to secure my future, trying to redefine myself while assiduously avoiding any mention of my exceedingly modest origins. Very few people in this world knew anything about the background of Morpheús the Hypatomancer, and I preferred to keep it that way. Whenever the obvious questions were posed, I sloughed them off, as one discards a worn-out garment. I avoided close relationships with others, both because I had no time to form or sustain them, but also because I wanted my previous life forgotten and purged, even by myself.

The Brothers of Saint Bronisláv had been the ones to rescue me, back in Zmyrna, on the west coast of Asia Minor. My father Kallíkratês had served with Emperor Belissarios II as the leader of a Hundred, until he'd been wounded at the Battle of Svetfantástika. Then they pensioned him off and sent him home, where he helped maintain the Lesser Julian Aqueduct, and later worked as a stabler and cart-keeper. It provided a modest living.

I was then known as Oridión *uios* Kallíkratous, being the eldest of four brothers and five sisters, and I had no desire to follow my father's footsteps into a life of unremitting physical labor. So when the good Brothers came to town, seeking young candidates to be tested for Psairothi training, I stepped forward, much to my family's consternation—for as the oldest male of the next generation, I was expected to enter the workforce at puberty, and help provide for the needs of the others. But they could not block my application, for under the law of the Byzantine Julian Empire, the needs of the state outweighed the needs of the few.

Brother Amandos's offer of a gold solidos to secure my father's permission did much to assuage his concerns. After all, he had other, more malleable children still at home who could provide for his old age.

From that point on, I worked as hard as I could to secure my place in the world, so that I would never have to return to that dusty, dirty, bug-ridden, chicken-filled, two-room stone house on the outskirts of the city. And now all of my efforts were threatened by events seemingly beyond anyone's control. If the Queen and her government couldn't find a solution, how could I?

I posed that question to Lord Gronos the next morning, amidst a light drizzle-*cum*-fog that made the hedgerows loom alarmingly at us out of the gloom as we strolled through the maze. They could have almost been the monsters that had been plaguing my dreams of late.

"If the problem could be solved by talking or negotiating or entreaty," the old councilor said, "it would have happened already. But something else seems to be at work, driving apart the existing factions in the Kingdom—and not just here, either. Old Emperor Stephanos II is nearing the end of his reign, and as the center of the Julian state weakens, his eldest son and heir, Prince Ioulianos, spends his days hunting and gambling and chasing young boys. He seems particularly ill-suited to sit on the Golden Throne of Julianople.

"And in the West, the Holy Roman Cæsars seem equally at sea. Pope Leo Magnus II has been fighting barbarian uprisings in the Maghreb for the past decade, and his three nephews are all striving against each other to succeed him. In Germania, Emperor Bernhardt IV is struggling to control his client states, with another outbreak of religious heresy directed at True-Pope Wilhelm III providing the flashpoint. Even the Poles, as dangerous as they've been in the past, are undergoing one of their periodic convulsions, with rival Kings Bentinck II and Iwon I tearing their country apart.

"Dissension, poverty, economic dislocation, political failure—all of these seem to be spreading throughout the civilized states of the world. It's as if an outside force is deliberately fracturing us, revealing the worst elements of our society and nature. Queen Evetéria may not be the freshest flower on the Tighris family tree, but she tries very hard, and she feels her lack of control just as painfully as any of her more capable ancestors might have. And she knows all too well—and understood the fact long before you emphasized it the other day—that her death could mean the end of all her family has struggled to achieve. The little men who want to occupy the Tiger Throne are none of them her equal. Only Lady Karlyna possesses, in my estimation, the intellect and ability to hold this country together, but she has the least chance of any."

"What do you suggest that I do, Lord Gronos?"

I heard the cawing of a crow somewhere off to my left, and then another, far away to my right.

"If you can contribute to the political stability of the state, you have an obligation to do so. If you cannot, you should leave, preserving what you can of your life and knowledge.

"For myself, I shall remain at Court until they inter my body under the earth—which I think is not long distant. But your recent revelation at the Council meeting makes you a target, Morpheús."

"But I thought the proceedings were secret," I said, startled at the notion that someone would want to harm *me*. I'd always eschewed training in the martial arts—perhaps I'd erred in slighting my education in this arena.

"Ha! Already the rumors have started, and they're wilder by far than your prognostications. The factions will want to confirm or deny what they've heard—and the only way they can do that is by taking you prisoner. You should return home today. You can better defend yourself there."

"What does the Queen say?"

"She agrees. You have her leave to go."

I sighed. "I just don't know what to do, Sir."

Having spent my life furthering my own ambitions, it seemed, well, unseemly suddenly to decamp—and lose all of the time and effort I'd put into the project of creating myself.

Then I heard a rustling in the hedges to my left, and I felt the Chancellor's bony fingers grab my elbow and pull me to a halt.

"Quiet!" he hissed. Then: "Listen!"

He did something that I couldn't see with his other hand and muttered a word that I couldn't hear, and then I discerned quite clearly the mumbling of two other low-pitched voices.

"Where are they?" one said.

"I can't see anything in this damned mist," the other man replied.

"Jocko's on the other side somewhere. Maybe we should call him."

"And tip off the marks?" the second man said. "Keep your

voice down!"

Slowly we edged backwards along the path, retracing our previous steps. Lord Gronos pointed at a mid-sized stone barely visible on one side of the walkway, and motioned me to pick it up. I threw it as hard as I could in the direction we'd previously been traversing, and could hear it crashing through the hedges.

"They're over there!" the first man said. "Come on!"

"That will keep them busy long enough for us to escape," the old man hissed.

When we were safely back in the palace, Gronos turned to face me in the entranceway before heading back to his quarters.

"Everyone says that you have a singular talent, Master Morpheús, one that has not been evident here in many generations. I've seen it displayed only twice, and on both occasions, I was greatly impressed by your workings. Can you do more with your ability than play parlor games with the Queen? Maybe you need to look within, before you can look without. If you can so clearly envisage the future, why can't you *shape* that future? Instead of being a Hypatomancer, perhaps you should become a Hyphainomancer, a Weaver of dreams—dreams that we can all share and believe in.

"But I'm just an old man living out his final years. What do I know, anyway?"

And then he kissed me on both cheeks and walked away.

I never saw him again in my life.

But I thought to myself then—and retain the thought even today—that he knew a great deal more than I, about most everything. The country of old men is visited all too seldom by the young, who perhaps envisage in those ancients' physical and mental decay their own Ultima Thule; but miss the fact that the fallen arches of elderly feet have trodden the very same paths that their juniors now traverse; and that, for the merest of kind words and a tad of patience, the latter could have derived much wisdom from their elders, and avoided repeating the mistakes of an earlier generation.

Such has been the saddest observation of our fathers and

grandfathers, but like so many other truisms of life, is forgotten anew with each washing of the spheres. All *I* knew after talking with him was that my own trial was yet to come—and I dreaded it.

CHAPTER FIVE
"'TWAS A VILE, VICIOUS THING"

Scooter and I transited home to Barstölný in Southern Kórynthia early that afternoon, and I wasn't sorry to go. People were now looking at me in very strange ways, to the point where even the wherret was commenting on their bizarre behavior.

"What's the matter with them, Master?" my familiar asked, after one such encounter with a comely lass, who made an effort to slink away from us as we passed by her in a Palace corridor.

"Maybe they think we're infested with cooties," I said.

"Cooties? What's that?"

"Blood-suckers."

"Wherrets don't tolerate such intruders."

"You're covered with fur, and you don't get cooties?" I reached around and plucked something off Scooter's right fore-limb. "Then what's that?" I asked.

"What's *what*? *What did you find*?" The creature frantically started examining itself, contorting its legs into seemingly impossible formations, until I could no longer restrain my mirth.

"Verrry funny!" Scooter said. "Ha...ha...ha. You humans have no perspective whatsoever. To willingly torment an intelligent being physically smaller than yourself...well, it displays, at the least, a lamentable absence of dignity."

I was laughing too hard to respond.

"Harrumph," it finally said. And then it started pouting. Wherrets can pout with a great deal of energy. It just makes them funnier.

＊ ＊ ＊ ＊ ＊ ＊ ＊

Upon our arrival, I began activating the more advanced features of my home's defensive system. This included blocking potential visitors from even reaching the house proper without my permission. My small estate was surrounded by what appeared to be a stone wall, but was actually more sophisticated than that. The main bronze gate, when secured, could not be forced by physical might, although any shield can be penetrated psychically, given enough time, energy, and knowledge. And if challenged, the wall would extend itself upwards almost indefinitely. Although based in the material world, it had dimensions extruding into other realities, and untangling those would be a task worthy of a Class VII Mage.

Similarly, the house was built into the side of a hill, placing the laboratory, transit alcove, and sleeping quarters securely underground; this enabled me to add another layer of protection to the facility. Even if an intruder somehow managed to penetrate the front door—an unlikely scenario—getting through the shield covering the solid rock bunker was nigh unto impossible. All of this would take even an accomplished magician a considerable amount of time—and while he was doing his damndest, I would be transiting to a safe house somewhere else. The knowledge of where such "back doors" were physically located were always kept very close to the breast. Mine was a rundown, rural hut in the remote mountains of eastern Asia Minor.

Mages tend to be somewhat paranoid about potential enemies, given their first-hand knowledge of what their powers can accomplish, and most of their abodes are built like miniature psychic fortresses.

While Scooter went to take care of its business, I greeted Mistress "Weasely," my housekeeper, whom I'd fashioned out of a weasel, broom, and several other implements. It kept the place clean, and all it cost me was a few live rats. It squeaked at me in return.

I gazed at my expansive front room, surrounded on three

sides by tall, broad windows of transparent silica overlooking a tranquil, well-tended garden. I truly liked my house. I liked it a great deal. And I didn't want to give this up, if there was any way to preserve it.

I fixed myself a light meal, which I shared with Scooter, and then I read a little Barlévin before turning down the light.

* * * * * * *

My dreams that night were filled with the monsters accumulated from a life of too many years—my sins of commission and omission, my loves (mostly lost), my undoubted success in my chosen profession—and my utter failure to find true happiness.

And so I sailed that boat yclept *Ye Night Mare*, being flung here and there upon waves of fiction and fantasy until I came to a shore that I had never before visited.

A great palace, mayhap, or just the dwelling place of a very wealthy man, some mighty structure inhabited by a potentate of potentates, filled with servants and slaves coming and going, like ants upon their hill, each to their purpose, unknowable to anyone save their ruler. I found myself drifting down long, dim passages, my spirit questing for…I knew not what.

And then I heard it again!

"Help me!"

The voice seemed to emanate from deep within the structure. I could feel its faint vibration, and I attuned myself to the sympathetic waves that it created within the æthersphere.

"Help me!"

It was a woman's voice, I now realized, now that I was closer to the source—a woman of power and puissance, an entity to be reckoned with.

"Oh, please: help me!"

There was almost a vibrato to the undertone, as if the speaker had long since given up any hope of a response.

"Where are you?" I cried, my words echoing down the passageway, with "…Are you?" bouncing back at me.

Suddenly God deafened all the sounds in the world but His, and I could hear the very heart beating in my chest, threatening to burst its bounds.

"Where *are* you?" I repeated, now almost whispering the words.

"Here!" came the faint reply.

I sent my soul in the direction of that voice, until I came to a blank brick wall that allowed me no access. It was interlaced with psychic protections of a sophistication and configuration I'd never seen before.

"Where are you?" I called out again.

"Here!" was her reply. "I'm a prisoner. In *here!*"

She was trapped somewhere on the other side of that barrier, but I couldn't penetrate that stone, no matter how hard I tried.

Then I placed both hands on the rough red structure and extended my consciousness to its fullest degree, pushing myself forward as hard as possible, until I could just barely feel a presence on the other side, just enough to know that someone was actually there, someone deeply immersed in her own knot of pain.

I was abruptly aware of a third entity, rapidly racing down the corridor behind me—and it was not a friend! I glanced back at the thing, and gasped at what I saw—and then....

* * * * * * *

...And then I woke up, choking for breath.

"Master," my companion said, jumping up on my chest. "What is it?"

I told the wherret everything that had happened to me in that foreign place.

"This was *real*," I said. *"All* of it. This was not a place of my imagining. It exists, Scooter."

"Tell me about the 'other'," the creature said.

"I saw very little of it, but what I could feel was like nothing I've ever encountered. It had the rough shape of a very large bird, but 'twas a vile, vicious thing full of malice aforethought, with claws on its wings, two spikes on its legs, and jagged, knife-like teeth. It would have killed me, had I given it half the chance."

"Yes, it would have," Scooter agreed. "I've heard of such beings, although I've never actually seen one. Master, this… creature derives from one of the distant Otherworlds, far out into the æther. You cannot go there and ever hope to return."

But I was not convinced. It is ever such with man, that he desires that which he cannot attain, and disdains that which is near at hand.

Although I'd had all the makings of a good life in Kórynthia, recent events had suddenly tainted my future—and that of the realm—with uncertainty. So, perhaps I would have better luck trying something else. Perhaps I could leave the Kingdom during its time of chaos, and return after things were settled again.

This captive woman might provide an escape from my troubles. The more I considered the notion, the more I felt energized for the first time in a great many years. There was something about her plight that touched a place deep within my soul. Why, I could go on a quest, just like the knights of eld! I could rescue the lady and make my fortune, and then return home, enshrouded in glory, a legend among mages.

My life here had become stale and static, unworthy of a scion of the great House of Parakôdês. My ancestor of that name had been known as a man of action, a man of principle, a man who wouldn't have hesitated to venture forth into the unknown void, oh yes! Rescue a damsel in distress—no problem!

I can *do* this, I told myself. I can find her. I can save her. I can find myself again in the process.

No greater fool does a man ever see than his own image in the mirror, reflected back at him.

In the end, all the worms really do ooze out of the clay. In the end, they consume one's being.

CHAPTER SIX
"I ONLY DOUBT HER HISTORY AND HER SINCERITY"

But to make such a change in my station, I'd first have to know a great deal more about the situation—not as I might envision it, were I writing this tale, but as it actually existed.

The sky-orb was such a simple device—really just a refinement and reduction of the old thro-mirror so popular in earlier days. It allowed limited communication across the æthernet—or could be used, as I had employed it recently, to scan for passageways into the Otherworlds.

I'd been taught at University that the Otherworlds were alternate realities to our own existence. No one seemed to know exactly how they were formed or organized, or even how many of them might fill the ætherspace; but we knew they existed because men like me had ventured both deliberately and accidentally into the void—and some few of these had even actually returned, bearing tales of grand adventures in the places "beyond beyond."

I'd ferreted out every account of these journeys in the Bibliotheca Magica during my student years, and had been stirred as never before by the glorious tales of these grand adventurers: the redoubtable Maximus Pomptinus, the unbowed Asinus Vetulus, the enigmatic Melanchthôn Malitiosus, the seeker-after-knowledge Doctor Scarabbaios, the sword of justice Prince Théodoric d'Aistolfe, the venturer-into-othertimes Elissa of Adrianople, and the accidental time traveler Don Cesarino

Copacabana, to name but a few.

Before I could join their ranks, however, I had to find some way of strengthening the communication link between myself and the woman, and confirming exactly where she was. Without such basic information, I was as helpless as she.

I'd once heard of a mage who'd taken several sky-orbs and strung them together as a linked chain. I asked Scooter for his advice.

"Master," it said, "what you propose is certainly possible. But why do this? You know nothing of this woman. She might even be a spirit seeking to ensnare a stray soul."

"I don't believe that," I said. "I could feel her pain through my dream. *That* was true—it couldn't have been faked."

"Even so," Scooter said, "even so…Master, she may regard you as her only possible way of escaping this…this trap, or whatever it is, since you don't actually know."

"I understand the risk."

"Do you? Do you really? You know nothing about the Otherworlds."

"And you know more?" I asked. "You're a creature of the *Spirit*worlds, Scooter. You've never even been to the *Other*worlds."

My companion looked at me then in that sly way it had. Its long whiskers curled up on either side, and I swear it grinned at me—except, of course, that wherrets can't really grin (I think).

"Very well," the creature said. "Yes, Master, you *can* connect two sky-orbs together, or even three, although balancing the energies of three would be difficult even for a Class VII Mage. I would suggest you try matching a pair of them first."

I'd never attempted this particular trick before, but I soon discovered exactly what Scooter meant. When employing a sky-orb, one must focus all one's attention on the *specus* of the thing—the center of its being—then seize hold of it while turning the stream of its essence elsewhere. Trying to control *two* of the spheres at once—coordinating their energies into one fixed probe to illuminate the æther—well, it proved nigh unto impossible.

I had to attempt the trick over and over and over again before I finally got it right—and just holding the beam true to its course required all my strength.

"Scooter!" I gasped. *"Help!"*

It swiftly moved into my consciousness then, loaning me some of its energy. With the wherret's assistance, I was finally able to send my soul deep into the ætherspace, looking for that unique vibration that I recalled from my dreamtime. But still it took me several hours of searching to find it.

"Help me!" It was that eerie voice once again.

"Where are you?" I asked.

Silence lengthened into eternity.

"Here." The reply was hesitant, almost timorous. "I am here. Focus on my voice. Are you the one who came before?"

I used the power of the conjoined sky-orbs to trace the sound of the woman's soul to its source.

"I am," I said.

And then I was there!

The room was large, I sensed, fashioned of the same red brick that I'd encountered before. Arrow slits in the walls allowed the sun to penetrate the darkness—so brightly, in fact, that I could not discern anything clearly.

Then I realized what the woman had done: she'd created a makeshift thro-mirror from an open container of wine or water. So long as the sun touched the still, slack surface of the liquid, the contact could be maintained. It was a brilliant artifice, one bespeaking a desperate situation—and a very high level of magical attainment. Sustaining such a link for even a small amount of time would require an enormous expenditure of energy.

In the searing beam of the sun I could barely make out the half-moon image of the mage hovering above the magic cup, her lower face enshrouded by an opaque veil, her dark hair pulled back from her forehead by what appeared to be a gold diadem impressed with arcane symbols. I could not see the eyes hidden in shadow.

"I see you!" she suddenly exclaimed. *"I see you! At long last! Oh, thank the Goddess Almighty, I see you! Oh...!"*

Then the link was cut, abruptly and without warning.

"Where are you?" I asked. "Are you there?"

Very faintly I heard: "I'm here. But the sun begins to wane. Try again soon...."

And that was all.

I closed down the orbs.

"You see," I said to my companion. "She's real. She's actually out there."

"I have no doubt of her reality, Master," Scooter said. "I have no doubt either of her desperation. I only doubt her history and her sincerity."

CHAPTER SEVEN
"YOU WANT TO DO *WHAT*?"

I needed help and advice, and I knew it. What I was contemplating could not be undertaken lightly or without consequence. I would begin with my immediate superior, Magister Geraklíd, the Minister of Magical Affairs in Kórynthia.

I asked for an audience, and when I received permission, transited on the next day to his home in Bizerte, leaving Scooter behind.

"You want to do *what*?" he said, when I told him of my plans.

"I wish to resign my position as Scanner Prime, Sir," I said, "Or at least take a leave of absence."

"Then the rumors are true."

"What rumors?"

"That you've predicted the fall of the Kingdom within the next year."

"That's *not* what I said, Sir." Since he already knew something of the Council's proceedings, I gave him a summary of my reading. "I was surprised that you weren't present, Magister."

"I was out of town, and failed to receive the notice in time."

"Really?" I found his answer puzzling. As a government official, he would have had to maintain contact at all times.

"We're here to discuss *your* business, not mine."

"Yes, Sir," I said. I didn't want to antagonize the man, since I needed his formal permission to proceed with minimal consequences to my purse, position, and person.

"So you want to abandon us at a time of crisis…if your prognostications are correct."

"They're true, Sir. I…uh…." The truth was, I didn't want to tell him the truth. "I need to go on a pilgrimage of reconstitution." Well, that was at least *part* of the truth!

"You want to go on a pilgrimage of reconstitution? Are you mad? The Queen won't let you leave, not when you're needed here, now more than ever."

"But truly, Magister, she has nothing to say about the matter. She maintains temporal authority over the Kingdom, to be sure, but wields no direct power over the magely class. If I *wish* to go, why, certainly I *can*."

Geraklíd began pacing on the rug in front of me, his hands clasped behind his back, his gray head and beard bobbing up and down like a hungry bird. Suddenly he stopped and turned to me:

"Morpheús…sometimes I wonder about you, boy, I really do. Yes, in theory Queen Evetéria has no authority over such as us. But the reality is far different. She can banish you from the kingdom forever—or at least until her own death. She can request that I set the dogs of war on you and bring you to account before the Court of Mages—and if I refuse, she can ask the Covenant to find a new Magister of Mages for Kórynthia. They may or may not agree, but the petition will have to be considered in any case. She can use the Lords Spiritual against us in the eternal three-way battle for power and influence in the State, and allied with the power of the Lords Temporal…well, the Lords Magical could not possibly maintain their position under such circumstances. She can withhold certain monies for the support of the Magical Estate. In sum, she can cause us unending trouble—and moreover, she is exactly the kind of ruler who *will* cause us difficulties, if we cross her in this matter.

"She likes you. That's both a curse and a blessing. It gives you a certain influence over the Lady, but nothing ever comes without its price. She has you by the short hairs, Master Morpheús, and you'd best acknowledge the fact. You can't leave, whatever the reason, and you specifically do *not* have my blessing.

"I have to admit, I'm disappointed in you. You were the first mage to be acknowledged as Scrutor Primoris since Doctor Scarabbaios. You're also a Dream Weaver, although you've never used that talent, to the best of my knowledge. We couldn't even measure your aptitude, because it was so high off the scale.

"Oh, you've done well, no question. You've risen very quickly in the hierarchy, and seem destined one day to take my place. But always I've had the sense that what you've accomplished has primarily and firstly been to promote the career of Master Morpheús. Everything that you've done has been carefully calculated to benefit *you* first. You've established no long-term personal connections with anyone, because (I think) you regard them as a potential impediment. And now that you see the inevitable collapse of the state, you're ready to run away at the first opportunity."

"Uh, that's not actually true, Sir." Although it was, of course. Who was I fooling save myself?

"Then tell me what's really happening."

I'd made a fundamental error, I could see that now. I'd asked a question for which I didn't know the answer—and I *should* have known the answer, if I'd just taken the time to think the thing through. Now I'd compromised one of my oldest supporters, someone who was bound to be hurt, both personally and professionally, if I followed my heart. Still, I was not swayed by his arguments.

"It's more than just my Council reading, Magister," I said. "It's...my life. I've been feeling for some time that I've failed, somehow, to find an appropriate purpose for what I do. Most folks just don't want to be told the reality of their futures—and so I have to lie to them. I didn't mind that, at least at first, but of late I've grown impatient with having to spew a rainbow-enshrouded version of things to come, when all I can see in most cases is old age, sickness, decrepitude, and death, sometimes interleafed with equal measures of poverty and loss of property, position, and posture. No one wants to hear that."

"Not all futures are bad," my superior said.

"But most contain bad elements, Sir. I'm tired of lying. I'm tired of having to be nice to everyone while misusing my craft."

"It's not a misuse of your abilities to reassure people," Geraklíd said. "You simply have to be tactful in what you say."

"No, Sir, *you have to lie!* All the time! I don't feel like I'm accomplishing anything worthwhile. There has to be some better use of my talents, whatever that is. Maybe this captive woman...."

"*What* woman?"

Oh, now I'd done it! I hadn't intended to reveal the connection I'd made in the æthersphere. Hellfire and damnation!

So I told him about my several adventures probing for links to the Otherworlds, one of them involuntary.

"You're not a neomage, Morpheús. I don't have to tell you that what you're doing is foolish and risky beyond belief. This being that you've encountered may not be human—or a woman—or even flesh and blood. You know nothing about it beyond the barest of suppositions. You have to stop this right away."

"That's what my familiar said."

"Well, your familiar is right," he said. "You said you actually Dreamed a connection. Has this ever happened to you before?"

"Well, no."

"You have that talent in your repertoire, the ability to shape reality through unconscious imaging. Perhaps it's finally beginning to emerge from your psyche. Such powers are little described in the literature, probably because they're so rare and elusive. Your distant ancestor, the Magus Magorum Parakôdês, was said to have been a Dream Weaver. But his life is the stuff of legend—he lived so long ago that the stories about his makings have become almost myths, and we don't know how his talent actually worked.

"But the real question is: why should your Dreaming emerge *now*?"

Why indeed? I'd thought about this for the past several days: "Something triggered the connection, Sir—and it had to be from the other end. I did not—*could* not—consciously activate what I can't control and don't understand. I think it was the woman who sparked a response—and that could only be due to her possessing a similar ability that created a resonance between us, even at this great distance. *That's* why I must find her. I have to know who I am and what I can do to make a difference. Otherwise, my existence is meaningless."

"I see," the Magister said. Then he sighed, long and loud. "Yet, my judgment remains the same: if the crisis will be as great as you claim, we need you here to cope with it—and to nurture the Queen. The needs of the many...."

"Yes, I know, Minister. I do appreciate your candor, Sir, and I understand your position; but in the end, I have to make my own decision, whatever the consequence. I'll let you know what I intend to do after I have sufficient time to think on it."

He gave me his blessing, and I returned home.

But in my heart, I'd already made my choice. I'd follow in the footsteps of my illustrious progenitor, and accomplish something significant with my life, instead of remaining a government functionary.

In my bedroom was a small alcove with a marble bust of Parakôdês. I lit the three candles—ebon, ivory, and emerald—that flanked his image, and bowed my head in respect. Then I spoke the words that my father the proud soldier had given me.

"I invoke the name of he who gave me flesh, faith, and foresight. Parakôdês of the Red-Lands, awake thou from thy sleep!"

The great bearded image shook itself slightly, straightened with a deep groan of stone, and then opened its eyes, in a startling, even blinding flash of blue-green. I avoided their twin gaze, as I'd been told.

"Is this my true path, o grandfather of my soul?" I asked.

"Yes, my brilliant son," came the reply, a hollow, heavy, hissing sigh with overtones of the æther. "This is what you must do, both to save yourself, the world in which you dwell, and the greater sphere in which your orb is a mere pearl littered upon a beach of worlds. The ætherspace has begun to fracture, and only you can make it whole again."

"But...but...why me? Why has this fallen to *me*, o Great Mage?" I suddenly felt overwhelmed by a burden that I neither desired nor felt capable of handling. I heard a small crack, and saw one ear flake from the bust.

"The son must rise to take his place in the cosmos," he said. "You were born at this time to do this one thing, whatever else you might accomplish. No one else can do it for you.

"But remember, Oridión the Morpheús, that there is a price to be rendered for every action that we take, and you must ultimately pay the ferryman his token, just as I did so long ago. That is why we hypatomancers may not envision our *own* futures, lest we breach the line that is drawn in the sands of eternity to keep us sane.

"Go now, flesh of my flesh, and do what must be done. Find the Eggs and restore the balance that has been lost."

"Eggs? What Eggs? Whatever are you talking about, Grandfather?" I was lost again in a mire of self-pity, trying to fathom what the old Mage was saying, and wondering how one man could do anything to save the entire cosmos. Another crack, and the back of the image's head crumbled into dust.

"The four Eggs of the Elephant—you must find and control them to restore order to the shattered spheres. The First Egg will open the Way. The Second Egg will show you the Way. The Third Egg will find the Way. The Fourth Egg will make the Way One."

"I don't understand." Grandfather's nose dissolved into eternity in a puff of dust.

"The knowledge will come to you if you let it. When you need some answers, twice more you may call upon me, and twice more will I respond. But should you call my name a fourth time, I will come for *you*, my child, and that will be the end of it."

And then he was gone, the statue disappearing like a breath that's been held a very long time and is suddenly exhaled. Perhaps it was *my* breath, for I seemed to have difficulty of a sudden regaining my wind. Then I snuffed out the candles in reverse order, and hearing the barest click of claws on stone, suddenly pirouetted.

Scooter was watching me from the doorway, its small, bewhiskered head cocked to one side.

"You humans—always full of surprises," it said.

CHAPTER EIGHT
"'THE OTHERWORLDS ARE NOT AT ALL WHAT YOU IMAGINE'"

I began making preparations for what I needed to do. I had the training and ability to seal my abode from every interference, both temporal and magical. Already I'd put in place a certain level of protection to preserve my privacy and possessions, some of which could have been dangerous in the wrong hands. No one could now enter my estate without my permission—and this was true even of the greatest Magi Magorum. But I went even further, and restricted access to my home to no one but myself and to those whom I permitted entrance, and even then, only with utterance of certain passwords and incantations. A magical seal of this type was almost impossible to penetrate, for it could be made to loop in upon itself, thereby increasing exponentially the energy required to break it.

I spent the next week doing those things that were necessary to prepare my house and life and laboratory for a prolonged absence. Just once was I called to Paltyrrha, and I dutifully reported to Her Majesty as required, and made those prognostications that were asked of me, politely and skillfully. The Queen was entirely satisfied, even if I wasn't. I assiduously avoided engaging with anyone else at Court.

I also tried several times to contact the woman held captive in the Otherworlds, but without success. My dream-quests were equally fruitless—and Scooter discouraged me from continuing them, saying that my soul could easily be stolen from me, unless

I was anchored to a waking reality.

But before I could proceed, I really needed more information about the Otherworlds, and the place to get it, I knew, was at the University of Julianople, my old Alma Mater. It'd been some years since my last visit—I marveled at the passage of time—and I found myself anticipating the journey with some excitement. Once again I left Scooter in charge of my home—there were things that it needed to do in my absence.

The great city of Julianople was dedicated by the Emperor Constantine I in the year 330, but it was his nephew, Julian I the Great, who built much of the edifice that we see today, making it the largest metropolis of the ancient world, with well over a million inhabitants at the time of its rechristening in the year 411 of the Christian Era. I'd spent six glorious years of my youth exploring its galleries and libraries and performance halls and architecture—and still I never touched more than a fraction of the whole. Who can forget the Bridge of Sighs or the Cathedral of Saint-Sophia or the Barrhônês Garden in the Autokratorial Palace? That time was the happiest of my life, I think.

The man I wanted to see was one of my old professors, Doctor Remírdas Árbogast, who'd been responsible for teaching that most dreaded of courses, Magical Philosophy. I remember suffering through that final exam, the worst I ever took, and having nightmares about it for years thereafter. There were nine students in that class. Three suffered breakdowns before the end of the term, two failed the course and had to retake it—one of them three times—and the other four, myself included, barely scraped by with passing grades.

But we learned—oh, did we learn! We learned about ethics and limits and choices and…so many different things. And we learned about the Otherworlds. Now that I'd had the perspective of working for many years in the field, I wanted to enhance my knowledge of such matters with a sprinkling of the good doctor's wisdom.

We met at the Three Wise Men, a tavern catering to the school's teaching assistants and professors.

"Oridión the Morpheús." The voice emanated from a dimly-lit corner near the back of the establishment. "You haven't changed very much."

I didn't know whether that was an insult or compliment—with Doctor A., it could be either—or both.

"Most of my students are glad to see the back of me," he continued. "Very few ever return for seconds."

He motioned me to the bench at the other side of the table. "This is on me," he said, "In honor of a rare, even subtle occasion."

I ordered the Menville Mash: it had an understated flavor, but as with many good things, it just kept on giving.

I sipped the frothy brew when it was delivered, and enjoyed the splash of pungent herb and airy ale against the back of my throat.

"I wish to know more about the Otherworlds," I said. Árbogast was not the kind of mage who favored the dillydallytant.

"Indeed." He buried his head in his mug, and then looked up again, his goatee flecked with white foam. "Why?"

"I want to travel there."

"So have many others. Very few have returned."

"That doesn't bother me," I said.

"Then it must be treasure of one sort of another," the professor said. "I never pegged you for a gawker after gold, so it's something else. Knowledge? No, you were never that much interested in the whys and wherefores, only the hows. Fame? I think not."

He looked at me more carefully then, studying my face and form and figure, as one might examine an insect under glass.

"Ah!" he finally exclaimed. "Now I see! You have, I note, been living on your own for quite some time. And time is the problem, isn't it? You are finally beginning to wonder if this is all there is, if time is leaving you behind. Were you a religious man, I'd say you were having a crisis of faith. But religious or not, it's still a crisis—of self, perhaps. So there must be a woman involved."

I admitted nothing. "I wish to travel to the Otherworlds," I repeated, "and return."

"Then you are a fool, Morpheús. Be content with what you have. You've done better than ninety-nine out of a hundred students. In mid-life you've already achieved high office. What more do you want?"

"Love?" I ventured.

"An empty gesture, a silly thing that prances and prattles and then goes pfft, a mere posture of lustration. What can love give you that knowledge will not?"

"Someone warm to ease the cold nights?" I said. I was beginning to get irritated, but Doctor Árbogast always had that effect on me. "In truth, I want to find a better way to live my life. I tire of the lie my existence has become."

He frowned, and then shook his head. "I see that you will not readily be amused," he finally said. "Very well: the best work on the subject is Probatikos's *The Music of the Spheres*. There's a copy in the library. I'd also suggest a little-known tract, *De Transmundis Aliis*, by Sillius Funambulus."

"I'll certainly look at these," I said. "But what can *you* tell me, Professor?"

"I would tell you not to go, but I see that such advice, however sound, will not be heeded. I still remember when Doctor Scarabbaios returned from the æthersphere a half century ago, and the stir that he created on the one occasion when he spoke to the assembled faculty.

"'The Otherworlds,' he said, 'are not at all what you imagine.'

"I questioned him closely during the days that followed, but he wouldn't give me many details of his experiences—and his memoir, which was published during the time you were taking classes here, while entertaining and at times amusing, revealed very few hard facts.

"My sense, however, is that nothing in his experience contradicted the general idea of the Otherworlds that has emerged in the last few decades.

"Travel through the transit mirrors is relatively easy on our own world, particularly for a mage with basic training. With a few precautions and some advanced study, most mages can master a transit to—and return from—the nearby Otherworlds, those that are most similar in nature to our own.

"The difficulty arises when the separation in time and space becomes ever greater. Accidental or deliberate passages to such worlds can happen infrequently, but returning to Nova Europa from them is extraordinarily difficult—and the measure of difficulty increases with each degree of separation.

"For convenience's sake, we class those worlds nearest to our own as being members of the First Circle or Sphere. Those created by the splitting of universes prior to one thousand years ago we place in the Second Circle. Those occasioned by splits occurring more than ten thousand years ago are part of the Third Circle. Those breaking off before one hundred thousand years ago are regarded as constituting the Fourth Circle. And those which derive from impossibly ancient times comprise what we call the Fifth Circle. There may be an infinite number of these—no one really knows.

"On each of these worlds, their geography may be the same or at least similar to ours, but their languages, histories, even their races may be entirely different."

"How can I reach a particular world?" I asked.

"I don't know." It was a startling admission from a man whose scholarly knowledge I respected above all others. "We've tried several experiments over the years, with many notable failures and no true successes. When I asked Doctor Scarabbaios the same question, he said: 'You really don't want to know'."

"You mean—he's still alive?"

"Yes," my former teacher replied, "but he has become reclusive in his old age, and will see no one without an appointment—and such appointments are not readily obtainable by anyone, even me. I've encountered him just once in the last few decades, when he came here during the Scriborial Festival two years ago—you know, the one where Apothecarius Magicus Franz von Jarmank was honored?

"However, there is a possibility. Doctor Scarabbaios once

served as the Librarian at the University, and he still maintains a passion for rare and odd tomes of magical lore. He'll do almost anything to find a new one."

"Even answer my questions?" I asked.

"If anything will gain access to his home and his knowledge, it's a book that he hasn't seen before. But I warn you, finding one could be a task worthy of the Labors of Hercules. His collection is said to exceed 35,000 volumes."

"35,000! So many?"

"Now you understand. Alas, I have to leave you, Oridión"—very few people in the world called me by my true given name—"to teach my next seminar. If you succeed in your quest, please do come back and talk to me once more. My lust, such as it is, has always been for understanding the nuances of *la philosophie magique*. Perhaps you can unveil a window or two to help enlighten this old soul."

"I'll do so," I promised. "Thank you for your time, Professor."

Afterwards, I located the two works that Doctor Árbogast had recommended, and found them useful, in a theoretical sort of way. Whether they'd provide any practical advice, however, seemed a bit dubious.

The good doctor had also given me the contact nodes to reach Doctor Scarabbaios. I returned home in good spirits. All I had to do now was to find a book that the old librarian had never seen. This would be easy, I thought.

Of course, I seriously underestimated the difficulty.

CHAPTER NINE
"FISHING FOR IFRITS?"

I was able to reach Doctor Scarabbaios quite readily. That was not the problem, as it turned out.

"Who the Hades are *you*?" he said, "and what do you want?"

I gave him my name and *bona fides*.

"Never heard of you." He spoke in an almost staccato fashion.

I explained my quest.

"Why would *anyone* want to go to the Otherworlds? I spent three decades there trying to find my way home. Do you think *that* was enlightening? Good day to you, Sir."

I caught Scooter laughing at me off to one side. "You humans," was all it could say.

The second time I tried a different tack.

"I have a copy of *The Old Mage and the Sea*, by Magister Terentius Callister," I said.

"The one about fishing for ifrits for one hundred and some odd years? Have three of them. Simplistic nonsense. Good day."

The third time, I thought, would be the proverbial "charm."

"How about Master Victor de Vannis's *De Verrucis Mysteriorum*?"

"Claptrap, although the notion of reading the splotches on some fat fart's fat ass was at least original." Then static.

And so it went, back and forth for over a month. I was getting more and more frustrated. I even spoke to Doctor Árbogast again.

"Well, you must realize," my old teacher said, "That Scarby's about three or four hundred years on, and he's had the time, money, and energy to secure copies of just about everything he wants. Of course, there's one book that he's been seeking for most of his life."

"Really? Which one?" I asked. Maybe this would provide the information I needed.

"*The Necropompeion* of Fredo von Schweitzermeister. According to Phôstêridês, the book was created in a half dozen identical renditions by the Associated Shades in Hades, under the direction of Johannes Kendrick de Sonipedis, and then smuggled across the Styx on a houseboat—and by its very nature, being linked to the Netherworld, it cannot be duplicated or printed in the real world. There's said to be a copy in the Bibliotheca Borgis, but, of course, the Avignon Papacy will not allow access to it, since they refuse as a matter of policy to allow magical practices within the Holy Roman Empire; and even its purported existence there is unverified. The other copies remain unaccounted for—either destroyed, lost, or perhaps in private hands. I venture to say that presenting him with one of these volumes would gain you unlimited access to his accumulated wisdom, such as it is."

"Then I shall locate one," I said.

But that was easier said than done, and my first feelers to bookmongers and private collectors were all unsuccessful.

In the meantime, I kept trying to reestablish contact with the distant female prisoner, but I had no better luck there than I did with the Hadish necrography. It seemed as if all of the omens were turning against me.

To compound matters even more, I was summoned to Court again a few days later, there to provide a round-robin set of prognostications at the Queen's Soirée of Soothsaying, with *moi* occupying the seat of honor, so to speak. Gad, I was getting tired of the utter trivialness of it all:

"Yes, Lady Kólményi, you have both love and riches to look forward to." I didn't mention that she'd be murdered within six months by a jealous lover.

"Ah, my dear Lord Düttermann, there is much about your existence that I envy." And there was much I didn't, either, since Düttermann was doomed to perish in a nasty house fire three years hence.

"Metropolitan Sygmunt," I said, "You will rise even further in the Church hierarchy." Yes, he would become Patriarch of Kórynthia, and he would always regret having advanced just one step too far. The burden would wear him down in the end.

"Of course, Master Krotz, you will attain great success with your epic poem set among the Angels"—but you will never be able to pen anything comparable the rest of your life, and you will come to rue that one great success with bitterness.

"Minister Jákman, how great to see you again! The treaty with the Liets will indeed be signed"—and be broken within the year by our faithless enemy. You will fall as a direct result, and ultimately go to the block, when your real nature is uncovered to the world.

And so on and so forth, *ad nauseam*. The problem with an innate talent is that you can never turn it off. It works whether you want it to or not. In the end, I could always see more than I wished—things about the frailty of human nature, about the fate of human nations, about the flaws in human nobility. I see and saw too damned much—that is and was both *my* curse and *my* fate, and I'm so damnably tired of it all. There has got to be some way out.

That night, using just the one sky-orb I carried in my luggage, but with Scooter's strength to assist me, I reached out from my quarters in the Palace to the æthernet, hoping beyond hope to find the captive woman again.

"Where *are* you?" I cried, putting my entire soul into the query.

"Here!" came the faint reply. "They took me away for a week."

"I've been trying to reach you for more than a month," I said.

"It has only been…days here," she said. She was fading in and out, and I could barely hear her words.

"Who are you?" I asked.

There was a long hiss of static, and I thought for a moment that our communication had lapsed again.

"I am...Niobë daughter of...," she said. "That is...not my birth name, but...."

I understood immediately. Within most worlds, even beyond Nova Europa, the same basic rules of magic always seemed to apply. Mages often adopted pseudonyms early in their careers, and their real names were then carefully put aside. There were many reasons for this, including the safety of the practitioner. Knowing an individual's real name can, under certain circumstances, grant another mage great power over that person.

"I'm called Morpheús," I said. "Morpheús of Kórynthia in Nova Europa. Where are you?"

"I am...held in...called Mirabö, in Naprimér. I...-ing forced to...my captor. I cannot...."

"What did you say?"

"I am being forced to foretell the future of my captor."

"You're a soothsayer? So am I!" I said.

"Oh, please!" Scooter interjected in my right ear. I shooed it away.

"Who was that?" Niobë asked.

"My familiar companion," I said, "Scooter by name."

"Mine is...Sable," she said. "It's the...friend I have."

"No, Lady," I replied, "you have another."

A long silence.

"Thank you...." I heard a rattling in the background. *"What's that?"* Then: "I must go! Goodbye."

"Goodbye," I whispered into the glowing crystal globe.

Imagine, I thought to myself: another hypatomancer! In its most refined form, this is a very rare talent in Nova Europa.

"Uh, she's using you, Sir," Scooter said.

"What? Oh, piss and vinegar, you weasely wherret! You can be such a negative entity at times. I've spent my whole life in study and work and brown-nosing the powers that be. Why shouldn't I begin enjoying myself for a change? Why shouldn't

I...?"

"No one's objecting to you having a bit of fun, Master," my companion said. "But this female isn't what she seems. Even under the best of circumstances, she couldn't possibly be a companion to you. You can't reach her physically, and you will never know her psychically. There's no future to this relationship."

"So you say."

"Have you ever even heard of this Naprimér? Do you have any idea of what Circle it's in? The fact that time for them runs slow is not a good sign. It means that her place is very distant from ours. She could be what passes for human there, whatever that is in her world, and still be very 'different' from you, both inside and out. She has to be inhabiting at least a Fourth or Fifth Sphere world. How do you get there? How do you get back? Do you have any notion at all of the difficulties involved?"

I'd known Scooter for a very long time. I'd given it refuge when the wherret needed it, and in turn the creature had had to indenture itself to me for seven times seven years—the usual term. I knew that it had my best interests at heart—if it had a heart, and I wasn't really sure of that, given its metamorphic nature—so I couldn't be cross with the wherret for very long.

"I do listen to what you say," I said. "I do understand the risks involved. But what I had to do today for the Queen is becoming unbearable to me—not just tedious, but dangerously irritating. One of these sessions, I'm just going to blurt out loud what I think—and that will be the end of me, and the end of you too, I think. Evetéria cannot be crossed without severe consequences.

"So let's do what we can to support each other. If I'm successful in reaching this Niobë's world, it'll at least be a grand adventure. And my life has become over-stale of late, dear friend—you know that quite simply to be true."

Its lack of response was an acknowledgment of the reality of the situation.

But we still had to locate a copy of that blasted book to gain access to Doctor Scarabbaios and his (we hoped) much-touted

window into wisdom. And I hadn't a clue as to where one might
be found.

CHAPTER TEN
"THE PRICE WILL BE VERY HIGH"

When all my efforts at securing the much-desired tome through regular channels had failed, I knew that I'd have to try other, less reputable means. Not all those with magical talents have safe, secure, and prosperous careers among the gentry. Those who've failed to complete their courses, those who've never actually been schooled in the arts, those who, for various reasons, have chosen not to walk the straight line, nonetheless have found ways to earn a living from their talents—which are, in most cases, all they have going for them.

I needed a Finder, someone with an ability to locate "things"—which could be people, artifacts, or a variety of odd objects, depending on the depth and breadth of that particular individual's ability. And one of the best Finders, I knew, dwelt somewhere in the bowels of Paltyrrha—Jécko the Mallet.

I'd had one previous run-in with dear old Jécko some years earlier, and it hadn't been a happy experience for either of us. I was trying to locate a Countess's lost, lamented, ne'er-do-well son, and Jécko was able to give me a lead that ultimately proved successful. However, the noblewoman very soon regretted having given me the commission, and when I paid the price that Jécko had demanded—a "real" reading of the future—that too proved unsatisfactory in many different respects.

How common it is for our talents to provide our prospective customers, whoever they might be, with tainted results. That was the second great burden of being a professional Forecaster.

Hypatomancy—the art of seeing the best possible future—is a hypocritical lie in most instances. Better not to know, I often think.

Be that as it may, each of our talents was equally seductive in its own way, and I knew the Mallet and I would dance our little *pas de deux* once again, with probably equally unpleasant results. But if anyone could find *The Necropompeion*, it was Jécko.

The problem was in finding *him*! He had no fixed abode, and he dwelt in some of the less desirable parts of the great capital. I decided to remain in Paltyrrha for another few days, even though that meant being at the beck and call of the Queen, until I could resolve this business. I needed to know right away.

So I put out the usual subtle feelers into the "Underground"—and soon had a "call" on the sky-orb.

"Master M.," Jécko's high-pitched voice said (he chose not be visible). "Heard you was lookin' for me 'gain."

"I have business for you," I said. "The usual place? Say, an hour before sundown?"

"Done! See you there."

A few hours later I transited to the Church of Saint-Kambros in the Hölleröll District, and upon exiting the building, found myself a bench on which to sit in the adjoining cemetery. I left Scooter behind; Jécko didn't like eavesdroppers. I was reading a grave when the Finder plopped down next to me.

"You ain't changed overmuch," he said.

I looked him over—the ragged hood, the dirty fingers poking holes through the ends of his gloves, the furtive glances—and said: "Ditto."

"What 'xactly is it you need?" he asked.

I told him.

"Um, not so wee a task this time, Morphy, no, not at all. So, what if I find you this, um, book, and you get it, and then the real, um, owner comes lookin' for you—and soon for me? What 'bout that, then?"

"So now you're only accepting 'safe' searches, is that what

you're telling me? Why do I know better?"

"The price will be very high for this one, Master M. Will need a foretellin' of the highest kind. No runaday rubbin's for this Finder. *Highest* kind, Morphy!"

"Agreed."

"Very well. Will take me some time. See you here 'gain 'xactly one week from today.

"Now, this is the question I pose for you: if I take Diyán the Goat out of this world, what will happen to *me* after?"

"Nothing good, I venture," I said, chuckling. But Jécko failed to see the humor.

"Do you have something belonging to this, uh, Diyán?" I finally asked.

He handed over a worn, ragged glove.

"This he owned once."

"One week," I said. "I'll bring my reading, you bring yours."

He nodded his head, and then disappeared behind an adjoining stone. I finished reading the burial plot of Æmilius Le Frenais, the old man who was buried there, and then went back home to Barstölný, where I found my abode undisturbed.

CHAPTER ELEVEN
"GOOD FLEAS ARE
SO HARD TO FIND"

A conditional reading is not to be undertaken lightly. It requires a great deal of preparation and planning in order for the results to make any sense. Well, I already had a piece of Diyán's apparel, always the first requirement—something he'd actually used and worn. Next, I needed the fresh blood of a mammal—one of my milk goats would do, if I couldn't buy a live rabbit at the market. Also, I needed hogbane, an herb that could only be obtained at great expense: it had to be fresh-picked, since the dried version just wouldn't do. The fourth necessity was worrywort, another costly item. Fifthly, I already had a stock of sulferox in my storeroom. I also maintained a small supply of the sixth item, gargoyle dung, in its sealed ceramic container. The last ingredient for the spell was coprolite, the pulverized grounds of the petrified remains of the scat of long-extinct dragons.

And so, the next day Scooter and I transited to Ye Olde Fleah Marquette in Asshyr, the most likely place where I could find all the missing materials. I started with Doctor Flox's House of Boxes, which consisted of a series of rooms folded in amongst themselves. The entrance to the place was an unimposing store front in a back alley of the rundown district of Doldrumu, surrounded by the weapon shops for which the city is so well known.

The good Doctor was there to greet us. He was a strange

little creature, covered in a piebald skin with patches of brown, black, white, and yellow (I never heard whether this was its original condition, or an affectation), a shaved head with two tufts of braided hair springing out either side, and a small gold ring dangling from the middle of his nose.

"How's business, Flox?" I asked.

"Ah, Master Morpheús—and Scooter—haven't seen you two in at least a year, maybe more. We've had busier days, Sir. Of late, there seems to be a miasma in the æther that's affecting both travel and transit, and we're getting fewer customers from abroad. But we're always happy to see those who appear at our door. How can we meet your magical needs, gentlebeings?"

I handed him my list.

"Ah," he said, "Yes, yes, I think we can help you here. The hogbane is not prime at this time of year, of course, but we do what we can. Worrywort, worrywort, um, let me see, I thought I had some of that around here somewhere. Hmmm.

"Kolkus! Kolkus! Here, boy!"

One of the magically enhanced fleas immediately appeared to the proprietor's left.

"Find me the worrywort," Flox ordered.

There was a puff of air as the creature darted off somewhere into the bowels of the store. I heard some crashes and bangs echoing off in the distance.

Flox shook his head sadly. "Good fleas are so hard to find," he lamented.

I acknowledged the truism. Scooter just scratched.

Finally Kolkus hopped back to the counter, and placed a battered can of Jarmank's Essence of Worrywort in front of me.

"Finest brand on the market," the shopkeeper said. "Straight from Transylvania. Now, let me see if I can find the coprolite. Back in a jiff'."

It actually took him a goodly time before returning with a bottle of Levons's Coprolitus Eruditus, manufactured in Germania.

"Potent stuff," Flox noted.

"Do you have any smaller portions?" I asked.

"Sorry, that's just how it comes, and I can't break down a container. As you know, this one has to be imported. There are very strict limitations on its use."

"Very well, then, how about the hogbane?"

"How fresh does it have to be?"

"Fresh!" I said. "Picked within a day or two at most."

"Maybe," he finally said. "As I noted earlier, this is not the best time to find good hoggies. You might say it's the bane of my existence, ha, ha!"

Scooter jumped from my shoulder to the counter, and said: "That's not very funny."

"Perhaps the problem lies with the perceptor," the proprietor said.

"And perhaps *not!*" my companion said.

Flox held up both hands. "No problem," he said. "No problem. At Doctor Flox's the customer is always right. *Kolkus!*"

When the giant flea arrived, his master said, "Hogbane!"—and off went the strange creature.

"Why do you use fleas to fetch and carry?" Scooter asked.

"Tradition," Flox replied. "Also, fleas are immune to many of the effects of the herbs and drugs they transport. That's not the case with certain other creatures, including man."

"What do you feed them?"

"Ha, ha, ha: non-paying customers!" the shopkeeper said.

Scooter decided at that point once again to seek the refuge of my shoulder. Flox was not the kind of man that you'd ever wish to cross. He had too many friends and too many options at his disposal.

Finally, Kolkus returned with the desired herb tied together in a bunch with a yellow ribbon. As Flox had indicated, it wasn't prime—the snappers were not as active as I would have liked—but it would have to do nonetheless.

"I've got a special today on Crap-a-Lot," Flox said.

"No thanks," I said. "I don't usually have a problem in that department."

"You never know! What about you, Scoot?"

But my companion had jumped down to the nearby counter once more, and was playing with a large, violet caterpillar that suddenly arched, hissed, and altered its hue to a very bright orange.

"Ooh, I would be careful there, my furry friend," the shop-keeper said. "Purplepillars are great for cleaning up horehound infestations, but you don't want to make them mad. They have a very nasty spray that'll make you wish you weren't covered with all that hair."

Scooter abruptly backed away from the foot-long creature after it started hissing at it, and hopped back once more on my shoulder. I paid Flox his fee, and then we went looking for a place to eat.

I remembered an inn in the Ishtar District, The Dead Kine, which featured the image of a steer on its back, its feet sticking straight up (a painting *not* drawn from life!). If the place was still there, it would surely be worth visiting anew!

CHAPTER TWELVE
"I'VE SEEN YOU
BEFORE, MY FRIEND"

"Morpheús!" I heard the scream echoing in my dreams. *"Morpheús!"*

I was back home in Barstölný again, after a day in Asshyria. It must have been the middle hour of the night.

"Scooter!" I yelled, "I need your help!"—and I ran straight to my *officina*—my workroom—where I had the double-orbs chained together.

"What's the matter, Master?" the wherret asked.

"Niobë's calling me. Something's wrong."

"Oh, fie and fiddlesticks, Sir! You're worse than a hungry hamadryad."

But I was already starting to synchronize the power of the sky-orbs, something that required the most delicate of controls. I'd made several refinements to the process to shorten the time necessary to attain enfoldment, and with Scooter's assistance, I was able to focus directly on the energy signature needed to reach the distant woman.

"What's wrong?" I asked Niobë, when I felt the link finally forged.

"Thank the Goddess you're there," she said, and I suddenly had a fuller representation of her personality—her soul, if you will—than ever before. I could feel her raw emotions pressing at me through the æther. "I'm losing control here. He's been pushing me to generate more forecasts. He wants to make a move against his rival, but I can't tell him anything more, because somehow it's tied to my own possible destiny. You know that hypatomancers can't access their own futures, but he doesn't understand this, and so now he's punishing me. What can I do, Morpheús?"

"Who? *Who's* punishing you?"

"My captor—Lord Sadokéy Drugániş. He has total power over me. I'm watched at irregular intervals, and my privacy is interrupted without warning. Now he's reduced my food to a barely sustainable level. What can I do?" she repeated.

"Can expand your link into a transit-mirror?" I asked.

Scooter shook its head "no" at me.

"What's a transit-mirror?" Niobë asked.

"What do you employ to move quickly from one place to another on your world?"

"Why, we use zip-ports, of course. It takes three individuals to operate the ætheroprobe—a foreseer-mage to pull the energy signature from the void, and two drones to help generate the beam."

"And we have transit-mirrors," I said, sighing. "I had no idea that magick differed so greatly from one realm to another."

"Master," Scooter interjected, "this is why it's almost impossible to both come and go via extremely attenuated links to the Otherworlds. Even if one can make the difficult transition from here to there, the problem of getting back again becomes almost insurmountable, due to alterations in the reality of the destination world."

"What about smaller objects?" I asked my companion. "Could I push something like a stone through the link?"

"Possibly—but what good would that do?" the wherret said.

"I don't know—yet! But maybe I can think of something that'd help. *Wait!* What about *me* foreseeing Sadokéy's future? There'd be no prohibition against that. Could you send something small of his, something that he once owned, through the link?"

"I don't know," she said. "I've never tried something like that with this makeshift setup."

"Do you actually have something of his that you could use?"

The æther was nearly silent for a brief interval, with just the hissing of the spirit-space to remind us that the aperture was still open.

"Yes," the prisoner finally said, sighing out loud, "Yes, I do."

"Then find and bring it to the cup," I said.

After another brief interval, Niobë returned and said: "I have it here."

"Now, concentrate all of your energy on reinforcing the link between us. Scooter, I need everything you have as well. I can feel the strands strengthening. Soon, very soon now! When I tell you to proceed, the connection will abruptly break as part of the ætheric counter-reaction, so be very careful."

"I will," both Niobë and Scooter said simultaneously.

"Drop the item into the cup and push it with your mind towards me!" I ordered.

I could feel the snap as the strands abruptly severed, and I jerked away from the twin sky-orbs, knowing what would happen next. The rebounding energy flung the object out of the link at high speed, but Scooter was still able to catch the thing before it smashed itself against the wall. Despite its high energy, it could not defeat a wherret's innate strength.

My companion brought it to me in one four-fingered paw. It was still smoking.

"It looks like a seal of some sort," I said, examining what appeared to be a dull green stone.

When it had cooled sufficiently, I took it from my familiar, and turned it over several times. It was designed to fit within a human hand—or something very much like it. On the flat bottom an image was etched right into the surface. I had some moving-clay in a jar on my shelf, and I rolled it out onto my workbench. Then I used the green stone to stamp-impress the surface, and stepped back to see the result.

The image thus revealed was the bird-creature that I'd encountered in my nightmare, with an obvious crown perched on its pointy little head.

"Well, well, well," I said, "I've seen you before, my friend."

CHAPTER THIRTEEN
"YOU CAN NEVER TRULY ESCAPE"

"What are these avian creatures?" I asked Niobë that evening, when we made contact again. I sent Scooter to bed so we could talk privily.

"They're our overseers," she said. "They came here through a rift created in the void, one they created themselves. They're few in number, but they had weapons superior to ours. They rule through fear, and through intermediaries who are willing to compromise their humanity. They've spread from world to world throughout this sector. If we could just seal the tear in the æther, I have no doubt we could drive them out, even with their fancy toys."

"And your captor is…."

"Yes, he's a human nobleman who willingly works with them to enslave his own people, I'm ashamed to say. I'm also sorry to ask this question, but I need to know—what's your interest in all this, Morpheús? What's your interest in *me*?"

Her question took me aback. I mean, what could I say? What did I understand of the situation myself? I was acting like an adolescent, going off on tangents to embrace an adventure whose dimensions were ultimately unfathomable. This certainly wasn't the act of a rational man. It wasn't even the act of a *thinking* man.

"I don't know," I finally said. "I…I'm tired, Niobë. I'm tired of my life and this world and my situation and my, my awful routine. I'm tired of constantly having to peddle lies to the

Queen, to the Church, to almost everyone with whom I deal on an everyday basis. I see pieces of the future of anyone I touch or reach out to—fragmented forecasts that I have to keep hidden within myself—and as a result, I can see nothing *of* myself, ever. I have no life outside of Court.

"In my world, the talent that I have is exceedingly rare. There are no others with whom I can share my work. The revelations that I see reflected back from my clients, great and small, are restrained from repetition by the oaths that I took when I entered into this profession—and I cannot usually repeat them even to those who seek the so-called 'truth'. They don't want the truth. They want me to tell them pabulum fantasies that they can imagine themselves living. And when I do have an occasion to exercise my powers, either the recipient doesn't believe me, or tries to find some way around the inexorable working-out of fate.

"I want to achieve something new, something different, something that will lend a little excitement and meaning to my life. I want to reinvent myself, if that's possible."

"You can never truly escape yourself," Niobë said. "I know—I've tried. Now I'm a prisoner, a plaything kept by my master to help guide him in his persecution of my own people. All I want is to get away—but if I succeed in escaping to another world, then I'd be abandoning my friends and family and all those I ever knew here. So, what's the right thing to do, Morpheús?"

"We're a fine pair," I said. "Each of us wants to flee our present situation for something better—only we don't know what that is. And our talent doesn't allow us to forecast our own destinies, so we really understand no more about our options than anyone else. Forsooth, soothsayer, heal thyself!"

She laughed out loud then, for the first time in my hearing, and it was as if the summer sun suddenly emerged from behind a cloud and lit the dark landscape of my soul. I abruptly felt young again, young and vital and full of good cheer. I could do anything. I *would* do anything!

"I'm going to travel to the Otherworlds, no matter what it

takes," I said. "I'm going to find Naprimér, and I'm going to rescue you and your people. I don't know how I'll accomplish this, but I *will* do it. I will make a difference in the universe, or die trying. This is my pledge to you, my dear demoiselle."

"I'm touched, kind Sir, to the very bottom of my heart. But you should know I'm no maiden lady. I've been married, though my husband is now dead. My children are grown. I retain a youthful appearance, as many mages do, but the scars are there for the discerning eye to see."

"But you keep your face enveiled," I said.

"That's our custom here. An unmarried lady, even a widow, may not be viewed by strangers. And I'm not such a libertine that I can readily dispense with years of inbred training. So forgive me this trespass, that I retain at least that much of my privacy."

"I do forgive you," I said, "If you will forgive my occasional ill humor."

"I don't find you...." There was a rattling noise off in the distance. "Oh, Goddess, I've lost track of the time! Someone's coming.... I must go. Goodbye, dear Morpheús, goodbye!"

Then the link went dead. I was left with a faint aura of hope tingling in my breast, for the first time in a great many years. I also had to ponder the ways and means that would be required to complete this long trek. For I was absolutely determined now: I would resign my commission of state and leave this place, if necessary for good!

But I had some things that needed to be accomplished first.

CHAPTER FOURTEEN
"WE'LL ALWAYS HAVE PARIS"

A conditional foretelling is the most difficult act that a hypatomancer can attempt, particularly when the subject is absent. That's why it's so important to have a physical object available that's been used or worn by, or is connected closely to, the person being analyzed. Under the proper conditions, it can provide a psychic link to the subject that's sufficient to generate an accurate forecast of the individual's possible futures.

Jécko wanted to know what would happen if his business rival Diyán was removed from the scene. What I was doing would have been considered by most soothsayers as an unethical or even illegal commission, since it was predicated upon the necessity of a crime being committed against another—but I was past the point where I cared very much. I needed the information that the Mallet could provide me, and I was willing to do the necessary to get it. After all, neither of these men would ever be missed from gentle society.

I put Diyán the Goat's glove and the rabbit cage to one side. I'd need them later, but now they were just impediments. Scooter hopped on my shoulder to provide me moral support—it could not actually abet or interfere with my forecasting. That wasn't its talent.

I began by lighting some coal in a brazier, and let it slowly grow and burn until it was good and toasty, an hour later. Then I added a smidgeon of sulferox over the top. An ochre vapor began swirling over the center of the concentrated heat. I intoned:

> "Double, double, toil and trouble,
> Fire burn and cauldron bubble,"

these being the classic opening words of the spell first written down by that great Magus Magorum, Gullielmus Shaking-Spear, just a few decades earlier.

I'd earlier chopped the hogbane into small pieces, and now I sprinkled some of the greens over the fire. It sizzled as it struck the hot coals, its snappers writhing, adding yet another bit of smoke to the mix. The next ingredient to the spell was gargoyle dung, again in small quantities (a larger dose would have been explosive). Then came the coprolite, some more sulferox, and the worrywort.

I removed the rabbit from his cage, being careful to avoid both the teeth and hind legs, and quickly slit his throat with a wavy stiletto, allowing the blood to spurt over the open brazier. The smell of burning copper joined the rest.

I put the Goat's glove on my right hand, and held it as close to the center of the heat as I could, without actually burning myself. Then I breathed in deeply, taking the mixed vapors within my lungs.

"Fiat prædictio!" I said.

I closed my eyes and let the miasma overcome me, my body sinking slowly back onto my bench. Images began to flood my mind, just as they always did. It was only a true Magister of the Art who could sort through and make sense out of the jumbled pictures of someone's future destiny.

Slowly, ever so hesitantly, I began to sift out the strands of Diyán's perverted life—for the future depends always upon the past, and one cannot know the workings of destiny without knowing precisely what has gone before. In essence, I lived his life of crime and perfidy along with him, moving through years, even decades, in an instant, until I attained the present—and beyond!

I reached out with my mental clippers, and snipped the root of the Goat's future life at the demarcation point marked "now" in my mind. All that would have been of the man collapsed into scattered threads of lifeless ectoplasm. But how would his untimely passing affect those around him?

I saw three main courses or paths emanating from Diyán's death. In one such possible future, his departure changed very little, with his chief accomplice in crime, Bániscu, assuming control of his "family"; in this scenario, Jécko was soon targeted and eliminated in revenge. In the second alternative, the Mallet stepped in and seized the reins of command—but was himself murdered by one of the Goat's associates within the year. In the third prospect, the Goat's criminous empire fractured within weeks of his removal, leaving a power vacuum filled by outsiders. These interlopers "cleaned house" by systematically slaughtering all of the deceased man's former colleagues—including, alas, Jécko himself. By killing Diyán, Jécko would, in effect, be committing suicide.

I thought about not telling him of the consequences of his action, but decided that fair was fair—he'd commissioned me to foresee his destiny, and I would do exactly that. Also, I might have need of his services again. Still, it would give me a great deal of satisfaction to see his face once I informed him of his potentially dire future. I really didn't like the little man.

Now I turned my efforts to Sadokéy, Niobë's jailer. No point in wasting a good stew! I picked up the curious emerald seal, and pushed the end of it into the coals, until it began warming. I added more sulferox to the mix, and began inhaling the fumes again.

A series of images flashed through my brain—one, two, three, four!—pictures of strange events and curious creatures.

I saw the bird-king perched upon his nest, with Sadokéy bowed down before him. Then the human lifted his head, and I got a clear glimpse of him for the first time.

He had the appearance of a man of perhaps forty years of age, with a long, pointed beard just barely touched with gray, and a face lined deeply with crevices of concern. The burden of office appeared to have weighed on him greatly. He carried in one hand a metal implement of some kind, perhaps a sign of his office—or a weapon.

I saw Sadokëy sitting on his own throne, judging his people; and when one man began arguing with him, he touched him with the device, and either killed or knocked him senseless on the spot.

I saw him with Niobë, whose face was partially enshrouded in haze (did this mean that our futures were intertwined?); her hands were bound behind her in chains, and he was obviously passing judgment over her, with the assembled lords and ladies bearing witness. What had she done to so provoke his anger?

I saw him standing over the prone body of an older man, perhaps a relative of some kind, with blood leaking from the corpse, his face a portrait of anguish.

I saw him as a young man at his wedding, filled with joy, and Niobë emerging from the crowd and planting a kiss upon his cheek.

What did this mean?

I probed further into his being, and looked at his possible futures.

I saw him being executed by the bird-ruler for rebelling against his masters. I saw him triumphing over his rivals and living to a very old age, reviled by his people for his willing-ness to serve as the bird-men's agent. I saw his prone body lying on the tiles of Niobë's room, and her hazy figure standing over him. In this scenario, I could barely make out her form—but I knew who she was. No one can hide from a determined hypato-mancer—no one save himself, of course.

And I knew something else, too: although I could not see my own destiny, I knew that the third prospect included some-thing of myself. That was the only possible explanation for my inability to discern the woman clearly. *I was part of that future.*

I closed the spell and doused the coals with antignis powder. The heat died within seconds. Scooter swelled up to ten times its normal size, and slowly blew the fumes away. The wherret was very useful at times, besides being my one true companion.

Because of the binding that I'd placed on the creature, it could never betray me.

What I'd seen was profoundly disturbing, in many different ways. It raised questions, both about my own motivations, and those of the woman captive. How far would I be willing to go to rescue her? Whom would I kill? Would I descend down that slippery slope already blazed with trails fashioned by the likes of Jécko and the Goat? Or would I, like Tantalus, be tormented by the prospect of something good and vital being dangled eternally just beyond my reach.

I looked down at Scooter, now returned to its normal shape and visage.

"We'll always have Paris," the wherret said, canting its head to one side.

I had no idea what it was talking about—but I laughed anyway.

Sometimes life was very good indeed.

CHAPTER FIFTEEN
"WHILST I LIVE, I HOPE"

Contacting Niobë was becoming increasingly easier, either because the causeway through the æther had now become sufficiently well-demarcated with frequent use, or just because I could find that sympathetic vibration so much more readily now. More and more I found that talking to her was like taking an opiate: it was both pleasurable and habit-forming at one and the same time. I looked forward to these irregular conversations with great anticipation.

They were irregular because time flowed differently here as compared to there, and because she was wont to be interrupted by her jailers on odd occasions. We had to be careful.

The first thing I told her, the next time we talked, was what I'd determined about her captor's possible futures.

"So he's doomed to a quick death—or a life filled with ignominy," she said. "I don't know which is worse."

"I thought you hated him," I said.

"No. I despise his casual cruelty, but men are often like that, and they don't even realize it on occasion. They think it's necessary to show people, especially women, that they're strong and determined."

"That's a cynical thought."

"I don't mean to be negative, Morpheús," she said, "But I've lived a life that's seen more unhappy moments than kind ones, and sometimes I despair of escaping the bonds of my captivity— and I don't just mean the physical restraints. You and Sable are my only friends at this point, and she, well, she has her limitations, not being human. You know what I mean.

"I crave *human* interaction. You have no idea how these distant meetings of ours have enlivened my existence. If you ever went away, I think the dark parts of my soul would overwhelm me. I have no resilience anymore."

"I feel much the same way," I said. "But I despair of finding a solution to our problem. I haven't even met with Doctor Scarabbaios yet. Everything seems dependent on something else happening first. I worry that I may have to wade through so many dung-heaps on my way from here to there, that by the time I reach you, I'll be layered with the stuff. You won't recognize the sad creature that stops before you."

"I'd recognize you in whatever guise you adopted. There's something about you that no one could mistake."

"But what about the forecast I just conducted for Jécko the Mallet?" I explained to her the bargain that I'd made with the Devil Minor.

She sighed then, and sighed again before responding: "I don't know what else you could have done. I sometimes think that life is a series of small compromises, and that the bottom line for each person is that point where he or she says, 'This much, and no more.'

"I've done things of which you would probably not approve. I had my reasons, to be sure, but even I now doubt whether the actions I took were worth the sacrifice of my basic character. You'll have to judge for yourself, when I finally tell you my story. However, I can't do that now. I'm too…unwilling to risk the loss of your companionship, as distant and fragmentary as it might be. I've become dependent on these sessions. I…."

There was a long silence in the æther, although I thought I heard a sharp intake of breath.

"Are you there?" I finally asked.

"I…yes, I'm here, Morpheús. But…I can't continue. Sorry."

And then the link was broken.

"What did I say?" I asked Scooter, who had taken the opportunity to pop in at that moment, seeking its supper. I dutifully went across the room, opened a small cage, and tossed a couple of wriggling mice in its direction.

"Thank you, Master," the wherret muttered, in between smacking sounds. "Tasty-goody, that! The lady likes you, Sir, that's obvious. You like her, that's obvious too. But there's many a slip 'twixt the cup and the lip, as you've often told me, and you'd do well to remember that. I've had my share of missed opportunities—not all of them my fault, either. You surely don't think I began my life hoping to become a slave to a human soothsayer? Still, these things happen. I'm glad to be alive, though. *'Dum vivo, vero,'* as one of your philosophers once said: 'whilst I live, I hope'."

"That 'old philosopher' is responsible for a great many worm-ridden bromides," I said, "not all of them worth repeating."

I laughed out loud. "We'll either do this or we won't, Scooter, that's how it always is. Are you with me?"

"Where else could I be, Master?" the creature said. It suddenly let loose a long, juicy fart.

CHAPTER SIXTEEN
"TELL ME 'BOUT THE GOAT"

I was called back to Paltyrrha the next day, and decided to stay there until my second meeting with Jécko. The Queen was in a royal funk, and I found myself biting my tongue to avoid responding in kind. Nothing I said seemed to please her this time, neither flattery nor effusiveness.

"What's going on with Her Majesty?" I asked Lord Dóbeldan, the Chamberlain.

"The States General are pressing her to name an heir," he said. "You know how the Queen is on that topic—she regards it as a commentary on her own mortality. And besides, after that last Council meeting…."

"But I thought the word had gotten around."

"Yes, but the factions are still bickering amongst themselves. The Lords Temporal prefer one of their own—Duke Zoltán. The Lords Spiritual, on the other hand, proffer the pious possibility of Count Víka Arkátch. And the Magisterium Magorum, well, they prefer Count Istiál Bogomilovich. So it'll probably be somebody we've never heard of before!"

"I very much doubt that she'll ever name an heir," I said. "She'd rather leave it to the Byzantine Julian Emperor to nominate a successor after she's dead, or…."

"Old Stephanos? Ha, he'll probably go before she does, and his son, July, is a real lightweight. I wouldn't look for much direction there."

I agreed with him and wished him well. It might be the last

time that I saw him. Dóbeldan was getting on in years, and this journey of mine could conceivably take decades. We mages don't measure time in the same way that mere mortals do.

That night I tried to contact Niobë again, but with no success. The psychic horns might announce my presence, but no one was answering at the other end.

The next day, the Feast of Saint-Pergamos, was a good time for visiting a church, I decided—or rather, a churchyard. And so about an hour before sundown I was seated at my bench once more when Jécko the Mallet came calling.

"You got my readin'?" he asked, as he plopped down beside me. He shot a glance at the gathering shadows on the stones. "Jeez, I really don't like this place. The dead, they never stay real dead, you know what I mean?"

"Yes," I said, staying on subject, "I have what you need. And you...?"

"Yeah, and 'twasn't an easy one, neither, let me tell you. Just didn't like one of them threads. 'T'ad a real bad taste to it, you know what I mean?"

I acknowledged that I did.

"OK, then, this is how I sees it. You said there were six copies of this book. Really, though, there's eight. One's at the Borgo—but I 'spect you already knew that. There's 'nother at that magic school down in Bab'lonia—I can't speak the name. Those are the easy ones.

"Four're in...some other place. Couldn't fix 'em 'xactly, 'cause I kept gettin' these crossed signals. Meself, think it's the Otherworlds. The seventh has gone back to its maker."

"You mean...?"

"Yeah, back to Hades, I think. That's the one that bugged me. There was a...a hook attached, and I just to hope to goddamned hellfire—pardon me the 'xpression—it didn't follow me all the way home.

"The last is owned by someone named Shah Ravivarma in Ko-Kopawalior, Indushia."

"Where's that?" I asked.

"Dunno. I just find 'em, I don't go huntin' 'em."

He turned sideways and looked me in the eye. "Now, tell me 'bout the Goat," he said.

"If you dispose of your friend Diyán," I said, "You have one chance in three of taking over his business. But no matter how it turns out, the chaos caused by his passing would likely destabilize the criminal world in Paltyrrha, and you run a severe risk of being lost in the shuffle, so to speak. You would do better to deal with the devil that you know than to exchange him for an unknown rival."

"'Bout come to that notion meself," the little man acknowledged. "Have a thing now that suits me pretty fine. What I do doesn't stir up many of my enemies, and I'd rather have that than the other—with the higher risk, you see. So what you've said makes a kinda good sense to me.

"Anyways, what's so goddang special about this book?"

"You know, Jécko, 'Curiosity killed the cat.' I'll just say this: if I can get a copy, it just might help me to help someone else. I wouldn't do it for any other reason."

"Glad to hear that. You ain't such a bad sort for a magee, Morphy. Been a pleasure doin' business with you 'gain."

"And you," I said. "Hope to see you again sometime."

He looked at me rather oddly then, as he pulled himself together and began shuffling down an aisle of headstones.

"Hope so too," he coughed back over his shoulder, "But I really sorta doubt it."

CHAPTER SEVENTEEN
"SO MOTE IT BE!"

"So it's come to this, eh?" Magister Geraklíd said, frowning up at me. He held my unopened resignation spell in his right hand. "And I can't persuade you of the foolishness of this course?"

"I've made up my mind," I said. "If I continue with my present position, I will say something or do something or be something that will bring shame upon myself and my profession. Better for me to leave while my honor is yet intact. Also, as we discussed previously, I must find some better way to live my life, some better way to contribute. I don't believe that's here."

"I disagree, of course, but you already know that. Have you told the Queen?"

"No. I'll leave that to your discretion, Sir."

"Coward!" He sighed and frowned again. "Very well. It's your life, Morpheús." The Magister spoke a word of power ("*Dice!*"), tore open the piece of parchment, and listened to my voice blaring its defiance:

> "I, Oridión the Morpheús of Barstölný, do irrevocably renounce my position as Scanner Prime to the Court of the Kingdom of Kórynthia, effective this xix[th] day of July in the Year of Our Lord mdcxxii, being the xvi[th] year in the reign of Our Noble Lady and Majesty Queen Evetéria i, Long May She Reign, and the xxxvii[th] year in the reign of His Imperial Majesty Stephanos

II, Autokratôr and Byzantine Julian Emperor. By the Lord God Jesus Christ, by Thunder and by Rain, by all laws and councils and traditions of Magick, so mote it be!"

"So mote it be!" Geraklíd intoned, completing the formula and resealing the spell. He snapped the fingers of his right hand, and a fetch-gnome appeared on his desk. "The Master Morpheús's account, Flick, if you please."

Within a man's breath, the fetcher was back, holding a slip of paper and a bag of coins. My magical overseer reviewed the numbers and said: "Everything seems to be in order." He then handed it to me for my evaluation.

I scanned down the page, and gasped when I noted the total written at the bottom.

"I had no idea...," I said—and truly I didn't.

"There was, of course," Geraklíd said, "the initial deposit you made on this office fifteen years ago, plus accumulated interest, and then the individual emoluments granted to you by the Queen for each service you rendered her. Despite your somewhat dyspeptic view of Her Majesty, she has always been careful to reward those who have rewarded her. Those thousands of pounds of herring add up, you know, particularly when they accrue on an annual basis.

"In any case, this is the sum due to you according to my office's calculations. Do you accept this accounting?"

I gulped. "I do, Sir."

"Very well. Here is payment in full"—and he handed me a sack of what I thought were gold and silver pieces, but turned out to be platinum chits for thousands of gold *aurei*. I was rich! For a man who had started his life with very little means indeed, I was stunned at my sudden good fortune.

"Magister...," I began, but Geraklíd waved his hand at me to stop.

"No time for rash sentiment, my boy," he said. "What's done is done. I sincerely hope that your decision will be a good one for you. I'll miss you, of course. I've followed and nurtured your career for a long time, and I had hoped that maybe, well, one day you would…but enough of such maudlin sentiments. Take care of yourself, and when you return from your journey, wherever it takes you, please come back and tell me about it."

Then he stood up and came around his desk, something that I had never seen him do before. He put his arms around me and hugged me just once, before stepping back and signaling that my interview was over.

CHAPTER EIGHTEEN
"GIVE ME A LITTLE KISSIE"

The very next day I returned to Paltyrrha, and requested an audience with the Queen—for of course the Magister was quite correct in saying that I didn't really want to face the consequences of my actions.

Strangely, I was ushered to her private quarters, where she shooed away her attendants when I made my appearance.

She wasn't wearing her wig—that was the first thing I noticed. Her neat gray hair was carefully combed back over her head. I dropped to my right knee. She held out her hand, and then helped me to my feet.

"Majesty," I began, "I...."

"You're leaving me, aren't you?" she interrupted. "I knew something was wrong. You know, people think that I'm such a simpleton because I spend all my time focusing on frivolities, but I'm my father's daughter, Master Morpheús, and you should never forget that. The blood of King Tighris runs through my veins."

She lowered her face and rested her eyes upon the mottled blood of the carpet.

"Everyone leaves me in the end—my father, mother, brothers, everyone. In the end, the burden always returns to me. I'm the only one in the entire Kingdom who doesn't have the leisure to walk away. For me, the only possible rescue is death."

Then she abruptly changed the subject: "Where are you going, Morphy?"

I thought about prevaricating, but decided that I owed her the simple truth.

"The Otherworlds," I said. "If I can find a way there, I'll try to rescue a woman who's being held against her will."

"How utterly romantic!" she said, perking up again. "I didn't know you had it in you! You've finally surprised me, soothsayer. I've never actually believed your forecasts, by the way—they were always too, uh, carefully crafted, if you know what I mean. All except the last one."

I nodded my head in acquiescence, before saying: "I've asked you this once before: do you *really* want to know what's going to happen, Majesty?"

She looked me squarely in the eyes then. "No," she finally said. "You carry a burden almost as terrible as mine, Morpheús. I can see that now. You can never tell anyone the truth, can you?"

"Rarely, Majesty."

"You may call me 'Eve,' my dear seer, for this one private moment. And as the first Eve once said to the first Adam, 'Partake now of this forbidden fruit'."

She reached down and opened a jewelry box, removing a small pin therefrom. It was fashioned into the shape of a small silver hand, holding upright in its grasp a stone unlike any I'd ever seen. It flashed in the glow light, its amber depths swirling and moving, almost as if it were alive.

"What is it?" I asked.

She reached up and fastened it to the upper left side of my chest. I felt a sudden tingle just over my heart, almost an itch that I couldn't scratch.

"I honestly don't know, Morphy," she said. "This was given to me by my great-great-aunt, Princess Kallista, who never married, but spent her days exploring the farthest edges of Psairothi science; she was a student of Queen Rÿna. Most people, including her brother, King Zakháry ii, were afraid of her, but not me. She was always kind and gentle to me.

"On the day after my tenth birthday, I found her sitting at

the center of the maze in the Hanging Garden, her legs curled under her, contemplating a book of glyphs created by Queen Grigorÿna.

"'I was sorry to miss your celebration yesterday,' she said, looking up from her reading and removing her embroidered shawl. 'But I'm not much for parties, as you already know. I find them...tedious and distracting.'

"'There were lots and lots of lords and ladies there,' I said, sitting down next to her. "Most of them I didn't really know. But they all seemed very happy to see me, and they gave me just oodles of presents.'

"'So why aren't you playing with them?' she asked, raising her left eyebrow in that expression that always meant, in our hidden language, 'We both know the answer to *that* one!'

"'I have no one to play with.'

"'What about your brother?' she asked.

"'Zacky's seven years older than me, and he says he's not interested in girlie things, and to just leave him alone. And the girls at Court, they'll play with me, because they have to, but they don't really like me much, I can tell. They say I cheat when I win all the games. I don't cheat, I never cheat, but I win anyway, even when I try to lose. Why's that, Auntie?'

"'Perhaps it's your talent, Evie. That's one of the reasons why I asked you to meet me here—that, and to give you *my* presents. Have you ever wondered about your heritage and what it means?'

"'Well, I'm from the family of old Tiger the Founder, aren't I?'

"She laughed: 'Something like that. Yes, King Tighris was our progenitor. He came here more than a thousand years ago from somewhere in the east—no one knows where—and established himself in a place he called Paltyrrha. And in his bloodline, from his day down to ours, runs a strain of the talent that helped give rise to the Psairothi race in eastern Nova Europa. But that talent expresses itself differently in each of us, to a greater or lesser degree.

"'So the first of the three presents that I give you on this, your first Decade Day, is the way to self-knowledge. *Your* talent, my dearest niece, is Survival. Whatever may come in your life, whatever hardships or sorrows you might face—and they will be many—you will survive the test intact. You will never be a leader in the race, but you will always be the one who wins— just as you now prevail in all the petty games you play in the schoolyard.

"'But there's a price to be paid for this knowledge, Evie—oh, Lord Above, there is always a price! So my second gift to you is this'—she suddenly dropped her book to the ground, reached around, and grabbed my head in both her hands before I could react or stop her, holding me so tightly that it almost hurt.

"'Auntie!' I yelled, now *very* afraid of who and what she was, and seeing her, perhaps, for the first time in her true guise. But she never let me go, and her dark brown eyes bored down into my soul as she did something to me inside my mind. Then she released me, but I was crying and shaking so violently by this point that I didn't have the strength to run away.

"'Wh-what did you do?' I bawled, rubbing my weepy lids with the backs of my hands.

"'You're not naturally a strong person, Evie,' Kallista said, 'But now I've enabled you always to say "No"—and to mean it and make it stick—and to understand when it's necessary, and also when it's not. And you will have to say "No" on a great many occasions in your coming days: "No" to suitors, "No" to advisers, "No" to those same lords and ladies who attended your natal day celebration. You will have to say "No" in order to prevail.

"'One day you'll be a Queen, and your one task, whenever that happens, will be to hold the Kingdom together. So long as you live, so long as you say "No," Kórynthia will stand.'

"'But...I don't want to be....'"

"'I know,' she said, rather sadly. 'You'd rather lose the games and be like everyone else. I'm sorry that that's not an option for you. The course of your life is tied to a larger skein already woven in the æther, and no one save the greatest of mages can alter that reality, even when things are fragmenting at the edges, as they are now.

"'But the third gift that I present to you will help you to cope.'

"And then she reached up and pulled a small leather pouch on a string from between her breasts, lifted it over her head, and opened the draw. She drew forth my left hand, and placed in my palm the artifact that I just gave you.

"'This is the Hand of Morlock,' Auntie said. 'It has very great powers. With it you'll always be able to tell who's lying to you, who's your true friend and direst enemy, and what course to take. All of these things you will "feel" instinctively, for you'll be able to translate the words from the gobbledygook thrown at you.

"'But, Little One, this is the kind of gift that must be passed on to another, as it was passed to me originally, and is now given to you. The Hand travels a journey outside of our lives, and we cannot forestall its departure. You will know the time and place, many years hence.'

"She could or would not tell me more, and she died the following year; but the Hand helped me on many subsequent occasions to sort out fact from fiction, and my life unfolded as she predicted. So I'm happy to present this to you to take on your quest 'out there' I'm told that its benefits accrue in different ways with different mages."

"This is much too much, Majesty," I said

"But it looks 'just right' from where I sit. So you must accept my gift: it's my royal command! I do wish you Godspeed, my friend. Try not to think ill of me in years to come.

"We have many powers of our own, the sons and daughters of Tighris, as well you know, and I have an intimation that this is the last time that you and I shall ever meet, at least in this fashion. My vision quavers with uncertainty. You have served me faithfully and well. You have my blessing for your venture, and you shall have this also."

She handed me a rolled-up scroll. I unfurled it and scanned

down the page. The parchment listed the award of a landed estate not far from my home.

"You have but to register this grant before the local magistrate in your county, and the thousand acres are yours. It's not much, but I'm told the place is forested and suitable for the raising of beefs and hogs. Better than salt herring, I suspect!"

Then she laughed—a real laugh this time, not the phony chuckle she maintained before her minions.

"Thank you, Majesty," I said. I was truly humbled by her generosity.

"Give me a little kissie before you leave, Morpheús," she commanded, and I leaned down and bussed her lips. "Now go! And do us proud, no matter what else happens!"

CHAPTER NINETEEN
"NO SAFE WAY TO GET THERE FROM HERE"

My next stop was Julianople, where I met again with Doctor Árbogast, my old teacher. I told him of my decision and what had transpired thus far.

"Do you know of this place in Indushia, Magister?" I asked.

"The subcontinent of the Indies is closed to magical transit except by permission of their Emperor—and that's rarely given. As a result, very few of us have ever traveled there; the great peninsula is enclosed on three sides by very high mountains, and is only accessible through the sea. The easiest way to reach there is via Serendip, the independent island kingdom lying along its southeast flank, which allows free and easy travel to and from its shores."

"I know nothing of these places," I acknowledged.

"Have you thought about what you're going to do when you get there?" he asked.

"Actually, no."

"You have to assume that the treasure will be closely guarded, with both physical impediments and psychic spells. This is not a one-man job, Morpheús. You're going to need a team to assist you, and you're going to have to get yourself trained in the art and science of weaponry and self-defense."

"It simply had not occurred to me...."

"Then you'd better focus your mind on the problem at hand, my boy!" Árbogast said, "And soon! You can't out-think an opponent you don't know. You can trick him, you can over-power him, you can overrule him, you can overwhelm him, you can do all sorts of things, you might even be able to mage him, but you better have a plan in place, and some options that you can rely on—including your own physical prowess.

"In the meantime, you can read Šalgü'ođ den'Alver on *Sailing to Serendip*, and Bromius Barlévin's *Indushian Days*. They'll be helpful as background material."

"Speaking of books, Sir, I looked up Phôstêridês, as you suggested, but he really says very little about *The Necropompeion*, and there doesn't seem to be any other source for the story." Then I told him what the Finder had said.

"Well, as I think I mentioned to you," the professor said, "I've never actually seen a copy myself, nor has anyone else that I know of. Even Doctor Scarabbaios acknowledged to me once that, while he was convinced that the thing existed, he couldn't confirm anything about it. It might not even be a 'book' in the conventional sense. Implements of great power can sometimes morph into various shapes, and this one has the feeling of being something like that.

"I just knew of the copy supposedly housed in the Borgo—but that Library won't even confirm the existence of the volume, much less allow anyone to access it. None of the magical Bibliothecas in Asshyria claim to own one, despite what your Finder indicated. And who knows who this ruler in Indushia might be.

"Whatever this volume is, if you're unfortunate enough to locate it, be very, very careful. These kinds of objects are inherently dangerous, even when you come well prepared. This 'thing' was created to accomplish something that you don't know or understand. Without being aware of its purpose or magical characteristics, how can you securely handle it?"

"I'll worry about that when I find it," I said. "Right now, I just need to get the information from Doctor S. about how to travel safely through the Otherworlds."

"Well, Morphy, there *is* no safe way to get there from here—

or back again, for that matter. If there were, it'd happen more frequently, and we'd all know about it, wouldn't we?

"And as for Doctor Scarabbaios, he was never well liked or respected by his colleagues. Some of my associates questioned whether he'd even *been* to the Otherworlds, since he had no proof to offer. I mean, there was one odd flower that he showed us that he'd inadvertently tucked away in a pocket of his vest— but it could have come from anywhere. He had a stone of power in his possession, but many such artifacts exist in the æther-sphere, and every charlatan from here to Serendip possesses such things. There wasn't a single thing that he showed us that could be demonstrated to have derived from a world other than our own. His stories were colorful, to be sure, and his adventures beyond, well, beyond anyone's experience. We had—we have—nothing to compare them with. So who knows where he went, and for how long. *I* believed him, but many didn't. I think it's one of the reasons why he became so embittered of the profession, and retreated to his mountain hideaway in the Alps.

"*The Necropompeion*, if it exists in any form, is unique in its characteristics and configurations. That much I can tell you for certain. So expect the unexpected, and protect yourself from its potential hazards, whatever they might be, as best you can."

"Thank you again for your advice, Sir," I said.

My head was swirling. My former instructor was right: I had a long way to go before I'd be ready for the trip. Fortunately, I now had the financial means to accomplish whatever needed to be done.

CHAPTER TWENTY
"LET'S HAVE SQUABS WITH EVERY MEAL!"

When I returned home that evening to Barstölný, I felt free for the first time in decades. No more classes, no more studies, no more obligations, no more requirements, no more *any*thing except what I wanted to do myself. I hadn't realized until now how much I'd resented my old life.

Well, things were about to change, and for the positive, too. I'd take control of my existence once and for all. Ha! As if Life, God, or Fate *ever* made that ever-present fantasy a reality.

I gave Scooter an account of my activities while munching on a chunk of roasted lamb that Madame Helena, one of my neighbors, had generously left for me. I think she fancied me as a potential suitor for her thirty-something maiden lady daughter, Susannah, since, by appearance, I was of a similar vintage. Alas, she had no notion of our *true* difference in age, which was considerable—although that would not have removed me, I suspect, from Madame H.'s rather short list of prospects. The sad thing was, I really liked Susannah, and vice versa, although we had nothing in common; and I knew the lady well enough to know that she no intention of marrying anyone.

The lamb was truly excellent, spiced with mint and covered with a sweet glaze. Scooter inhaled several live squabs it'd harvested from a garden nest—crunch, crunch, crunch.

"You ought to be ashamed of yourself," I said between bites, "Stifling the pitiful squeaks of those poor, defenseless pigeons."

"Master, 'those poor defenseless pigeons,' as you so prosaically put it, are taking over the entire property by the hundreds, pooping all over the roof, lintels, and sills, and attracting flies and other vermin. They're like rats with wings:

"Squabs, squabs, the musical fruit.
"The more I eat, the more I toot.
"The more I toot, the better I feel.
"Let's have squabs with every meal!"

Then it belched out loud, a surprisingly massive sound emanating from that compact, cylindrical body.

"Puh-lease," I said. "Be nice."

"Why?"

"If for no other reason than to please me." I then related an account of my day's activities.

"We haven't even met this Doctor Scarabbaios yet, Sir, and I already dislike him," the wherret said.

"He is a hypatomancer," I said, "Although I don't believe he's actually practiced in many a decade."

"Then why does he want this book?"

"I don't know and I don't care," I said, "so long as I get the knowledge I need from him on how to traverse the Otherworlds quickly and safely."

"I think you're chasing a pipedream, Master," the creature said. "There are no free rides to the Otherworlds."

"'Men go and come, but Earth abides,'" I said, quoting *Ecclesiastes* and the Stewart.

"Nothing abides forever, not even this lovely place, Sir. You should know that from your own observations. When the roof fails, you'll be dashing for shelter just as fast as the other roaches that've been uncovered."

I got up from the table to summon Mistress "Weasely," my ever-present cleaner-upper, and felt a sudden dizziness as the light from the chandelier caught the amber gem tucked between the fingers of the silver hand the Queen had given me.

"What's that?" Scooter asked, twisting its head to one side back and forth to get a better view of the glittery interior of the stone.

"Her Majesty called it 'The Hand of Morlock,'" I said. "It's an artifact given to her by Princess Kallista many years ago, and now presented to me for our journey."

"May I see it, Sir?" it finally said.

"Of course." I unfastened the gift, and handed it to Scooter.

"Oh, my!" the creature said, when it touched its right front paw. Its whole body stiffened briefly. "That's...different."

"Different...how?" I asked.

"Well, Sir, most implements, even those with magical over-tones, have resonances that are predictable within certain ranges. Some may be more sophisticated than others, but most can be categorized by type, origin, and imposed powers.

"But this one—this isn't like anything else I've ever encoun-tered. It has multiple levels of...of...the word doesn't exist in your language. It's very ancient, and so far above the average power stone that there's no comparison. I have no idea what it's capable of."

"Let me see it again," I said, and the wherret placed the thing in my left palm. I lifted it as close to my eyes as I could, trying to fathom the details etched into the small silver image.

It was a nude man of about thirty years, I finally realized, its anatomical detail perfectly realized, poised as if leaping for the heavens, and holding between its two outstretched arms, high above its diadem-crowned head, an amber gem. There was something about the face that seemed familiar to me—and then I realized that it somewhat resembled that of my ancestor, Parakôdês the Mage, although for some reason I didn't feel that it actually *was* him.

I turned the mini-statue over as I examined every facet of the exquisitely sculpted image, and realized that the bottom of one bare foot had a slightly rough surface. I held it up to the light, but I couldn't make out what was there, if anything.

"Scooter, my view-glass, if you please," I said.

When the wherret brought the small square piece of framed glass, I spoke a word to activate the spell it contained, and placed it over the silver foot. Etched in minute archaic Greek letters from the big toe to the heel was a name:

ΜΑΘΟΥΡΕΙΝΟΣ

…or Mathoureinos in transliteration, or Mathurin in the common tongue.

I repeated the name out loud, and then said to Scooter: "Never heard of him."

The wherret's eyes opened wide in a brief look of startlement.

"What? You know something?"

"Master, the name is roughly similar to one I heard a very long time ago, but it can't possibly be the same being, for the context is all wrong. No, it simply cannot be."

"Then let me check further," I said, and walked across the room to the bookshelves there. I was looking for Adrian's *Mages of Antiquity*, which I found remarkably quickly. I laid the volume open on the reader stand, and intoned, "*Inveni*! Mathurin-*cum-varietatibus.*" Nothing happened for a moment, and then pages fluttered back and forth quickly, until they settled again, a dim light illuminating one paragraph on the right-hand page.

"This is very interesting, Scooter:

> "According to an account in Zélénÿ's *Con Brio*, Parakôdês derived from the Other-Places, being a scion of the House of Matyrinos the Maker. And it was back to those realities that he ultimately returned, having sired a son to act in his stead on New Europa.

"I've never heard this tale before. I wonder if there's anything else on the subject."

I expanded the spell, this time to include my entire library of 456 volumes, and several more tomes flopped onto the stand, their pages riffling to and fro until the appropriate references were found. I checked them quickly.

"Well, look at this: Dûn-Pålestal states:

> "Today I presented a paper on ætherial order to the group [of mages], but Denormo countered by pointing to the *Sixth Dialogue* of Parakôdês, who stated that 'chaos is the normative state of ætherspace; without some imposed structure, such as that provided by Aulax or Maturin, regular transit through the ætherial realms would become exceedingly difficult, if not impossible.'"

I looked at the next item spread-eagled before me, and shook my head: "Nothing new in this one." The fourth book was written in a language that I didn't understand, so I commanded, "*Converti!*"—and got another reference to the House of Mathurin. The fifth tome was more interesting, but the pages were cracked and crumbling, and again had to be translated. I read the section out loud for the wherret:

> "In his *Last Dialogue*, Parakôdês says that he has been recalled by his [ancestor] to the Heart-World, that all [__] are needed to fight the incursion of the outsiders, lest Chaos return to the [__]. He leaves his successor, Phôstêridês, to guide their development until he can return. He will carry the group's good wishes to Overlord Mathoureinos.

"Evidently," I said, "Many of these early mages were connected by blood, as well as by study and inclination."

"That may be, Sir," Scooter said, "but how does that affect our proposed journey into ætherspace?"

"If *this*"—I held up the amulet—"is indeed a representation of the ancient mage Mathurin, perhaps the implement was either created by him personally, or imbued with some of his power or authority by Parakôdês. In either case, it might give us an edge in finding our way through the difficulties that we're sure to find in transiting to the Otherworlds."

"Yes, but how will you access whatever power's there—if, indeed, it has anything that could help us?"

"I don't know," I admitted. "Perhaps we need to try a few experiments."

"And perhaps not!" the creature said. "This…this thing is chock full of energy, Master. You just don't go probing something with such huge potential without enormous fail-safes in place."

"Uh, I know that, of course," chagrined to be read the basic rules of magical experimentation by my familiar. I was just frustrated by having something quite literally in hand that might be useful to us—and having no easy way of assessing its potential utility.

I finally shook my head and reattached the pin to my chest. I'd sleep on the problem, and maybe something would suggest itself. So I retired to my quarters, and settled down with Barlévin, *Musings and Meanderings*, Volume XLI. That was as efficacious, in almost every instance, as a sleeping draught.

And so it proved to be.

CHAPTER TWENTY-ONE
"THE TENTH DAY
OF BLOSSOMING"

I received the message, astonishingly enough, while I was sitting in my *officina* the next day, contemplating whether or not to try contacting Niobë. Suddenly I *knew* she was there at the other end, and I had only to focus on the sky-orb to reach her almost immediately. The more we talked, the easier it became to traverse the ætherweb.

"I wondered if I could reach you from my end," she said, when the wavy picture of her veiled face appeared before me. "I created a bigger pool of water this time, using a small bowl that I had Sable beg from one of the handmaidens who serve me. It gives me a larger stage from which to launch my soul through the void."

I immediately tried focusing on the practical. "Is there any way you can broaden the contact sufficiently to facilitate the transit of a greater object—or even of yourself?"

"Not possible," she said, her voice downcast. "The container doesn't allow me to stabilize the image sufficiently. Even now, you can see how wavery the outline of my body seems—I perceive yours in the same way. If I could freeze the water and polish the surface, it might be possible—but I can't do that with the limited materials I have at hand. Perhaps during the winter months...."

She had a slight hitch in her voice. "I...I was just wondering what you were doing today."

I told her of my recent adventures with Queen Evetéria, the Magister, and Doctor Árbogast, but for some reason said nothing about the Hand of Morlock. "So you see," I said, "With each step forward I take, I open the way to others that must be taken before I can make any progress. So I now know where I can find the tome, but I don't know how to retrieve it. Why are things always so difficult?"

"I wish I knew," Niobë said. "My whole life has been like that—and now I wonder whether any of it amounted to anything. All those pretensions…gone! All those posturings…worthless!

"Here I am, rotting away in this prison cell—a nice prison cell, you understand, but still a confinement against my will— and I have no freedom to do anything but converse with you. That's the only real pleasure I have left, Morpheús, and I do treasure these moments, few as they are.

"Yes, Sable does provide me with some company, bless her little being, but I'm not allowed to socialize much with any of the servants—in fact, I've been told that if I do so beyond the level of everyday conversation, *they'll* be the ones punished. I can't allow that. So I talk to Sable, and she talks back (within her limits), and I talk to myself (a lot!), and I talk to you (all too infrequently)—and of all these things, the one that gives me most hope and pleasure and even occasional laughter—well, that's you, my distant friend.

"I wonder some nights whether I've made you up to keep myself from going mad. Have I, Morpheús? Do you really exist somewhere? Please tell me that you do, that I'm not crazy."

"How long have you been held captive?" I asked.

"I don't know for sure. Ten years? Fifteen? I was taken by Lord Sadokéy in spring of the year 4422—the Tenth Day of Blossoming, just when my flowers were starting to show their faces. I've not seen them since. Oh, how I miss the garden and the open air and the three moons and the whirring of the insects and, and, just all of it! I miss everything."

"We're in the midst of summer here," I said. "Such a beautiful day outside. Not too hot, as it often is this time of year.

Hmm. I think I'll try an experiment."

I picked up the pair of sky-orbs, trying to maintain the psychic link between the two globes, while keeping the distant contact with my far-off lady.

"What are you doing? I'm losing you!" she said.

"Just hold on, if you can."

I walked very carefully out the open doorway of my laboratory, putting one careful step in front of another, and yelled at Scooter to help me. When the creature appeared, I was waiting at the outside exit to my garden.

"Open the door, please," I ordered.

When it complied, I walked slowly out into the sunlight, and sat down on a stone bench next to a fountain. A slow stream of water trickled from the mouth of a fish-sculpture down into a small pond where guppies and tadpoles and minnows swam. Then I laid the orbs down next to me, firming up the ætherspace connection once again with my distant friend.

"Where are you?" she said, her voice coming through the link with an almost hollow echo.

I didn't reply, but concentrated my essence and let myself drift, releasing the restraints on my soul—and letting her see with my eyes and hear with my ears.

"Oh, Goddess!" she suddenly exclaimed. "Oh Great Goddess Above! I...I can...." Then she started to cry. I could almost feel the tears coming through the link. "To...be...outside again! To be free again! Oh thank you, thank you, thank you! Such a gift of light and life and liberty! No one has ever done anything like this for me! No one! Ever!"

I said nothing, but just sat there, seeing the world recreated anew through her starved eyes and parched being, and knowing that this was the best thing that I had done in a long, long time. I remained stationary for just over an hour, until the moment came for her supper to be delivered (time ran differently there), and we had to break the link.

Then I sat by myself until the sun started to set, and hunger and desire drove me inside once again.

"I think it's real," I told Scooter. "I don't know how else to measure this, this hollow I have left in me when she's gone."

Scooter usually had a wry response for everything, but it made no reply on this one occasion, just continuing to munch on its salted herring. Crunch, crunch, crunch, was all I heard. So I began peeling and eating a piece of fruit, spitting out the rough pips one by one.

What the bloody Hell was I going to do? How was I going to get from here to there? And what would I do once I got there?

I had many questions, but no answers.

CHAPTER TWENTY-TWO
"I DON'T HOLD NO STOCK WITH THEM BELCHERS"

His name was Sergeant Strook. He was an ex-soldier in the Byzantine Royal Guards, and he'd been recommended to me by a former classmate, Brén the Single-Minded, as we used to call him. Strook had retired from the ranks after a particularly vicious campaign, and had used his savings to open a small studio in Julianople, where he trained the sons of the gentry in the use of epée and saber and the basic military arts—everything, he said, except guns.

"I don't hold no stock with them belchers," he stated, standing up straight. "They're fine when you're just a-shootin' at a mass of idiots a-marchin' right at you. But when the shit has to be shoveled, Sir, well, you gotta know how to use a bow and lance and sword and knife, both a-comin' and a-goin'. That's what I do."

It sounded good enough for me, and so I hired him to put me through an intensive self-defense course for six weeks. When I told him I'd had basic calisthenics and weapons training as part of my schooling decades ago, he just laughed.

"You ain't done nothin' with that stuff since, right, Sir?"

I nodded.

"Then you gots to be put back into shape again. I can't work the monkish miracles, man, you gotta understand that. I can teach you a few basic moves, even get you into an exercise thing—but the rest is up to you. And you're never a-goin' to be more than barely basic, even under the best of times. You know that."

I did, alas, and so I underwent a month and a half of sheer misery, presaging the agonies of the afterlife if I didn't straighten up my act. My muscles were just not designed to perform the kinds of motions that Sergeant Strook put me through. And it didn't seem to get any better, even after I'd learned a few basic defensive moves.

I told Niobë about the agonies of Hades that I was suffering, and she commiserated by just laughing at me. "So now you're paying for all those sins of yours, eh, Morpheús?" she said, in between chuckles.

"I guess," I said. "I must be paying extra for the privilege, that's for sure. I'm so sore some nights that I have a hard time getting to sleep."

This was hours after sunset by my time, although it was still afternoon in Naprimér.

"Well, maybe I'd better sing you a lullaby then," she said.

"So now I'm just a baby, eh?"

"Most men are, when you come right down to it. They want to be stroked and told how great they are, and have their hands held when they hurt. Yes, you're all pretty much alike in that regard."

"You have to give us some credit," I said. "We hunt and we provide and we certainly cherish our beautiful women…."

"Yes, you do all of that, but that's only what's expected of you. You don't ever do anything extra, not without prompting."

"You know me all too well," I said, yawning out loud.

"See, I'm putting you to sleep already."

Then she began humming a tune—a strange little ditty it was—and there must have been a hint of magick behind it, because it took hold of me in spite of myself, and I felt my consciousness slipping slowly away, the cares and stresses of the day sloughing off my soul. I fell asleep with my mind and heart completely open to her, and yet she closed the link herself without violating any part of my being. I would have known of such an intrusion—we *always* know, we mages—but she tiptoed away and left me resting, giving me the best sleep that I'd had in a month.

* * * * * * *

The next morning, I was back at my routine, parrying and lunging, lunging and parrying, blocking and thrusting, thrusting and blocking—over and over and over again, the endless pantomime of lust. During a break, I asked Sergeant Strook whether he'd agree to take a short leave of absence from his studio.

"I'm leading an expedition to the East," I said, "and I need someone to put together a small group of fighters to assist me."

"Now then, just what is it you're a-plannin' to do there, Sir?" my trainer asked.

"Something that I don't want generally known," I said. "I'm trying to take a certain object from a certain secure location, and I can't do it on my own."

"I see. You'll be a-payin' well then?"

"Oh, yes. There'll be ten gold pieces for each person that survives—or his wife or child or parents—and fifty for the leader."

"And how long would we be gone, Sir?"

"Not long, I think. But understand, Sergeant, that I require complete discretion on the part of anyone who accompanies me. No boasting afterwards, no loose tongues, no nothing. I want professionals who'll do the job they're given, without complaint, and then keep their lips zipped when they return."

"And you'll have them, Sir. I can easily put together a team of, say, six men, all recently retired from the army, but still in good physical shape. They can all use the money, and I've worked with them before."

"Very well, Strook, quietly begin assembling the group," I said. "And don't tell them anything about me. Can you have them ready to leave within the month?"

"Of course, Sir. And you might think of a name for yourself, Sir, something to be identified by—you know, when we're hangin' with the boys."

"Good idea. How about Owl? It's a large, silent, and strong predatory bird that's also renowned for its wisdom. And I'll call you Hawk. You'll have complete military command, but I'll set the agenda. Is that acceptable?"

"Yes, Sir, I'll get on it right away." Then he motioned me back to the training room. "Now, let's get back to it, Sir. Try to kill me once again—and this time, let's use a little more force, eh? Maybe we can actually work up a sweat?"

I tried, but I could never penetrate his defenses. I knew, however, that with each attempt I was getting a little bit better at protecting myself and those around me. We didn't have much time, and I was willing to do whatever necessary to achieve what I wanted.

CHAPTER TWENTY-THREE
"THE CURIOUS CASE OF
THE MAGICAL MAGPIE..."

I spent my evenings in Julianople roaming the stacks of the University Library, for which I'd obtained a pass from Doctor Árbogast. This was something that I'd always enjoyed doing in my student years. There is enormous satisfaction to be gained from a random encounter with the great minds of past and present, and I would spend hours just cruising through those endless shelves, looking for small treasures.

Now, of course, I was seeking something else entirely. The Library was not really organized in any kind of rational fashion, beyond a very general segregation of materials on similar subject matters, which were usually shelved or pigeon-holed together.

You really needed a guide to find anything specific, so I sought for my old friend, Master Barít, whom we students used to call the "Muse of News." He was a funny little creature, to be sure, a man who'd spent his entire life surrounded by books and incunabula (many of the ancient manuscripts had never been produced in printed form). I was never quite certain whether or not Barít was a trained mage. At times I thought that he demonstrated an almost preternatural ability to locate obscure items within the collection; but on other occasions he seemed quite an ordinary man, beyond showing certain personal eccentricities—farting, for example. He could be a regular gas machine after lunch.

"It's, uh, it's, uh, Mordy, isn't it?" he said, when I located him in the Theosophical Collection.

"Morpheús, Sir," I said.

"How're your classes going, Mordy?"

"Well, I graduated some years ago, Sir."

"Really? I never noticed. What can I do for you, son?" Everyone was "son" to Barít. And, truth be told, he might have been the oldest man in the building, for all I knew. No one there, even Doctor Árbogast, could remember a time before Master Barít.

"I'm looking for some information on a place called Kopawalior in Indushia."

"Really? Well, no one's ever asked for anything about *that* before. Fascinating country, you know. I remember hearing a story about the Yamatha Holkarvarma II, who burned his living wife on a pyre because she had smiled once too often at an overly handsome male gardener. He came to a bad end himself, as I recall, being murdered by his cousin, Prince Bodrivarma. And that reminds me of…."

"If you please, Sir," I interjected—because I knew Master Barít all too well from previous experience. "How do you actually get there?"

"Well, as you know, the King of Kings of Indushia banned all transit to and from the land a hundred years ago—save, of course, for necessary travel by the country's chief Magi. This law was promulgated after the Eye of Shivaji was stolen by the thief Khalid ibn Bitri al-Buni, who employed a transit-mirror in a highly creative way to bounce the stone through a half-dozen sites before lifting it, shall we say, into obscurity, never to be recovered again. Of course, Khalid did not actually profit from this transaction, being…."

"Sir, if I might interpose, could you just tell me where Kopawalior is located?"

"Of course, of course, sorry for the digression, which reminds, however, of the curious case of the magical magpie of Prince Dervivarma…."

"Uh, Sir, the location, if you please?"

"The Principality—or the Yamathaship, to be precise—is situated on the southwest coast of the subcontinent. It forms a long, narrow strip of fertile countryside against the hills that delineate its eastern boundary. At times the rulers have controlled considerably broader stretches of the interior plateau, but today their sphere has been much reduced by the Panchan States."

"Do you have any notion of who Shah Ravivarma might be?" I asked.

"Why yes, he's the uncle of the present Yamatha-ha-ha, Kunundramvarma IV—and since his nephew is underaged, actually serves as Regent of the country, governing from his capital of Tellalye. He's said to be a master of the eastern magical arts, a man who's used his powers gradually to increase his control over the smaller neighboring states."

"How do you know all this?"

"Ah, well, I tend to read a lot—there's not much else to do here. But I also talk to the travelers who pass through our fair city from east to west, and I often exchange stories with them. Even though travel to and from Indushia is not easy, commerce does occur, with caravans finding their way through the Badlands into the northwestern part of that country, and then back again, at least during the summer months. So I receive regular reports of the goings-on in that part of the world."

"I don't want to spend months on the road. How do I get there more quickly?"

"The island of Serendip allows regular passage through their transit-mirrors with the payment of a small fee. From there you can catch a boat to the mainland. The Emperor doesn't ban foreigners from his country—he understands the necessity of maintaining business connections with the outside world—so you should have no trouble finding your way around the tip of the subcontinent and up the other side until you reach Kopawalior. What exactly do you plan to do there?"

"I enjoy fishing," I said, smiling—but the man thought I was telling him the straightforward truth.

"Really? Oh, you should find the place a veritable paradise. I don't think there are very many people in Indushia who fish for sport."

"Probably not." In truth, there weren't all that many anglers in Kórynthia either—and I certainly wasn't one of them! "I also like exploring libraries in various parts of the world."

"How fascinating! Oh, I should really like to see the Emperor's collection in Gudandthabad. They say it numbers over a hundred thousand volumes. But Shah Ravivarma's library in Tellalye is equally renowned for its inclusion of many rare tomes of magical lore."

"Really? I hadn't heard that."

"Yes, he's always eager to show his treasures to a fellow bibliophile. You should really inquire about the books when you're there."

Then I thought of something. "My dear old friend, would you be willing to write me a letter of introduction, as one librarian to another?"

Master Barít almost bubbled over with joy as he said, "Of course I would! So happy to oblige. For one of my students, everything is possible. Just write your name down on a slip of paper so I don't forget who you are. Always glad to be of great assistance. Wish I could go with you, but…."

"Yes, I know, your duties here prevent you from doing much traveling anymore. What a shame too!" I clucked my tongue in commiseration.

"Ah, well, we who labor in the vineyards of obscurity, so to speak, must be content with fermenting on the vine—which reminds me of the story of the farmer, his wife, and the twice-plucked grape…."

I promised to visit him again soon—after all, his missive of recommendation might provide me with just the access I needed to Ravivarma's collection.

And then it was back to Sergeant Strook again—or perhaps I should now use his *nom de guerre*, "Hawk."

He was happy to see me.

I was not, however, happy to see him!

The truth is, I didn't particularly like calisthenics as a lad, and I surely didn't favor them any more as an adult.

Thrust and parry, parry and thrust, and then a jog around the studio ten times at full speed, and then back to the infernal practice again. Why, a man could damn near kill himself exercising so hard!

CHAPTER TWENTY-FOUR
"THIS ONE I JUST CALL BIRD"

Wanting something, even wanting it badly, doesn't make it so. You have to plan properly and pick a good team to execute your plan.

"Sir, this here's Sparrow," Hawk said, pointing to a short man of five-and-twenty with olive skin and long, black hair. "Now, he's about as good with bow and knife as anyone I know, and he can climb any wall that I ever seen."

I stepped forward and shook his hand.

"This one we call Eagle," my squad leader continued. "He's got the far-sight, both with his eyes and with his mind. He sees things no one else sees, stuff the rest of us would ignore."

He actually sported a feather tied into the braid dangling down his back. His arms and shoulders were knotted with hard muscle.

"Ah, ole Raven, he ain't so much to look at, see, with one eye gone and that scar down his face, but he's the best man in a fight I ever seen, and he's got a nose for a-findin' things."

The tall, black-skinned warrior bowed at me, his oiled skin glistening in the lamplight, a patch over his left eye socket.

"Gull—he knows all the secrets of water and swamp. He knows just where to strike—and when."

He was a thin, midsized man of perhaps thirty years, with a beak of a nose and narrow brows.

"This one I just call Bird. Not much to look at, eh? But he sings a merry tune that others will follow, and he's good at a-findin' the vital bits."

The small, ugly soldier was covered with scars on his face and arms and fists. There was a flute tucked into his waistband along with several curly knives and stilettos.

"This is Roc. Look at them muscles! But like the rocs of yore, he has two heads, and sometimes two heads are better than one, specially for a-catchin' the enemy off-guard."

Another huge fighter, this one wearing a loose leather vest studded with colorful beads over an undershirt, neither of which at all disguised the ripple of muscles on his chest and shoulders.

"And finally, boys, our leader's the one called Owl. He's the brains of this bunch, and he's the man with the money!"

"That's true," I said, "but I want you to know that if I don't return, you'll still be paid. All you have to do is contact Doctor Árbogast at the University of Julianople. I'll also make arrangements for your families to be rewarded if none of us survive—just give a list of your folks to Hawk. But I'm hoping that we all return with our bodies and spirits intact.

"By the way, my companion's called Scooter. It'll be traveling with us. You'll be surprised at how useful a wherret can be. However, it only takes orders from me. You don't want to cross it."

I could hear the creature chuckling quietly in my right ear: "No, no, no, you don't want to cross me!" I think it was looking forward to this trip even more than me.

"Any questions?" I asked.

We were gathered at Sergeant Strook's studio in Julianople. I could hear some of his instructors practicing with their patrons in the other rooms.

"Sir, what about the lingo there?" the Sergeant said.

"Most folks understand a bastard form of Greek, although the accent's sometimes difficult to penetrate; the language is the closest thing they have to a *lingua franca* on the Indushian subcontinent. It's a legacy of Alexander the Great's second invasion.

"When we get to Serendip, I want to look for another addition to our team who can act as a guide to, in, and from Kopawalior. I plan to pack a collection of rare and unusual magical tomes that I'll try to peddle to the Regent—that should at least gain us access to his palace. I understand he has a large library of esoteric literature."

"When do we leave, Sir?" Sergeant Strook/Hawk spoke for the rest of them.

"Tomorrow morning," I said. "Wind up your affairs, gentlemen, and meet me here again at the third hour."

CHAPTER TWENTY-FIVE
"IGNORAMUSES, ALL OF THEM!"

I hadn't finished putting together my own "kit" for the trip, so I transited back home in early afternoon. But the first thing I did upon arriving there was to contact Doctor Scarabbaios again, because I wanted to make certain that if we were successful in obtaining the book, he'd accept it as payment for the information I required.

"*The Necropompeion*, you say? You've actually *found* one? Where *is* it?" The old man was almost beside himself with excitement.

"Never mind about that," I said. "If I get it for you, will you tell me what I need to know in order to traverse ætherspace safely to and from the Otherworlds?"

"Yes, yes, of course, anything you want," the elderly mage said. "I've been looking for that blasted book for several hundred years. You get it for me, son, and I'll give you the directions to reach as far as the Fifth Circle itself! I've been there, you know—been there and came back again, which very few Nova Europans have ever done before."

"Why did you return?" I asked.

"I was a goddam fool, that's why. I thought my friends would welcome me, would even honor me for what I'd done. Instead, they just laughed. They didn't believe anything I said. Ignoramuses, all of them! I followed in the footsteps of the greatest mages of ancient times, and they just pooh-poohed my accomplishments."

"You could have gone back."

"To what? Without the…but I've said too much already. You get me that ancient tome, and I'll tell you where to go and what to do to get there in one piece. Then it's up to you. You got the balls, boy, you can make the trip."

"I'll get you the book," I said. "I'll be back in a few weeks, and then I'll be in touch again."

"Wait…."—but I cut him off. I didn't really like the old fart that much—didn't trust him at all, and wondered about his motivations. I indicated as much to Scooter.

"I wonder about *all* their motivations, Master," the wherret said. "But if this is what you want to do, I have to go along with it, against my better judgment, I should add."

"You're always noting your exceptions," I said, "and I do appreciate your contributions to the discussion—so long as you understand who has the final say in the matter."

"Yes, oh sahib!" the creature said, bowing its head to the floor in front of me several times. "I hear and I obey, Mogul of Moguls."

"Cripes! I thought you were supposed to be subservient."

"That's not what it says in my contract," it said. "'Obey,' yes, that I must do, according to Clause 57. 'Nice'—nope, don't recall anything about that."

"Great! That's just what I need—a sarcastic familiar."

"You get what you pay for, Sir," the little beast said. "At least you have the benefit of my great wisdom."

"Great wisdom?" I said. "Great wise-ass, maybe. Why don't you do something practical for me, like find me several obscure magical tomes to offer in exchange for *The Necropompeion*. That Oriental potentate probably doesn't have any notion of what he's got."

"I wouldn't bet on it," Scooter said, "but I'll see what I can do." And it went flitting off to the bookshelves, jumping from one to the other, and occasionally knocking some old tome off onto the floor.

"Hey, be careful there!" I shouted. "Some of those volumes

are actually rare and valuable."

"And some of them haven't been opened in years," it said, sneezing in the midst of a giant dust cloud, "Maybe decades. Gad, I haven't seen so many bugs since I went rooting around in your garden this morning."

Finally the wherret piled up five volumes for me to examine, and I acknowledged that they were sufficiently obsolete and/or uninteresting for me to be willing to part with them. I tucked them away into a pocket of ætherspace from which I could retrieve them easily in the future—that way I wouldn't actually have to tote them on the journey to Indushia.

Then I got down to the serious business of deciding which magical implements and potions and such that I actually needed to take along on our expedition. With the wherret's help, I sorted them into stacks of "maybe yes" and "maybe no," and finally chose the ones I really needed.

"Pack 'em up," I ordered my helper, and it went scurrying off to obey.

Then I stuffed some extra clothes, boots, and hats into a bag, plus the Hand of Morlock, of which I'd grown rather fond in the last few weeks, and a couple of specially ensorcelled knives and other artifacts. One can't be too careful, after all!

CHAPTER TWENTY-SIX
"GODDESS, MY HEAD IS KILLING ME!"

That evening, I finally made contact again with the captive Lady. We'd more or less figured out a rough schematic to help measure the passage of time between Nova Europa and Naprimér, but it wasn't always accurate, for no reason that either of us could fathom. The sun had to be shining at her end in order for her to empower her makeshift thro-mirror, and she had to be undisturbed. I'd even tried plotting it out on a chart, but there were times when I got nothing but static in return.

But this time I was lucky.

"It's good to hear from you again," she said. "It's been quite a few days since your last contact. I was beginning to worry about you."

I sighed. "I wanted to tell you that I'm leaving for the East tomorrow, and don't know when I'll be back. I can't take the double-orbs with me, so I'll be out of touch. However, if things go well, I may return within a week or two my time."

"Do you have to go yourself? I thought you'd recruited some mercenaries to help you."

"My companions will handle any of the rough stuff," I said. "I'll just stand back and let them do it."

"But what if you don't return? There's got to be another way," she said.

"I'm the only one who knows what to look for. I can't send men into danger without sharing the risk."

"But what if you don't return?" she repeated. "If I didn't hear from you again, I think I'd lose whatever little grip I have on reality. Please don't do this, Morpheús. There has to be an alternative."

"Doctor Scarabbaios is apparently the only man alive who's traveled to the Fifth Circle of the Otherworlds, and returned to tell the tale. I absolutely have to have the knowledge that he possesses. And he won't even talk to me—not as a rational human being—without a *quid pro quo*. I've already asked—no, begged—the man several times, and he's said repeatedly that I shouldn't even consider the trip—and because of this, he absolutely won't help me unless I bribe him with something he wants. A copy of *The Necropompeion* is the only leverage that he respects. He's a bibliophile *par excellence*, and he won't turn down what's likely to be his only opportunity to acquire the book."

"What about one of the library copies? Surely they'd be easier to filch."

"Yes they would, if I could find them, but none of the institutions that are supposed to have them will admit to their presence. Also, while I have no problem removing the book from a man who's hoarding it for his private use—whatever that might be—there are limits beyond which I won't go."

Niobë rubbed her forehead. "Goddess, my head is killing me! If I lose you, even this wavy semblance of you, I think I'll reach an end to all hope. I'd rather share a part of you every so often than risk…."

"I'll be very careful," I said, "really! I still intend to come for you, Lady. I'll find a way to reach you. You must have faith."

Imagine *me* saying something like that! What had happened to the old cynic?

"It's not that I doubt *you*," she said so faintly that I could scarcely make out the words. "I just sometimes doubt the world itself, I think. I've lived way too long."

"Ah, but not as long as I," I said, chuckling slightly to alleviate her fears. "I take very good care of myself, and I'll continue to do so, you can be sure of that."

"Do you have any idea why this book is supposed to be so important?"

"I honestly don't know. The title means something like *The Dead-Procession* or *Procession of the Dead.* Fredo von Schweitzermeister, the so-called Maltesian, is the purported author, but he's otherwise unknown, completely unmentioned in any other context. The one account that I found describing the volume—in Marcus Menvillius's memoir, *So It Goes*—says that it consists of a series of apparently fictitious quotes from well-known and obscure historical figures. Fredo supposedly implies that these statements were made after these people died—from the very depths of Hades itself, I presume. But Hades was the pseudo-Hell of the ancient Greeks, and is generally regarded by most theologians as a construct, nothing like the real place at all."

"Uh, so you've seen Hell yourself then?"

"No, of course not! But I can't find any other mention of the book anywhere.

"I wanted to ask you something else as well. During my last visit with the Queen, she gave me an artifact called the Hand of Morlock"—I described its physical appearance—"Have you ever heard of such a thing?"

"No," she said, "Never. It's not something I would have likely encountered on this side of the universe."

"I didn't think so, but I wanted to ask anyway. There was something else about it, too. Inscribed on one foot was the word 'Mathoureinos,' apparently the name of the man whom the silver image was intended to represent. Does that sound at all familiar?"

"Now that's a strange coincidence," Niobë said, after a long pause. "The mythology of Naprimér mentions a great mage, Matrin, who came here from the Otherworlds during a time when the states of my world were warring with each other, and threatening to destroy our civilization. This was many thousands of our years ago—no one's sure exactly how many.

"This Matrin established a new order in which the women were placed in positions of authority, as they have been ever since—and the men relegated to other roles more appropriate to their nature. He did this in partnership with a hypatomancer named S'rënë, one of my ancestresses, who possessed the unique ability of reshaping another's imaginings into realities.

"After he left, S'rënë gradually remade our civilization into what it was until the Bird-Men came a generation ago. Since then chaos has been spreading throughout our societies."

"Do you know anything about this Matrin?" I asked.

"No more than I've told you. He's a very shadowy figure lurking behind some of our most powerful myths. No portrait of him survives, and no first-hand account of his visit to our world. He's just 'there' behind everything that made our culture sane and safe and worth living for. At some point he departed and never returned. We didn't need him by then."

"I think he may be the same person as my distant ancestor—and maybe the connection with these two families explains, at least partially, why you and I have been brought together now in such an unlikely confluence of interests. Maybe we're supposed to follow in their footsteps—or something like that. I just don't know. I can't find any clear signals pointing me in the right direction.

"Well, I really do need to go," I finally said, sighing audibly. "I have to rise early tomorrow to make the transit to Serendip. I'll contact you again when I return."

There was a brief pause before she responded.

"Wait!" she suddenly blurted out, *"wait!* Morpheús, I'm… sorry if I was short with you. I don't—I didn't—I mean…. Like you, I was raised with a certain set of principles. I've lived all my life that way. I…what's important, I think, is that we both seem to share a common belief in the need for some higher order of things, whatever or whoever that might be.

"I can't go back to what I was, ever again. I have to find some new way of living. I get the same sense from you, that perhaps you too are unwilling to continue down your present path.

Maybe together we can find some third way. At least I hope for that possibility, and as long as I have some small hope to cling to, I remain sane and alive and open to the future. Just—just come back alive, please."

What could I say? The truth was…I *was* getting a shade tattered around the edges. My life was fraying away from me, thread by inevitable thread, just like the society I could see around me. Unless I found some better purpose for my existence, I risked becoming meaningless in my own eyes.

The rest of the world scarcely cared about Morpheús the Seer. All they wanted from me was blandishments about great success and greater love. Everyone wants reassurance, even the worst of them.

So what about *moi*, eh? I couldn't even see around the corner where my own existence was concerned. Blind as an old alley cat, when it came right down to it.

Quo vadis, Morpheús? *Where are you going?*

I'm sure my quasi-friends would say, "Why do you have to look halfway across the æthersphere to find the answers? What's wrong with Paltyrrha or Julianople or Asshyr?"

I have no answer for them. Whoever rules the universe, if there is one, has a decidedly odd sense of humor. He or She makes us want things that we can't attain without great sacrifice. Maybe *that* was the key. I had to want it badly enough to make the supreme effort—or it wouldn't be worth anything to me.

"I'll come back," I finally blurted out. "And I *will* find you, Niobë! I'll *never* give up!"

And I meant every word.

CHAPTER TWENTY-SEVEN

"I HEARD IT FROM SILPHUS THE SNAKE"

Early the next morning, Scooter and I transited to Paltyrrha again, emerging from one of a series of public alcoves located four blocks from Strook's establishment. Then we headed down the nearby avenue towards his studio. The sun had risen perhaps an hour earlier, but the streets were relatively untrammeled at this time of the day.

Suddenly a man emerged from an alleyway in front of us, blocking our advance—and when I stopped and turned sideways, I saw another coming up behind us, and a third crossing the street to join the others.

"What do you want?" I asked, pulling a dagger from my belt, and waving it out in front of me.

"You think that little thing will stop us?" the third man said, grabbing a short sword from its scabbard. "We want *you*, mage, and will settle for nothing less. Come on, boys!" he yelled at the others.

I backed against the brick wall of the building behind us, trying to keep my eyes on all three assailants. The leader lunged at me, but I somehow managed to block his attack with my knife, although he scratched a long furrow sideways across the top of my right arm. This was the end of all my adventures, I suddenly realized.

"Shalákh!" I clearly heard the words uttered *sotto voce* from somewhere down on my chest.

I paid it no mind, having other things to worry about just then.

"Shalákh!" came the whisper, more urgently this time.

All three men began closing in on me for the kill.

"Shalákh!" I shouted out loud—and a rush of energy surged from my heart across my chest, down my outstretched limb, and into my dagger. It suddenly came alive in my hand, twisted around the leader's sword, and plunged into his right eye right up to the hilt—and then abruptly yanked the life out of the man's soul while pulling itself loose with a sucking sound, my outstretched hand still attached to the haft; and slashed out—snick, snick!—at the second and third attackers, leaving them gasping their final breaths into the caked filth of the detritus lining the avenue.

I slumped back against the rough bricks behind me, barely able to stand, my entire right arm throbbing from being stretched and pulled into odd contortions it wasn't designed for. Blood was dripping from the deep cut the lead ruffian had made in my sleeve and flesh.

"Master!" Scooter hissed in my ear. "Are you all right?"

I had to force myself to keep from passing out. I heard somebody shouting for the gendarmerie from somewhere further down the road.

"Master, we need to leave this place. Right now!" the wherret said.

I groaned myself upright again, and then gingerly stepped over the still-twitching bodies of my trio of attackers, accidentally treading in a pond of blood left by one of them; and then staggered slowly down the street, before being urged into another alleyway by my familiar. It took forever and a day (or so it seemed to me) to reach Strook's studio.

"What happened, Sir?" Hawk said, when he spotted us stumbling through the main entrance.

He yelled for Eagle to help, and the olive-skinned warrior quickly stripped away my torn and bloodied shirt, cleaned my wound, laid some powder into it that burned even more fiercely than the slash itself, and carefully wrapped a bandage around my arm.

"It looks worse than it is, Sir," Eagle said. "It should heal just fine."

I thanked him and the Sergeant, and when the group had gathered 'round, told them what had happened.

"Then the rumor's true," Roc said, shaking his head.

"What rumor?" Hawk asked.

"There's a price on the Master's head," he said. "I heard it yesterday from Silphus the Snake in the bazaar. The sooner we leave, Sarge, the better for all of us."

"I agree," Hawk said. "Where we do need to go, Sir?"

I wanted nothing at this point but to go home to bed, but I would never reveal such weakness in front of these tough men that I was supposed to be leading into "adventure," so I just sighed and said: "Doctor Árbogast's apartments at the University of Julianople. We'll have to transit there from the main station."

"They'll be laying for us again, Sarge," Bird said.

"Indeed they will," Hawk agreed, "but they won't see us." He turned around and yelled, "Bastian!"

One of his attendants came running out of the back room.

"We still got that chair that Lady Elvira left here last month?"

"Yes, Sir."

"Then get it cleaned up! In the meantime, you men strip down to your loinies, and stash your stickers and prickers in the carry-cage 'neath the trap. You're now become slave bearers to the high and almighty of Ye Olde Paltyrrha."

Gull just grinned and said, "Aye, Matey!"—dropping his duds in a pile while the others followed suit. I just gaped at them, not really understanding yet what they were about—until they brought the fancy travel-chair into the room.

The contraption was a throwback to classical times, with two long poles stuck through an upright seat covered over by a canopy on top and privacy screens on either side. They were rarely used or seen these days, and only by scions of the old nobility who wanted to display in an ostentatious way their roots in the early kingdom.

They carefully laid me and Scooter onto the cushions inside the vehicle, drew the blinds; and then two men each grabbed onto one end of a pole, with Bastian and two others of Hawk's employees making up the sixth, seventh, and eighth places. The Sergeant led the way. They smoothly lifted the contraption into the air, and headed out the doorway into traffic.

"Clear the street!" Hawk shouted, brandishing a long staff of authority, a pennant trailing from the top. "Make way for the exalted Lady Elvira of Vostok!"

Many of the pedestrians and horsemen looked long and hard at this unusual and colorful spectacle, some of them even pointing at us as we trotted by, but none of them saw anything beyond what Hawk wanted them to see—a fat old noblewoman out for a jaunt in the morning sun. With my left hand I tossed a couple of coppers out through the window shade, leaving the crowd scrambling in the dust behind us.

And so we made our stately and ponderous way down the twisting city streets for a mile or so, until we reached the central transit station in Paltyrrha. There we quickly got in the line for first-class travelers, paid the fare, and immediately found ourselves on the University grounds in Julianople.

Doctor Árbogast was waiting for us in his office.

"What happened to *you*?" he asked, when I disembarked from the travel-chair and he saw my bandage.

I told him about the attack.

"I'm not surprised," he said. "The factions supporting each of the potential successors to the Queen are maneuvering to get the Estates to back their particular candidate. Most of the delegates, however, remain unmoved, at least in public, realizing that it's a far better situation right now *not* to reveal their preferences—at least until they know who's going to come out on top.

"Are you going to be able to continue this venture, Morpheús?"

"It hurts like the Devil himself," I said, "But I'll be safer away from here, I think—and I have my men to help protect me. So I think the sooner that we transit to Serendip, the better for all of us."

"Very well, then," Árbogast said. He motioned us into an adjoining room, where eight containers of books and supplies were already assembled. Some of these had been collected during the previous week by Strook and his friends, and the magical lore by my former teacher and by my familiar, putting some of my newfound riches to practical use. We'd already decided not to tote a large cache of weapons with us, beyond those personal items that every man of action seems to cherish—a particular dagger or a short sword, for example.

We "saddled up," so to speak, each tying one of the packs onto one another's backs. Even Scooter had a little harness that it wore on such occasions, lined with small tools and weapons suitable to its tiny paws.

"Everyone ready?" I asked.

One by one, they nodded their heads.

I thanked the three men who'd helped us with the travel-chair, and paid them a bonus for their assistance.

Then the good Doctor unveiled a large *rubraurum* mirror in one corner. We employed these red-gold structures for longer jaunts through the aethersphere, while their *viridaurum* (green-gold) counterparts were confined to quick, short, local trips. For some reason having to do with their composition (and I don't pretend to understand the science behind the construction of transit-mirrors), the *rubrauria* could be more readily focused on very distant targets.

"You have the coordinates?" I asked.

Árbogast held out his arm and allowed it to be scratched by Scooter, who took the information from his mind and passed it along to me.

"Then let's proceed!" I said.

I instinctively reached out my right arm to touch the surface of the metal, but stopped short with a bark of pain as I stretched my recent injury beyond the limits allowed by the wrap.

"Cripes!" I exclaimed, doubling over while I tried to shake

off the excruciating ache that rolled up my limb.

"Are you OK, Sir?" Hawk asked, immediately coming over to help me.

"Just stay back, Sergeant," I ordered, standing up straight again and using my left hand this time. I allowed myself to become psychically entwined in the ley lines that permeated the æther, seeking the proper "tune" on the surface of the transit-mirror with which to focus. When I found the right vibration, I twisted space and sent us helter-skelter through the void to Serendip.

We emerged on the other side to a scene out of Dante's *Indago*, stumbling amidst the hordes of travelers clustered 'round a row of smooth, giant, upright structures—only to be shepherded like cattle through lines of wooden partitions that led slowly but inevitably to the slaughtering-pens—actually a series of tables flanked by Serendipi guards and officials.

"Next!" I heard, and put my attention back where it belonged.

"Owl of Byzantion," I said, "Bookmonger and trader in magical devices and lore, together with my familiar, Scooter, and my septet of guards and servants."

"One gold piece, plus seven and a half silver pieces for the passage of the personages, and two gold pieces for the goods," the magistrate intoned.

I counted them out without questioning.

"You can stay or go from the Kingdom for one month from this date," I was told. "Then you'll have to pay the tax anew." The official motioned me to put my left hand forward to allow the mark-imp to nip me on my little finger. It would leave an indelible magical impression, I knew, that would fade in twenty-eight days, the length of a month in Serendip. Each of my companions followed suit, all except Scooter, who refused.

"It's a spirit," I said, "You can't mark it without causing yourself harm."

"Very well, very well, pass it through, Deepseedoo! Next!" the man bellowed.

We gathered our little expedition together, and strode out the main doorway into the heart of the Vavúm District of Pondiporc, the capital city of Serendip. We headed down the Grand Passage towards the Royal Crest Inn, where we'd previously reserved lodgings for the night via the sky-orb. Once safely ensconced in our rooms, I finally collapsed into a comfortable bed, utterly exhausted by the day's events.

Scooter carefully unwrapped the bandage covering my sword slash, and slowly licked out the wound with its long tongue. The spittle of wherrets has remarkable healing properties, and also contains a narcotic that puts the recipient to sleep—which I quite desperately craved by this point.

Then I knew nothing more until mid-morning of the next day.

CHAPTER TWENTY-EIGHT
"AT THE SIGN OF
THE LEGLESS TOAD"

We rested for several days at the Royal Crest, to allow my arm to regain its flexibility again. With the aid of Scooter's magical tongue, the slash healed remarkably quickly, with no infection or residual soreness, and I was soon able to use it again with relatively little stiffness.

Meanwhile, Hawk secured passage for us on a merchant ship that was leaving Serendip in a few days, and planned to stop at a series of ports on the west coast of Indushia—including the capital of Kopawalior.

And so, a week and a half later, we furled our sails in the great harbor there, and disembarked on our grand adventure to steal *The Necropompeion* from the state's Regent.

The city of Tellalye, also sometimes called in its fuller, more archaic form, Dunnoto-Tellalye, is an enigma wrapped within a puzzle, with the old walled town encircling an even older citadel perched atop a great stone monolith rising a hundred feet into the air. It reminded me of the *bundesbread* made by the peasants of Maltésia, in which a circle of dough is molded around a large sausage, and then baked until the bread forms a crispy blanket of golden brown crust surrounding the thrusting, fiery hot cylinder of meat. Scrumptious!

But most of the business of the kingdom was actually conducted in New Castle, the government building that had been erected by the Regent in New Town or Alsander, the section of the city that had overflowed the old walls. It was there that the eight of us appeared on the morning of the seventeenth day of Annasarrah, to make our petition for an audience with Shah Ravivarma.

"Why do you wishes to misencounter the Exalty One?" the turbaned official asked in broken Greek.

I could barely understand him through his heavy accent, which broadened the vowels and slurred some of the consonants of the *koinë* (common) language, as well as utterly mangling the grammar.

"We understand that he's interested in literature of a certain esoteric nature," I said. "We've brought some samples of rare and unusual books from the West to offer him for purchase or for trade."

"Uh, what it is that you was said?"

I repeated myself.

"Uh, let me, uh, possess them, and I would pass them among His Supremal Regentude."

"I deeply regret," I said, "that that won't be possible. We've made a solemn oath to our masters not to let these extremely valuable materials wander from our protection. However, we can tender a list of our offerings written in the Greekish tongue, if that would suffice."

I stepped forward and unscrolled a parchment itemizing several valuable tomes.

"Ah, hmm," the functionary muttered, "hmm. Very well-so, Mastery Owl. I will, uh, throw your missive among and through the proper cannolis. Whence would you be sleeping?"

"At the sign of the Legless Toad," I said.

He motioned us to move on. "Next, tell!" he yelled.

* * * * * * *

The Legless Toad was a higher-class establishment in the Pithpoorah District of the old city. Emblazoned on the wall over the main entrance was the stylized painting of an amphibian amputee, dangling over (or escaping from) a boiling black pot with steam rising from the top.

"Classy," Scooter said. "Wonder if they have any live ones."

I rented a double suite of rooms on the third level, back left, with two beds to a room, and two of us per bed. Only the wherret objected, but I pointed out that it didn't sleep much anyway.

"We still need to find someone local to add to our team," I said to the Sergeant.

"You think, then, Sir, that you won't really be a-sellin' these things?" Hawk said.

"Of course not. These books are rare, but not *that* rare. The Regent'll probably have copies of these already in his collection. And if he's missing one or two, he'll likely make us a cash offer—or try to take them from us in exchange for something else—or just try to seize them!

"No, in my estimation we're still going to have to find a way of breaking into the library and locating the book ourselves. I hope I'm wrong about that, but I doubt it."

"Very well, Sir. I'll begin a-makin' some feelers in town. There are usually lots of men 'round who'll do anythin' for the gold," Hawk said.

That evening I decided that we should sample the local cuisine, and after making some inquiries of the proprietor, headed to the Prickled Pear, named (I understood) for a local fruit or something like that. We had to wait a bit for a bench to come open, but finally we were seated, all eight of us, in a row, like so many birds lined on a rail.

"We don't serve them kind," said the wench who appeared at our table. She was pointing, of course, to Scooter.

"It's just a pet," I said. "We don't expect you to feed it." I could feel the wherret's little paws digging into my shoulder.

"Jus' so's you know, Sir. We has our standards here. Now, this night Chef Bokh-li is prepared to serving the splendid dish we call the kooleemooree, which takes the cake and puts the fish in it, with the sauce we call the fahirantsy. Goodness gracious, goodee yum-yum eats! You try, yes?"

I looked around at my comrades-in-arms, and they all just nodded in my direction. No one wanted to make a decision. So I told the server to proceed: when in Julianople….

First, however, she brought us a strong brown ale that had a rather musty odor about it—and a kick like the sneaky butt of a ram. It only took a couple of mugs of that hearty brew to get us in a much better mood, let me tell you!

Then came the kooleemooree, served in round wooden bowls with large spoons and elongated slicers, accompanied by loafs of light, crusty bread. Some kind of pastry shell lined the base of the dishes, covered with a concoction that looked like a brown beef stew filled with veggies, noodles, and…and then something moved just beneath the surface, I swear to God! I poked the opaque film with my knife, and saw a little mouth filled with sharp, pointy teeth reach out and try to nip it.

"Whoa!" I said. "Be careful, men! The broth bites back!"

"Ha, ha, ha!" exclaimed another patron sitting across the bench from us. "You not have the kooleemooree 'fore? Ho, ho, ho! Lotsa fun to eats!"

He quickly jabbed his knife down into his sludge, and pulled out a small, narrow eel impaled on the tip. He banged the wriggling head on the hard table, knocking it senseless, and then bit off the end of the still-living fish and avidly chewed it up, swallowing it all down with a swig of the ale and obvious great gusto.

"Hokhém!" he shouted, and the rest of the restaurant's patrons joined in with hearty *"Hokhém!"* of their own.

We did the best we could, but only managed a half-dozen not-so-hearty *"Hokhém!"*'s before we called it a night. The addition of the fahirantsy sauce, which had to have been created in the bowels of Hades itself, and had the flavor of something that had sat in the sun one day too many, didn't help matters any. At least the bread was good.

Although I have to say that Scooter enjoyed the eels as much as anything we consumed on that entire trip—our serving wench's prohibitions notwithstanding!

CHAPTER TWENTY-NINE
"WE PUT IT UP YOUR NOSE"

The next morning, we were very slow to rise, due to our exploding heads and rumbling tummies.

"Oh," was all I could manage until midday. I couldn't even raise my head off the pillow without wanting to spew my insides all over the outside of my bed.

Hawk thought this was very funny.

He was up at the crack of dawn as usual, and then vanished until early afternoon. When he returned, he brought with him three candidates to stand before the rest of us; and although I surely didn't feel like interviewing possible assistants for our expedition, I forced myself to get up and get functioning again.

I lined them up in a row, and looked them over carefully. None blinked an eye; indeed, no one even fidgeted. Each of the trio seemed young, full of energy, and knowledgeable. One was tall, one was short, and one was medium-sized. I nodded at Scooter.

The wherret hunched over his little body and began to cough—long, body-wrenching convulsions that gradually subsided. Finally it spit something out into one of its hand-like paws, and displayed it to everyone.

A hard, shiny, yellow grub perhaps a half-inch in length was squirming there among its claws.

"What that?" one of the new men asked, looking at the ugly little bug with more than a passing interest.

"A truthworm," I said. "We put it up your nose, and so long

as you tell us the truth, nothing happens. But if you should lie to us, by commission or omission, well, let's just say that you'll have a very unpleasant couple of weeks.

"One of my late acquaintances described it as an itch you just can't scratch—that wasn't long before he took his own life. You see, truthworms don't kill people—their victims do the job for them. So which of you wants to be first?"

"Uh, uh, uh," the tall prospect muttered—and then he turned and ran out the door, leaving just two behind.

"What about you?" I asked the next man, the second in height, but the largest in strength.

"What 'bout what?" he said.

"Do you want to answer my questions truthfully?"

"No fear," he said, standing upright and pushing out his chest. "Bring bug on. I strong."

"What's your name?"

"Badhdhay," he said.

"Badhdhay what?" I asked.

"Badhdhay Bahlahkrokh."

"Why do you want this job?"

"I want money," he said. "Many, uh, many kittens to feed."

"You have many children?" I asked.

"Yes, yes, say that so."

"What kind of experience do you have?"

"Kill bad men, chop, chop, chop! Much fun!"

"Working for whom?"

"For Regent. Kill bad men!"

"Why aren't you working for the Regent now?"

"Uh...dunno," he finally said.

"Scooter!" I indicated, and the wherret raced across the floor towards the big man. Before it got there, however, the candidate jumped back, pulled out a stiletto, and waved it at the creature.

"No, no, no! You...you thing, you, you stay back!" he said. "No bug on me! No bug!"

Then he backed his way towards the exit, and quickly departed.

"Well, so much for Door Number Two," Scooter said.

I turned to our last candidate.

"And you are?" I asked.

"Singh Singh," the shorter man said.

"So you're not afraid of this little critter?" I pointed to the truthworm.

"No-uh, Sir. Nothin' here t'hide."

I went through the same list of questions, and got back similar answers. It seemed that the Regent was the principal employer of ruffians-for-hire in this region, which was only what I'd expected. I just didn't want them to be reporting to two masters simultaneously.

"Scooter?" I said.

The wherret ran over to the man and quickly swiped a sharp claw through the skin on top of his big toe, where it poked out the end of his sandal. The creature bent down and licked the blood oozing from the cut. Then it looked up and nodded at me. The candidate never flinched during the entire procedure. He might have been the most petite of the three possibilities, but he was also clearly the most honest and the bravest.

"Very well," I said, "you'll do. Sergeant Hawk will tell you what you need to know: follow his instructions. I think we'll call you Warbler. And please make an effort to learn some basic words in our dialect of Greek."

So now we were nine!

CHAPTER THIRTY

"I MIGHT HAVE
THE *MARROWBONE*"

The summons from the Regent arrived on the third day.

I don't know what I'd expected of Shah Ravivarma, but this certainly wasn't it: a prissy little man of about five-and-thirty years, the complete antithesis in appearance to the hard-nosed ruler he was supposed to be.

I presented him with my letter of introduction from Master Barít, the librarian.

"You come highly recommended," the ruler said. His Greek was flawless, albeit a trifle archaic in tone.

I bowed my head in acquiescence.

He cleared his throat. "One of the books on your list…," he began.

"Yes, Sir?" I said.

"It's this one: *The Old Magus and the Sea*, by Terentios o Kallisteros. Do you have it here?"

"No, Sir," I admitted. "We were not foolish enough to drag such valuable items thousands of miles across the world. I assume you've done business with *bibliopolae* before."

"Yes, I have," he said, running a hand through his wispy hair. "Most bookmongers of the *ars magica* community have some means of retrieving their merchandise through the æther."

"As do we," I said. "Once we've reached a bargain, the trans-action can readily be secured to both parties' satisfaction."

"I am also interested in the volume, *Pomphólux o*

Ánthropos"—which roughly translates in the common tongue as *Man Is a Bubble*.

I have to admit that I'd never read this one, and had no idea of what it was about, so I said: "A very rare and highly prized work, Sir."

"So I am told," the Regent said. "I would prefer to trade, if that is possible."

"Of course, Sir. If you will permit...?"

I very carefully and slowly reached inside my shirt, watching my watchers all the while to make certain that one of them didn't unduly or unexpectedly twitch a dart or arrow in my direction; and then pulled out another small piece of parchment. I handed it to an intermediary, who passed it to a magical "Sniffer," and so on and so forth, until it finally reached the hand of the Exalted Personage himself.

I had five titles on my list of "wants":

The Effusion of Affectation, by Reginald de San Bernardino
Measuring the Marrowbone, by Flaccus Kohlmeinie
The Necropompeion, by Fredo von Schweitzermeister
To the Stars Through Difficulties, by Sagan the Asturgian
Change You Can Believe In, by Cain bin Eric

What the Regent didn't know is that four of the volumes were fictitious—I'd invented them myself. The only book that actually existed was the one in the middle.

"These are what my buyers are seeking, Sir," I said.

The ruler frowned. "Hmm," he finally said. "I might have the *Marrowbone*, but I don't recognize any of the others. They must be very precious indeed."

"Well, Sir, my clients specialize in very unusual and hard-to-find items," I said. "Some of them have been looking for copies of these books for decades—or even longer. They're willing to pay top coin, of course, although most would prefer to trade."

"Hmm," he said again. After a long pause, he finally sighed and said: "No, I can't do a trade. I'd be willing to buy the two volumes I mentioned, if we can reach an agreement on price. My seneschal, Lord Kalimane, is empowered to negotiate on my behalf."

Then he dismissed us.

"Well, that's about what I expected," I whispered to Hawk as we were exiting the room.

"He didn't even admit that he had the book, Sir. D'you think he forgot?"

"Not a chance," I said. "No real bibliophile loses track of the treasures in his collection. No, he didn't want us to know that he owned a copy."

"So we move down the other path?" Hawk asked.

"Yes. We need to find out everything there is to know about the place."

"If we do get inside, how will you locate it?"

"That's where Scooter comes in," I said. "You just get us through the back door, so to speak, and I'll do the rest."

CHAPTER THIRTY-ONE
"JUDGING BY WHAT HAS *NOT* BEEN SAID"

But getting us "in there" was not a simple process. There are a myriad ways to hide and protect one's valuables, and I was certain that Shah Ravivarma had had both the foresight and the resources to do a particularly good job. After all, no one else had been successful in securing this particular treasure during the time that the Regent had owned the volume.

Which led me to wonder, of course, just how long *that* had been, and how he'd obtained his copy in the first place.

"Perhaps, Master," Scooter said, "He stole it from someone else."

"Perhaps," I said. "But who...?"

"Maybe 'what' is the more appropriate question. Remember, Sir, that there are two institutions in Nova Europa that supposedly have copies on their shelves—at least according to your Finder—and neither, strange to say, is now to be found. Perhaps one of them wandered its way to Indushia."

"But then Jécko should have known that."

"There might have been a residue of the 'odor' of the original copy still lingering in the collection where it had been housed. That can sometimes confuse a Finding, I believe."

But determining the location of the Kohlafaloor Library presented no difficulties, of course. The Regent had cleared away several city blocks within the walled portion of Old Town, and built a simple, solid stone rectangle perched on a mound within a beautifully sculpted garden, the entire complex being surrounded by a metal fence ten feet high.

The structure had no windows, and the only way in or out was through the main entrance. During the day the open ground surrounding the building was paroled by armed guards, always marching in tandem. And at night—well, at night, it was said, something else roamed the grounds, something that no one wanted to talk to us about.

So that was our challenge.

Hawk and his men began the process of surreptitiously gathering information about the structure, while I continued to negotiate with the Seneschal on a "fair" price for the sale of the two books we'd proffered Ravivarma. Of course, I initially proposed an absurdly high figure for the items, as everyone expected, and over the course of a week, the amount was gradually reduced by offer and counter-offer to a reasonable level.

Finally Lord Kalimane was satisfied.

"Very well," he said in perfectly understandable Greek, crossing his hands across his fat belly. "My master will be well pleased. Can you have the items ready on the morrow?"

"In two days, Sir: you bring the gold, and I'll supply the tomes," I said.

We had a deal, but I intended to vacate the country before it could be consummated.

That afternoon I gathered together our seven men and lone wherret, and we reviewed Hawk's plans for penetrating the cube.

"We need to get up to that roof," he said. "There gotta be shafts up 'bove, or the folks inside would choke to death. One door ain't enough to move the air 'round, and there isn't no holes in the walls themselves."

"Can we do this tonight?" I asked, looking at each of them in turn.

"Yes, Sir, but the key is defeatin' the guard he's posted outside after dark. Whatever it is, the city-folk utterly fear it."

"Judging by what has *not* been said, I have a pretty good idea of how to deal with it. We'll leave at the third hour of the night."

In the meantime, Scooter and I had some business to conduct as part of our preparations, so I dismissed the others and told them to relax in the tavern below us for a couple of hours—but not to become inebriated.

Then I pulled out my "bag."

Every mage worth his saltpeter always carries with him the basic tools of his trade. In its minutest rendition, this consists of just a leather pouch strung about one's neck, but for journeys such as ours, much more is required; and so I'd brought several carrying cases full of spells, tools, and implements, not to mention a small sky-orb, a brazier with scented coals and oils, and a pack of sealed vials containing various potentials and potencies.

I spoke a word to unlock the fastenings, and then selected what I needed: tenax, peduncle, maser root, flagellor, and barf beetle, plus frankintense and myrrth. Scooter pointed to something else—a tincture of Iovine—and I agreed. Io was always a great help, one way or the other!

I packed these with a small burner and some charcoal into a pouch, and we were ready to go. Then I lay back on the nearby bed to get some rest.

CHAPTER THIRTY-TWO
"SAINT MISOGYNA!"

By the time we reached the iron fence, the town had mostly gone silent, other than a few drunks, some barking dogs, and the occasional click-click-click of the patrols of the gendarmerie. I picked out an area of the perimeter that was shadowed with a few trees, and with a muttered "*Fiat flamma rapida*" and a twist of my wrist ignited the brazier.

"Keep a close watch on both sides of the fence," I hissed at the men, as they spread out under the overhanging branches. "Tell me if you see or hear anything."

Within just a few minutes, the coals were burning nicely, so I added the barf beetle concentrate, knowing that the noxious odor would attract whatever creature was roaming the grounds, while repelling just about everything else.

"Someone's coming!" Eagle whispered.

Sure enough, I could hear a rustle of the brush within the gardens as something very large pushed or slithered its way through. It was heading right for us.

I popped a pinch of maser into one side of my mouth, and chomped down hard on the root, releasing its sour and bitter flavor. I almost choked on the stench and foul taste. Ah, what we mages have to endure in the name of science!

I would have about eight or ten minutes of enhanced vision as a result. That should be quite enough.

I got as close as I could to the metal fence posts without actually touching them, and peered intently in the direction of the critter's ongoing progress. Gradually my eyes cleared, until I could finally see the thing for what it was.

"Saint Misogyna!" I exclaimed.

"What?" Hawk and Scooter both asked.

It was a paleofrey, a creature of the Otherworlds, which had the appearance of a shaggy, squatty horse with an oversized head and way, way too many buck teeth. It had the ability to hide itself from the sight of man, which was unfortunate indeed for any individual who happened to encounter the critter. I knew of such things from my studies of magical fauna, but had never actually seen one in the flesh, so to speak.

I picked out a prickly stalk of peduncle, and sprinkled it with tenax to affix the spell and flagellor to sting the beast; and then dusted the stick with a speck of barf beetle on its end to lure the creature to me, frankintense to heighten the stench, and myrrth to fix the ultimate "bite" of the weapon. I took a swig of the Iovine myself, both to strengthen my vision and steady my hand.

I waved the wand in front of the iron palings, and waited for the thing to approach, as I knew it would. Paleofreys can never resist a bad smell.

The rest of my crew couldn't see anything, of course, but they could certainly hear it moving, and I could tell that they were becoming increasingly uncomfortable with the notion that something as large as whatever that was could get so near to them.

"It can't cross the line," I told them. "Its governing spell restricts it to the grounds after dark. Just don't touch the fence, or you'll allow it to breach its confines!"

The paleofrey opened wide its huge mouth, and put it flush against the iron bars. As soon as it came within range, I shoved the tainted peduncle right up its nose. The night suddenly shook with the bleat of a frightened beast, as it reared back and tried to dislodge the pokey thing. But then the flagellor began to bite, and the cry of fear became a howl of pain, as it shook its great head back and forth, back and forth.

"Ow-roooo!" blasted our ears, and the sound surely must

have awakened half the town, leaving the citizens cowering in their crumpled beds.

The paleotrey ran at full tilt through the trees and plants, flattening them beneath its broad feet, raging at the spear firmly affixed to its nose, bellowing constantly. I almost felt sorry for the beast: the tenax would not release its grip until morning. But one thing was for sure: no one else would bother us in the interim. Even the Regent would think twice before dealing with his out-of-control guard.

"That should hold it for a few hours," I said. "Let's get to work, gentlemen."

CHAPTER THIRTY-THREE
"OH GREAT GRYPHON-DUNG!"

Sparrow was already perched in a tree overhanging the fence, and as soon as our "impediment" had been cleared, he dropped onto the other side, and anchored a rope that enabled us to go up and over the palings very quickly and easily.

From there it was just a short trip to the side of the monolith that Hawk had judged the easiest route to climb. Sparrow led the way, of course, but even he had to take his time, feeling for small protrusions that allowed him to inch his path up the fifty-foot-high walls. When he finally reached the top, he anchored the rope he'd been carrying to a chimney emerging from the roof, and let it down the side. Within minutes, the rest of us had joined him.

Our team fanned out over the top of the slightly canted structure to look for possible access points into the building below.

"Sir," I heard Gull call, "I think I've found something."

We rushed over to examine a curious structure fashioned from metal bars and awnings.

"Air shaft," Hawk said. "See, Sir, they've covered it up to keep the rain from a-comin' in, but these openin's allow the breeze to be pulled down inside. If we could get through somehow, we could enter one of the rooms down below."

But the rods were as thick as my arm, and embedded deep within the large stones that anchored them on either side. We tried to move one with our joint physical strength, and got nowhere.

"Scooter," I said, "Can you fit between the lattice-work? I'd like to know what's down there before we proceed any further."

"Of course," the creature said, and then stretched itself out until it could "scoot" between the bars, disappearing down the hole.

"Amazing," Gull said, shaking his head.

A few moments later, the wherret reappeared and pulled itself up through the opening.

"There's a second set of ironwork at the other end," the wherret said, "But if we can pass *that*, we'll find ourselves in the main reading room of the library."

"You're confident you can stretch yourself through that barrier as well?"

"Yes, although it's a ten-foot drop from there to the floor."

"What about magical traps?"

"I detected none."

"Very well," I said. "Gentlemen, we have a situation here that requires a particular kind of solution. I must make this final part of our journey alone—or rather, with Scooter. You can't accompany me because you're not as attuned to my familiar as I. However, you still have an important function: to guard the roof from any intruders, and to warn me if the Regent should appear."

"What about that paleo-creature?" Hawk said.

"It won't bother you up here, and if you don't go near its blunderings in the garden, you'll all be able to leave without danger before dawn. If we don't return by the time you see a lightening of the horizon, depart this place immediately and return to our quarters at the inn. If we don't appear within another day, vacate this kingdom immediately and return to Kórynthia. Is that understood?"

"Yes, Sir," they all replied.

Then I turned to Scooter. "Are you ready?" I asked.

"Yes, Master," came the reply. "You'll need to remove your clothing."

I stripped down to the skin, and huddled over the grate. Then the wherret stretched itself up and out into the air, and wrapped itself completely around me. I released my consciousness into Scooter's control, because any stray thoughts on my part would make the alteration impossible. Drifting into the æther, I vaguely felt myself being attenuated into a different form, long and thin, that would allow me to pass the barrier.

"Morpheús!" I heard the call from a far distant place. *"Morpheús!"* came the cry once again. Then a choked-off scream of pain.

"Niobë?" I whispered deep within my buried mind. "What…?"

But I could not realize the link before I was suddenly yanked back into my body by the wherret.

"We're here," it said.

I was standing on a cold tile floor on one side of a large, domed room. A single soul-light cast a flickering, pale luminescence over the scene. I shivered and shook myself fully awake, and then staggered as the expenditure of energy suddenly made me light-headed, forcing me to brace myself against the wooden shelves behind me. The entire wall, save for the arched entrance-way, was lined with books.

"That was…unsettling," I finally managed to say. Slowly the blood was oozing back into my extremities. "Let's find what we need and get out of here."

I pushed myself upright, brushing away a cobweb that had somehow adhered to my bare arm and back.

"He must never clean this place," I muttered to myself, while trying to shake the silk loose from my fingers. "Bloody damn cold in here."

"How do you propose to find it?" the wherret asked.

"Find what? Oh, yes…*The Necropompeion* was produced in Hades, according to the tale, and so cannot be copied in the real world. This strongly suggests that the volume has a spiritual component that links it to the Netherworld. Since you derive from the Spiritworlds, an analogous place, you should be able to sniff the volume out quite readily."

There was an extended silence.

"Well, shouldn't you?" I finally asked.

"No, Master," Scooter said. "Despite what you may believe, I am not that sort of creature, not at all. I have a physical nature, albeit one possessing certain unusual abilities, at least by human reckoning."

"Oh," I said.

"That's all? 'Oh?' You have no other plan?"

I coughed slightly to hide my embarrassment.

"I see," the little creature said. "You brought us all the way to Indushia, thinking that *I* could find this book for you? And you never asked?"

Another extended silence.

"There's got to be a way," I finally said.

"Look around this room," Scooter said. "There must be ten thousand volumes here. How do we separate one from another? It's very easy to hide something in public view."

"Is it? Or are we making matters more complicated than they are?"

I still had the pouch that I always wore around my neck; even my recent experience in elongation hadn't dislodged it. I pulled out the small silver Hand of Morlock that Queen Evetéria had given me, and unwrapped it from its protective silk covering. The amber that was grasped between its fingers winked at me in the dim light.

I used the pin to scratch the palm of my dexter hand, and touched the gem to my blood. I closed my fist around the smaller silver image, and forced my essence into the heart of the old amber, finding there the small creatures that had been embedded in the sticky goo when it was made stone.

"Come forth!" I ordered. "Find me the spirit-ensorcelled book!"

I heard a buzzing in my ear as a cloud of almost invisible mites emerged from between my fingers and headed to the nearest shelf. Around and around the room they flew, faster and faster, until the whistling of their passing beat up the scale into an almost unbearable whine.

And suddenly they were back again! I reached my mind into the essence of the resin, and found the answer that I sought. I carefully reclothed the silver hand in its silken pouch and put it away. Then I walked across the open space of the great domed reading room, dodging the seats and benches placed there, reached up to the sixth shelf, and pulled down the copy of *The Necropompeion*. It was covered with cobwebs, and tingled within my grasp. I tried to brush them away, but the more I pawed the volume, the dirtier it seemed to get.

"I have it!" I yelled across the room at Scooter, still attempting to clean the precious tome.

"Uh, Master," came the reply.

I quickly looked around, and then felt the webbing suddenly enshroud me, tangling my arms together with the book.

"And I have *you*!" Shah Ravivarma said from the doorway, smiling very sweetly. "And so we have each other. Isn't that all just grand?"

"Oh great gryphon-dung!" I exclaimed to the wherret.

But Scooter had already fled up the spout, and was nowhere to be seen. I, on the other hand, was bound quite tightly by the Regent's silken trap.

CHAPTER THIRTY-FOUR
"THE PULLING-OFF OF WINGS"

"The time has come," the Regent said, "To talk of many things. Of *Necropomp* and gryphon-dung and the pulling-off of wings."

This did not have a really good sound to me, and I wondered when and if Scooter and Hawk were going to rally the troops, so to speak—I hoped "real soon now." Because in the meantime, here I was, strung up with chains in Shah Ravivarma's cold, dark dungeon in his pokey palace on the pedestal, and the future did not look very bright to me at just that particular moment.

"So, soon-to-be-wingless Owl, who are you and whom do you represent?" he asked. "You *will* tell me in the end, you know."

Oh, I knew very well that I would talk, talk, talk rather than be tortured to death. Unfortunately, given the way these scenarios usually unfolded, probably both events would occur more or less simultaneously, since talking too early tended to lend a certain aura of disbelief to the words being spoken.

"My name is irrelevant," I finally said. "I represent someone who desires *The Necropompeion* for his collection, and is willing to pay a...."

"It is *not* for sale," the ruler said in his high-pitched voice. "I thought I made that clear to you, although *why* he would want that particular volume is quite beyond me. The text is utterly frivolous."

"Like you, he wants to be complete. That's all he told me. I'm just his agent."

"Really? I wonder. No matter: I *am* willing to trade for the item in question."

"But you said…."

"You offered me nothing of interest. No. I'm willing to trade *this* volume"—he held it up before my face—"for one of three things: first, the death of my nephew, Kunundramvarma IV, in such a manner that no blame can ever be attached to me; second, my advancement to the throne of thrones of Indushia; or third, the Nose of Nagha'aïd. Give me one of these, and you'll have your book in return. I do so solemnly swear, by the groping hands of Shiva, the big balls of Brahma, and the ever-moist valley of Vishnu."

The dungeon shuddered and rumbled under the impact of such a mighty oath, although it certainly didn't do very much for me.

"Very well," I said, "but you'll have to release me if you want me to meet the terms of our agreement."

He sighed. "I suppose I must, although I'd really rather play with you for a while. Will you give me your word that, should you prove unable to meet one of my stipulations for the exchange, you'll return to continue our *tête-à- tête*?"

"No, of course not. Do you think I'm a fool?"

So two hours later, cleaned up and dressed in a new suit of Tellalyean clothes, I was released from the main gate at the top of the great pedestal, and allowed to walk down the winding stone road that led from the walled city to the citadel. Life certainly takes some very strange and unexpected twists and turns at times.

My friends seemed happy to see me, although they were forced by my appearance to postpone their rather frantic packing.

"Weren't you going to save me?" I asked.

"We talked about it," Hawk said, "But couldn't see any possible way to rescue you."

"Scooter?" I said, looking at the downcast wherret.

"Yes, Master?" But it wouldn't look me in the eyes.

"Oh, never mind," I finally said. "We have some thinking to do, gentlemen," and I explained the terms that had been presented to me for obtaining the rare tome.

"Do you know what this Nose-thing is?" Hawk asked.

Warbler, a native of Tellalye, cleared his throat, and spoke the words that I eventually translated as: "The god Nagha'aïd is the local deity of the Sukh sect in the Kingdom of Bukwatherpoo. His statue adorns their holiest shrine in Banisia. There he's displayed as an upright, rampant ram, with a large ruby representing his nose, so that he can illuminate the path of righteousness for his people. Of course, in Maiharsia he's depicted as a slimy lamprey glowing in golden goodness. This slight difference in theological interpretation has long been a matter of contention between the two states, and...."

"We don't need to know the particulars," I said. "Can the jewel be stolen?"

"Well, that would bring a great curse upon the thieves, and also upon the recipient of the gem. The temple is closely guarded at all hours of the day and night, and would be difficult, I think, to penetrate."

"What about our other options?" I asked.

"Killin' or deposin' the old Emperor of Indushia would be nigh unto impossible, Sir," Hawk said, "But even if we were successful, the Indushians would never stop a-lookin' for us, and would eventually track down and kill anyone involved. That would not be a good outcome."

"And the Regent's nephew?"

"He would have to die in public in a way that could only be seen as an accident. But I have qualms about killin' an innocent lad just to advance the uncle. I mean, I've killed a lot of men in my time, but they all deserved it, more or less. He's just a kid."

All the others agreed.

"There's also a fourth option," Eagle said in his soft, measured voice.

"What's that?" everyone wanted to know.

"Kill the Regent."

Hawk smiled. "You know, I really like that idea."

CHAPTER THIRTY-FIVE
"BUT THEY'RE *YOUR* TRASH!"

And so we finally came to a less than firm conclusion, after much animated and even distressing discussion: we would assassinate Shah Ravivarma, and then advance his teenaged nephew to his early majority. Our price would be the book—and a million gold pieces, if we could get the boy to give them to us.

Everyone thought that that was only fair, but we hadn't reckoned on the Yamatha-ha-ha himself.

"But I don't *want* to be in charge," the sixteen-year-old ruler said, when we'd arranged a clandestine meeting with Kunundramvarma in the Glorious Gazelle Gazebo. "I'm perfectly OK with Uncle Ravi running things. I have my wenches and horses and games and...just everything! Why would you ruin that? Everyone wants me to do this and that and the other, and all I want to do is have some fun. What's wrong with that, eh?"

"Nothing, Your Majesty," I said, "But isn't it time that you assumed more responsibility for your people?"

"Why? What difference would it make? The people will still be there. They're all just trash anyway. That's what Uncle says."

"Yes, but they're *your* trash!"

"Then I should be able to do what I want," the Yamatha-ha-ha whined. "That's why I've got Uncle running things—and he does such a good job of it too."

"You're right, of course," I said, shaking my head slightly at the others. "And we respect your decision, Majesty."

"What are we going to do?" Bird asked, as we left the giant cabbage garden.

"We could still try killing the Regent—he'd be no great loss," I said. "However, I think he'd be very difficult to get to, particularly being forewarned—and the boy will surely tell him of our meeting—and without the support of the Yamatha-ha-ha.... No, we have to go after the gem. It's the easiest solution."

"But how do we steal it?" Eagle asked.

How indeed?

The Kingdom of Bukwatherpoo was located several hundred miles north of Kopawalior on the western coast of Indushia. The dominant Sukhee ruling class, according to Warbler, was a religious gerontocracy centered in the small town of Bumpeerodh in the interior. The Sukhees had erected three shrines there to their chief deities—Nagha'aïd the Noxious, Pekhari the Portentous, and Bakhshi the Breathless.

The Raja of Bukwatherpoo, Sharshavan Singh Shah, tolerated the sect because they provided a steady stream of cheap but effective recruits for his army.

Getting there was not a problem, since the main coastal highway was patrolled by the Federals of the Emperor, and was heavily traveled in any case. We set off the next morning, and arrived at the capital city of Bukrhojeera a week later. Bumpeerodh was located a day's journey to the east, but we wanted to rest our weary feet and make our final plans before proceeding.

"Oh, I do miss our transit system," I said, as I soaked my blistered heels in a pan of warm salt water. "Ahhh."

Although the Indushians maintained an internal system of instant-travel through low-level *argentaurum* mirrors, these were tightly controlled by the federal bureaucracy, and individual possession of such magical implements was a crime punishable by death. Even the rulers of the autonomous states that comprised the Empire were not exempt. Hence, most of the travel most of the time took place on foot or by beast, slow as that was. And even if we'd had access to one of the mirrors, their low power levels meant that they could only be used for short hops of no more than a hundred or two hundred miles, depending on the geography.

The layout of the great green temple of Nagha'aïd was well known and quite simple: it consisted of an immense dome stretched over a large open space lined with stone benches, with the twenty-foot-high statue of the deity mounted at the far end of the room opposite the main entrance. The shrine was open all day and all night except for one brief period just before dawn, when the huge bronze doors were shut, and a cleaning crew swept and mopped the interior floors and seats, collecting the cumulative garbage of the preceding day. This usually took about an hour.

"It has to be then, then, Sir," Hawk said, after we'd reviewed all of the possibilities. "Since the main doors are closed and locked, only a few guards are left on duty, and they're tired from a-standin' there all night. They want nothin' more at that point than to be relieved. We just relieve them slightly early, grab the jewel, and get away before anyone knows what's happenin'."

"There's a Federal post station just outside of town," Warbler said. "It has a transit-mirror, but only one person there knows how to use it. Most of them regard it as a kind of sacred mystery—something to be feared, not employed. It's almost never activated."

"We can use that to escape," I said. "It'll take us back here, at the least, and then we can decide the best way to proceed thereafter."

That was our plan, and it worked just fine until we actually retrieved the jewel. Then things started going wrong. Hellfire—maybe it really was cursed!

We dressed ourselves in the uniforms of the local gendarmes, and entered the side door of the temple, shooing the handful of guards and the cleaning crew into a small back room, where we locked them up tight.

I could see the large shining ruby that marked the great Nose of Nagha'aïd, some fifteen feet up the statue.

Sparrow led the way, of course, scaling the side of the great monument without difficulty. He hung by one hand from the snout of the image, using a knife to pry the gem loose.

"Beautiful," he said, holding it close to his face.

And then, completely without warning, the man who never lost his footing slipped, perhaps from lack of concentration, and fell straight backward right onto the marble floor. He lived just long enough to hand me the Nose.

We could do nothing for our comrade, so I quickly cast a light preservation spell over the body, and tucked it away into a pocket of ætherspace for later retrieval. Then we proceeded to the transit-station just outside of Bumpeerodh.

We burst in through the front door, disarmed the men on duty, and found the mirror without difficulty. I reached out to activate it, and was immediately knocked to the floor by a sudden surge of energy.

"What the...?" I said, slowly making my way back to my feet. It took me a moment to regain some clarity. Then I tried again, this time much more gingerly.

"It's got an ætherlock," I said, utterly disgusted by the situation. I should have thought of this. Even the Indushians weren't complete idiots.

"What's that, Sir?" Hawk asked.

"It prevents unauthorized users from accessing the leys. It's usually disarmed by a set series of phrases, or sometimes by a charm that's been attuned to the particular mirror in question."

"Can you do something with it, Sir?"

"Not quickly," I said. "Bring me the director of this station."

He was a mustachioed man of perhaps forty-five years, sporting a pointed hat striped in yellow and black, rather like a bumblebee.

"Give me the key," I said, pointing to the *argentaurum*.

"But I do not have the thing, Great Sir, goodness gracious, no."

"Who does?"

"Why, no one does, Great Sir, oh me, oh my."

"Then how do you activate this device?" I asked. I was beginning to lose my patience.

"We do not make it go 'pfft' by ourselves, oh no, no, not at all, Great Sir. Someone else, he can make it work by coming through the other way—from theresome to heresome, as you see—and sometimes, whenever that does really happen, that great and exalted individual has also been given a key to return back through the gate, and then he makes the mirror light up from this side. But I do not have that key, by Nagha'aïd's great whiskers."

"Great," I said.

"They've got horses out back," Hawk said from the doorway.

"That'll have to do," I said, and sent the manager back to the closet where he'd originally been confined.

Soon we were pounding down the road towards the capital.

Warbler, however, moved up next to me, and said: "Sir, there was something odd about that situation back there."

"What do you mean?" I asked, while trying to keep my rump firmly planted on terra horsey.

"Well, according to what I'd heard, these places do use their mirrors sometimes."

"He explained that."

"Yes, well, but…."

"I think it would be wise, Master," Scooter whispered in my ear, from where it was sitting on my shoulder, "To consider what this man says."

"I wonder," I said, putting my lips together in a thin frown. "I know the director wasn't actually lying to me—I would've detected it in such a simple creature—but perhaps he didn't tell me the whole truth. Maybe he has a communication link, a small sky-orb or something. He could then receive an activation code, if necessary, from somewhere else. We can't take that chance."

I slowed my steed to a walk, and then motioned the others to gather around. I explained the possibilities to them.

"If you're right, someone may be waiting for us at Bukrhojeera," Hawk said.

"Indeed. We probably should avoid the main roads and cities."

As a result, it took us nearly two weeks to return to Kopawalior. I never did learn whether my surmise was right or not.

CHAPTER THIRTY-SIX
"THE JEWEL, SHE IS CURSED"

I didn't trust the Regent. Once he had the jewel in his sweaty little hand, he might decide to keep the book as well—and dispose of our little band of adventurers. He certainly had the power to do so.

So I had to devise some way of making the exchange that would allow us to escape his grasp while maintaining control of the all-important tome.

"Sir, we must do this as quickly as possible," Warbler said— or rather, I translated what he said to the rest before I realized its import. "The jewel, she is cursed, and if we hold her too long, anything could go wrong."

Now, whether or not the ruby was *actually* cursed is a matter of speculation, but certainly my intrepid and brave young men *believed* it was cursed, which amounted to the same thing really. I carried it in the now-overstuffed pouch dangling from my neck.

The problem was, I just didn't feel safe while we were still in Indushia, much less Kopawalior. I outlined the pros and cons of our situation to my group of merry men.

"Sir," Eagle spoke up. "I think we should take the jewel back to Serendip. We can set up a trade there where we could control the setting. If we stay here, the Regent will be much tempted, I think, to take everything."

We all agreed with that sentiment, all except Warbler, who was concerned about the curse again.

"Do you wish to remain in Tellalye?" I asked.

"No, Sir," he said, in his somewhat warbled speech. "I've always wanted to see something of the world outside this place, and this is my best chance of doing so. Also, I think that the Regent needs to forget this incident before I can dare return home. So, if you will permit me, I'll stay with your group."

I nodded my acquiescence.

"Gull," I ordered, "Find us a discreet vessel to ferry us back to safety."

"Aye, Sir," came the reply.

He was gone several hours before reporting back again.

"I found a fishing vessel, Sir, that's willing to take us south, if we pay them two pieces of gold."

"Can we trust them?" I asked.

"I know the master," he said, "And I sailed with several of the 'boys' over the years. Yes, Sir, we can rely on them."

An hour later, he introduced us to Captain Bheebheejo, skipper of the low-slung dhow, the *Water Crest*, which had once (perhaps) seen better days—in someone else's lifetime.

That night, we finally departed the shores of Kopawalior, and spent a week slowly tacking southeast back and forth along the western coast of the subcontinent, until we finally left Indushia for good. By then I was thoroughly tired of all the fish.

CHAPTER THIRTY-SEVEN

"DO YOU HAVE THE
NOSE OF NAGHA'AÏD?"

Pondiporc, the capital city of the Serendipi Kingdom, is located halfway down the western side of the island. We were able to transit there directly from the port of Serendipi-tee-Doohdaah on the northern shore, although we did have to pay an extra entry fee. Of the collection of taxes and assessments there is seemingly no end.

I was able to secure rooms once again at the Royal Crest Inn in the Vavúm District. This establishment was not the fanciest lodge in town, but its location was ideal for our purposes: it was perched on a pile of rocks in the bay, and connected to the city by a long earthen ramp. We could easily watch the comings and goings of strangers, and, if necessary, defend ourselves from any intruder. Of course, Hawk pointed out that we could also wind up being trapped there, but he tended to be more pessimistic than I.

The proprietor was named Kundalini Yogi, a wiry little man who could wrap himself into truly remarkable contortions, intertwining his legs with his arms—although why he should want to do this, I have no idea. On at least one occasion, I had to assist him in regaining his normal posture when he became stuck in one of his "exercises."

I handed the Nose of Nagha'aïd to Scooter, telling it: "Tether it someplace in the æther where no one but you can find it."

That afternoon I paid a visit to the same great transit-station at which we'd entered the island, and bought each of us new exit passes, good for ten days. Then I visited the trans-orb station.

"Do you deliver messages to the mainland?" I asked.

"Of course," came the reply.

I paid the fee and gave him the written note that I wanted sent.

"Can I access the reply via sky-orb?"

They gave me a code with which to enter their æther-base, and then I returned to our inn. I figured it would take five days to receive a reply, but was pleasantly surprised when it was only three.

What I'd said was this: we had the Nose, and we'd make the exchange for *The Necropompeion* in the public forum of the main transit-station in Pondiporc, which was always filled with security guards and state police, under the official eye of the supervisor of the facility—who would receive his usual fee, of course, for handling the transaction. Basically, if the Regent wanted the jewel, he or his agent would have to be there to make the switch. The exchange would take place on the ninth day hence.

Although I knew the Regent would try something sly, what I hadn't expected is that he'd push his nephew out front.

* * * * * * *

I had our men posted around the area where the trade would take place, and I'd also bribed a number of the police officials to watch our backs, so to speak. I had no idea how and when the Kopawaliors would come.

Shah Kunundramvarma was the first through the transit-mirror, but he was immediately followed by a contingent of guards and attendants, who milled around between the partitions separating each entry point. The Station Supervisor waved them through, but required them to set aside their weapons first.

I nodded to Hawk and Gull on either side of the floor, telling them to be alert.

"So, Your Majesty," I said, "Are you ready to proceed?"

"I am," he said, holding out his hand. One of his aides placed what appeared to be *The Necropompeion* in his fingers.

"May I verify that the merchandise is genuine?" I asked.

When he nodded, I stepped forward and touched the book's cover. I'd gathered a feel for the thing when I'd briefly held the volume in my hands in the great library of Ravivarma, and I immediately recognized its aura.

"Do you have the Nose of Nagha'aïd?" the Yamatha-ha-ha asked.

I held out my hand. Scooter spoke a word under its breath, and the jewel suddenly appeared on my palm.

The assembled guards and officials gasped at the sparkle of the thing. It was quite simply…huge, larger than any comparable ruby that either I or anyone else there had ever seen.

"Let me have it!" the ruler demanded, abruptly reaching out to grab it from my grasp. But he miscalculated, instead knocking it from my hand. It rattled across the floor, skipping and jumping as if it were alive (maybe it was!).

The Shah dropped the volume and threw himself after the rolling stone. I scooped up the precious book, whistled out loud, and headed for the transit-mirrors. But the lanes in front of me and the others to either side suddenly filled with an influx of armed Kopawaliors flooding through from the other side. Ravivarma must have ferried a troop to Serendip from the mainland, and then bribed a transit-official to allow his men to access the system *en masse*.

"Shut down the mirrors!" Scooter shrilled in my ear.

I grabbed the pouch beneath my shirt, and spoke a series of rapid-fire incantations. The last of the soldiers in front of me was cut off in mid-section as the mirror went dead. I pulled a long knife from my belt, and rushed at the other half-dozen enemy, just as the wherret ballooned itself up from my shoulders, making me suddenly look ten feet tall. They dived away to either side to avoid the giant shadow-monster thus created. I heard Scooter roar at the men in the other lanes, scaring them into submission.

"To me!" I yelled to my comrades. "To me!"

I ran to the great *rubraurum* and reached out with my mind, skewing and activating the leys. Suddenly the path was open to my laboratory back home. One by one my comrades evaded their potential captors and found their way to safety—only Gull was injured, having been cut on his left arm. Then Scooter and I ducked through the opening into the æther, transited to Barstölný, and I shut down the link before anyone else could employ it.

We were safe once more—or so I presumed! And I had the book, the precious book!

CHAPTER THIRTY-EIGHT
"AN EQUAL-OPPORTUNITY WHORE"

"Don't touch *anything*!" I ordered my men, as soon as I'd caught my breath again. Then to Gull: "How badly are you hurt?"

His face was pale and his breath was quick, and the sleeve of his upper arm was soaked bright red. I was not well versed in the healing arts, so I needed to secure professional attention.

"We need to get him to Paltyrrha," I said, and prodded my weary men to their feet again. I left *The Necropompeion* at home with Scooter to stand guard, and then moved everyone else from my *officina* to the main transit-station in the capital city.

There I contacted Doctor Oscito, a young but rising physician, and transited to his house in the Evon District.

"What have we here?" he asked, when I led Gull into his examination room. "Bad slice, that."

He cleaned the wound, doused it with Virilox to kill any *animales*, and bound the cut together with *Adstrinxit*.

"You've lost a lot of blood," he told Gull. "You need to eat plenty of red meat and get a lot of rest for the next several weeks, at the very least. I want to see you back here daily so I can examine the course of healing. Do you understand?"

When Gull nodded his head, the doctor gave him a sedative to put him to sleep.

"Can he remain here overnight?" I asked.

"I'll insist on it," Oscito said. "This is a serious wound. You don't want it to go sour."

I paid the man and asked him to keep me informed. Then I took the others to the Greenbriar Inn to celebrate our safe return.

This wasn't the fanciest establishment in town, but it better suited the kind of folks that comprised my merry little band, serving good food in plentiful quantities, and barrels of beer and ale salted with a little fleshy entertainment. Every evening at midnight, the proprietor, one Master Timotheus, would conduct the "drawing of the dark," the *crème de la crème* of the tavern's alcoholic offerings—and dare any patron who was then left standing to quaff a triple mug of the frothy brew down to its dregs. Very few individuals survived that particular rite of passage, although there were many who tried.

Tonight the renowned belly dancer, Shah'rah, a native of far-off Andalusia, was exhibiting her luscious limbs, while enveiling the lower part of her face, Musselman-style.

She writhed to the music of the pipes, darting around and among the varied patrons of the inn in the dance known as "snake-arms," thrusting her shiny great bosoms in their faces— and I must admit to enjoying this spectacle along with the rest.

"Would love to have a few hours with that one, eh, Sir?" Hawk shouted in my ear. Shouting was the only way one could communicate in the noisy bar.

"You couldn't afford her," I said. "And even if you could, no man, they say, can last even one night with her. She drains them dry. She does better with the ladies."

"The ladies? What do you mean, Sir?" Roc said, scratching his lower lip.

"She's said to be an equal-opportunity whore," Raven said.

"I still don't get it," Roc said.

"Oh, I'd surely be a-willin' to accept *that* challenge, Sir," Hawk said.

Meanwhile, Shah'rah had been moving ever closer to our table, somehow weaving in and out of the benches and sprawled legs and drunken bodies and barmaids with nary a mishap—and still grinding those hips up and down in a perfectly marvelous measured fashion.

"She does have a certain *savoir-faire*," I said, gulping down another chug of the strong ale.

And then she was upon us, and she seemed to be paying particular attention to me, for some reason I honestly couldn't fathom. I mean, I'm not a particularly handsome man, and in the midst of all these muscular types, I "stood down," so to speak. Nevertheless, she seemed to hover over my spot on the bench, touching me with her hands, her hips, her flashing eyes. The fragrance of her perfume was like a summer night in Serendip. I felt a wisp of paper slipped between my fingers—and then she was gone, off to entertain another rowdy bunch of overgrown boys.

"Hey, she really liked you, Sir," Bird said, and the rest of the group joined in his raucous laughter at the idea of *me* attracting someone like *her*.

A few moments later, when their attention was drawn by the flit of another female butterfly, I glanced at the note in my hand:

"Meet me 2nd hr. post-mid-n. behind inn."

After the nightly "drawing of the dark," my lads really got down to business, while I sipped my brew more carefully, wanting to keep my wits about me. I had no idea what this woman desired of me, and I was very suspicious of her motives. I didn't know her from Eve—indeed, had never actually met her, although I'd seen her perform previously at several other establishments in the great city. She'd never before paid me the slightest attention, even when I'd wagged a gold minim in her direction. So why now?

I was lounging near the rear exit to the Greenbriar when she scurried around the far corner of the alleyway. I could smell the faint fragrance still lingering in her hair when she approached me.

"You are the one dey call...*el brujo*, the...soot-sayer?" she asked. Her accent reminded me of a gypsy I'd once met.

When I nodded my head slightly, she gasped and said: "I...I need have *fortuna* told. *Real fortuna*, not make-up."

"Why?" I asked. "In my experience, no one wants to know their true destiny."

"Must...know. Must know if *el amor*, he is real."

"Believe me when I tell you, fair lady, that you do not want to learn such things," I said. "Please take my word for this and go away."

"I...can...not, Señor."

"Very well," I said. "You know that I cannot refuse you under Kórynthian law. What will you pay in return?"

"I...have coins, many coins," she said.

"I don't need or want your money," I said. "What else?"

"I see you look at my body with lust in eyes. I give you my body."

"No," I said, for I was not angling for a quick liaison, even with this beauty. "What else?"

"Not know what else you want. You tell me thing, I give this thing to you."

"Yourself in service to me for a period of seven months." For some reason, many things in magic must occur at intervals of seven. "Whatever I require, you will undertake, without complaint, without fail, so mote it be."

She looked down at the damp dirt of the alley and sighed. Then she gazed straight up into my eyes.

"This I will do," she said, "By mine very own 'mortal soul."

I pricked her finger with a magic sting, causing a small spot of blood to ooze forth, and then grabbed her hand and touched the red spot to my tongue.

"It's done. Follow me," I ordered, and without even bothering to see if she trailed behind, abruptly turned and headed back to the main street.

I was angry and upset at being so easily manipulated, but I had no choice in the matter, for mages are required to accept all commissions, unless they can demonstrate that the execution of such an agreement will cause harm to another, or if the contracting party cannot or will not pay the fee demanded for the service.

Still, I sensed something unseemly about this particular request, and I was not looking forward to its resolution. I'd been practicing far too long to expect anything other than grief to come from this charge. And I wasn't wrong, either!

CHAPTER THIRTY-NINE
"IS SHE TRAINED TO USE THE BOX?"

I took the girl with me back to Barstölný, leaving Hawk and the other recruits to continue their celebration. They wanted to remain in Paltyrrha until (and if) I should have some further need of their services.

She brought with her a small bag of clothing and personal effects, gathered from her room at the Greenbriar Inn, after she'd changed out of her performance costume. Although she still displayed a decidedly ripe figure under the sedate, light blue dress that now covered her body, without the veil she seemed almost ordinary to me. Her dark hair drifted down around a face that was etched with worry lines. The top of her head reached no higher than my shoulder—and I was not considered a tall man.

"What's your real name?" I asked, as we strode down the Avenue du Saint-Constantine to the main transit-station.

"What…yours?" she retorted, and after a long pause, finally said: "I have used the Shah'rah for very long time now. You not need know any other thing else beside."

"Speaking of which," I said, "Who's this 'El Amor' of whom you speak?"

"Sevastiano Belloto," she said. "My, uh, darlin'."

"Do you have something of his that I can use in my reading?"

"*¡Sí!*" she said.

"Very well." We walked in silence the rest of the way.

When I took us both through the *viridaurum*, she reacted like someone to whom fast-travel was alien—but then I realized that she emanated from a part of the world that still disavowed magic in all its forms. The Holy Roman Cæsars controlled only a fraction of their original realm by the seventeenth century Anno Domini, but the peninsula known popularly as Espania was one of the three remaining slices of their diminishing pie, the others being Francia and Italia. I had never traveled there myself, but had heard many stories from those who had. I pitied the people who chose to live in such primitive conditions.

When we exited the mirror in my home, she abruptly stopped, dropped her bag, and screamed when she saw Scooter.

"So who have you brought home now, Master?" the wherret asked.

Shah'rah screamed again when she realized the creature could talk.

"Another playmate for you, my little friend," I said. "At least for the next seven months."

"Oh, joy! Is she trained to use the box?"

"Box?" the woman screeched. "What…is…this box? You mean I have…go in…box?"

"Scooter was just tickling your sensibilities," I said. "You can use the outhouse like all the servants."

"I no servant!" she said.

"You just indentured yourself to me for seven months. You did this of your own free will."

"I no servant!" she repeated.

"Can you cook?" I asked. "I don't do that very well myself, and Scooter here prefers its food still mobile."

"What…kind place…is this?" she yelled. "What you…do here?"

"Mostly, I blow up things and torture lost souls," I said. "But, to pay the bills in earlier days, I also once told the fortunes of a different kind of 'lost soul.' Just like you want me to."

"What's her name?" Scooter asked.

"She won't tell me. She calls herself Shah'rah."

"This…this…terrible place," she said.

"So I've been told," I said. "But it's home—for me, for Scooter, and now for Shah'rah—for at least for the next seven months. And if you give me any trouble, woman, any trouble at all, that time can be extended, per Paragraph LXXXV, Clause XXI of the *Lex Magica*. So long as you're bound to me, you have no rights. Do you understand what I'm saying?"

Her face suddenly flushed with anger, and her dark brown eyes darted this way and that, as if looking for a way out, and she almost said something then, but managed to restrain herself. I nearly made the mistake of laughing at her.

"I…'derstand," she finally managed to choke out. "I…do what…you say, *Maestro*."

"Good. Now, answer my question, please: do you cook?"

"I…cook real good," she said.

"Excellent. Then do so, if you please. Scooter, please arrange for Martana to come by again. Shah'rah, she's a local peasant woman whom I've hired to assist with cleaning and maintenance, for which I have neither the time nor energy nor interest personally, and which Madame Weasely can't handle. I've cursed her so she can't reveal anything of what she sees here. She's well-compensated for her efforts."

"You…you…terrible man."

"Very probably. However, this terrible man also reads the future, and you contracted with me to read yours—and this Sevastiano's. This I shall do, but not until the morrow. In the meantime, follow me to what passes for a kitchen here, and see what you can do with whatever remains in the larder."

"I did order some supplies, Master," the wherret said.

"Excellent. Then we shan't starve."

And Shah'rah actually turned out to be a fairly competent chef, within certain limits. She had a tendency to overcook and over-spice everything, but she put together a quick and tasty meal that first night from just odds and ends. She was utterly enthralled with the freeze-box.

"How…this work?" she asked, opening the door and watching

the chill fog pour out into the room. "This...'mazing."

I pointed to the back side of the container, and then opened a small hatch there. She leaned over to peer into the dim alcove, and screamed again.

"What...th-that?" she said, visibly shaken.

I closed the cover, hiding the gnarly little critter running frantically on the treadmill.

"A gnasty gnomette," I said. "They infest the Æthernet like viruses, often causing transmission problems. They have to be cleaned out every once in a while, and when that happens, you can buy their services for specific periods of time. Kind of like an indentured servant." I smiled at her very sweetly.

"You...nasty, nasty man," she said. "Not...nice 't-all."

"Nope," I said, "not nice at all. That does smell good, though."

She was fixing a mixture of fresh vegetables and lamb sautéed with oil over an open flame. I wondered why she hadn't used the gar-coal, and then realized that she had no way of knowing how it worked. I'd show her tomorrow. We had no bread in the house, but that could also be remedied the next day, whenever Martana appeared. She usually did the shopping for us, and the nearby town of Barstöl had a thriving marketplace.

I cleared off the "dining table," which I'd long used for other purposes, and even gave it a swipe with a cloth to swish away the stains. Then I retrieved a flower from the garden, and made it stand on end in the very center, embedding a "false flame" on top to cast some light. It looked almost "homey," if I say so myself.

I moved two proper chairs—not benches—to either side of the wooden structure, and plopped myself in one of them. When Shah'rah brought our food, she was again "'mazed" by what I'd done.

Scooter hopped down from my shoulder to the third spot.

"What did you get for yourself, my friend?" I asked the wherret, as Shah'rah sat down in her place.

"Escargot with a mouse chaser," it said, bringing up the small lacquer cage.

"Sounds scrumptious—but not as scrumptious as this," I said, easing a spoonful of the hot stew into my mouth. It was a fiery brew—and not just because it was hot. I grabbed my mug of ale and doused the blaze.

"Is…good?" Shah'rah asked.

"Is very good," I managed to choke out between bites.

I could get used to this, I thought to myself.

But what about Niobë?

CHAPTER FORTY
"A LITTLE SHORT OF COLDDUST"

What about Niobë—*indeed*? I hadn't consciously thought of the Lady, as I called her, during much of our expedition to Indushia. Nor had I had any contact with her since leaving my home in the first place, other than fleeting impressions. Was I growing tired of my quest, even before it was launched? I suddenly felt very guilty.

After dinner, I linked together the pair of sky-orbs and attempted to contact her, but received no response, not even a tingle from the æther. It should have been morning on her world. However, even a light cloud cover on her end could interfere with the transmission of messages, so I wasn't especially worried by her lack of reply.

"What...you do?" Shah'rah asked.

"Trying to contact a friend," I said. "She lives very far away."

"Oh. She...you *amor*?"

"No," I said. "Just a friend."

I put away my contraption.

"Oh."

"Really, she's just a friend. You want some music?"

I wasn't used to entertaining females, as one might have guessed by now.

"*Sí,*" she said.

I snapped my fingers twice and said, "*Fiat musica,*" and the little buggers poured out of the hole in the wall where they lived, and began playing "Old Paltyrrha."

"Yeek!" Shah'rah screeched, when she saw the wee critters.

Some years earlier, as a kind of experiment in applied magic, I'd enhanced a group of crickets, roaches, and bagflies, increasing their size and augmenting their ability to produce audible and pleasurable sounds. The only problem after that was preventing them from being eaten by something else, or seeing them die too quickly because of the biological limits of the medium.

Oh, and there was also the yuck effect, for those individuals that couldn't abide large insects. Ah, well!

She was about to stomp the mini-band into oblivion when I grabbed her arm and pulled her back.

"No!" I said. "No!"

"You…'orrible *hombre*!"

"Yes, horrible and terrible and all those 'bull's. But you will not kill or damage or otherwise mar any of my property, not without my permission. Do you understand?"

"Or…or…what?"

"Or I will turn you into one of *those*," I said, pointing down at the musical creatures.

"Oh, no!" Then she started cursing in rapid-fire Spanish.

Of course, I had no such power, but Shah'rah didn't know that. Transforming one type of beast into another is extraordinarily difficult and energy-consuming, and requires special skills that take years to hone—unless, of course, you're already an animorph like Scooter. I snapped my fingers again, just once, and the wee players all retreated to their dens.

Then I showed her the alcove that would serve as her room during her stay in Barstölný, complete with a bedroll on a stone shelf, and a small wood dresser in which to store her clothes and other personal items; and I also led her to the commode that was used by servants and guests (I had my own private privy elsewhere), and took her around to the several water pumps installed inside and out. Finally, I told her that she was not to enter my laboratory for any reason unless I was present, showed her how to lock the outside doors and windows, and ordered her to keep all external openings locked at all times if I was absent.

"No one is to be allowed in, unless you know who they are," I said.

"But…know no one here."

"Yes, that is correct. The world can be a dangerous place. You will not leave these grounds and buildings without my permission. Do you understand?"

"'Derstand," she said, her voice very muted now.

"Good." I pointed to the kitchen. "Please clean up the mess, and then the rest of your time is your own for the evening."

"But…what I do here?"

"That's up to you," I said. "I have work to attend to and materials to read. I do not wish to be bothered again until morning. Good night."

"*Buenas noches*," she said, her head downcast. Then she began slowly clearing away the dirty pottery. I could hear her banging and clanging in the kitchen for perhaps an hour, and then the sound of silence.

* * * * * * *

Back in my workroom with Scooter, I checked my supplies for the exercise we were going to conduct with Shah'rah.

"We seem to be a little short of colddust," I said.

"Let me check the supply room, Master," the wherret said, and scooted quickly out of the building. We had several secure structures out back, including one that acted as a long-term storage area for basic magical implements and supplies. It wasn't wise to keep some of these materials too close to one's living space.

The creature was back in a jiffy. "Yes, Master, I thought so." It held up a jar of the goop. "We still have a few of these in stock."

"Good. Then, assuming that our subject can provide us with something belonging to the other party, I should be able to conduct my reading without difficulty."

"Why does she want this done?" the little beast wanted to know.

"She wouldn't say. Only that she had to know whether or not this Sevastiano was true to her. I assume he's her paramour."

"This task has a very strange feel to it, don't you think, Sir?"

"Yes, I wondered about it from the very beginning, particularly after I placed so high a price on the service—a price that she was quite willing to pay, I might add. That in itself I find quite odd."

"Still, it's not as if she's a stranger in this world. She's been working the higher-class taverns and establishments of Paltyrrha for several years now, and is well-known as a professional dancer and prostitute, charging premium prices for her services."

"What about her background, Master?"

"No one knows anything about her except that she hails from Andalusia. She refused to tell me her real name or life history—these may seep through the net when we do the reading.

"By the way," I said, "Did you look at the book I left you?"

"Yes, Master, and that volume is very, very *outré* indeed. It consists of a series of dialogues between the various shades of Hades, dealing with life, liberty, and the pursuit of happiness—or was it life, the universe, and everything? In any case, none of it seems to make much sense.

"One section is labeled 'Catalytic Quotes,' while another is called 'Quæstiones,' and yet another 'Under Egypt.' The Maltese Cat figures into some of the stories, and the Mad Mendicant Monk, Marcus Menvillius, wanders through some others. Certain apparently real individuals such as Barlévin the Beleaguered make an appearance in passing, but to no effect that I can see. Some of the other names are unknown to me.

"I suspect, Master, that we could study this volume for years and never come to any conclusion as to its utility."

"Then why can't it be copied?" I asked, "If it has so little value, it should yield what small secrets it contains most willingly. No, there's something else we're missing here. Doctor Scarabbaios must want it for a very specific reason, and I wouldn't be at all surprised if it doesn't have something to do with his travels to the Otherworlds.

"Well, my friend, 'Sufficient unto the day is the evil thereof,' as Barlévin says." I laid the book to one side. "It's almost time for bed." I yawned in slow counterpoint.

"You know I don't sleep much," the wherret said.

"Yes, and I always assumed that was due to your spiritual component. Now you tell me you're not from the Spiritworld."

"Those kinds of questions do not yet require answers, Master. I bid you good evening."

"And to you."

I took a jar of glowbugs with me to my bedroom, together with a copy of Kallistos Probatikos's *The Music of the Spheres*. It was good to be home again. I read till I fell asleep, and woke later that night to find the book cradled on my chest, face down; I had the impression that I'd heard the voice of the Lady calling me.

But there was no one in the æther that I could find.

So I snapped my fingers and extinguished the light.

CHAPTER FORTY-ONE
"WHO'S WHAT'S-HER-NAME?"

I'd barely put my head down (or so it seemed) when I again felt Niobë calling to me.

I was in the midst of a dream in which I was trapped in a maze, similar to that of the Hanging Garden in Paltyrrha, but also different in several respects. I was searching for the four eggs of the Great Elephant that had been mentioned by my ancestor, the mage Parakôdês; but every which way that I turned created some further difficulty.

I would find one egg tucked up against the side of the hedge, and pick it up; and then spot the second—but I had no place to store them, and they were large enough (larger than any *real* eggs that I'd seen) that I could only carry two, one in each hand. My garments contained no pockets. I would put down one egg to pick up another, and then find that the first egg had disappeared.

I spent hours and hours (I thought) wandering through the turns and unexpected jogs of the shrubbery, but never actually getting anywhere. I could never control more than two of the eggs at a time, and I knew that I needed all four to accomplish my task (whatever *that* was).

Finally I came to the center of the maze, and in place of the statue of Queen Landizábel I found a living, breathing woman standing there, the lower half of her face enshrouded by a veil— and I knew it was the Lady herself.

"What do you want?" she asked.

"The four Elephant's Eggs."

"Are you sure it isn't the Fourth Elephant's Egg?"

"I don't understand what you mean," I said. I held out my hands, palms up. "I have two of them already."

"These look like birds' eggs to me," she said. "Do you take everything so literally? You should know better, hypatomancer."

Both cracked and began leaking their yellow dew over my outstretched fingers.

Then she canted her head to one side: "Ah, my better half is calling me. Perhaps you should wake up now."

I stumbled out of my dream-drugged somnolence, forcing my eyes open and relighting the glowlamp.

"What?" I mumbled.

"Morpheús!" Niobë said. "Are you all right?"

"Lady," I said, gradually regaining my senses. "I tried contacting you earlier, but couldn't get through."

"It's mid-morning here now," she said. "I've tried to reach you at this time for the past week."

"Sorry, I just returned." Then I told her all about my trip.

"So you found the book? Why, that's utterly marvelous! What does it do?"

I sighed. "I don't know yet. Scooter and I have just started examining the thing, and it appears to serve no function. The content is meaningless without some context. Maybe…well…." Then I related to her the dream that I'd just had.

"What are these eggs?" she asked.

"Something that I have to find—or so my ancestor indicated—to accomplish my task (and I'm not really sure what that is, either). Niobë, I'm just so tired right now, I can't think straight."

There was a long silence from the other side of the æther. Then she said: "What about the boy who was killed?"

"Sparrow? What about him?"

"You have to do something, Morpheús, to commemorate his passing. You can't just let him die unspoken. After all, he was one of your men. He gave his life for you while on your service.

You have to treat his memory with respect. All of your group will expect that."

I sat up abruptly in bed, causing the wherret to scoot out from its hidey-hole underneath to see what was happening.

"You're right, of course," I said. "I knew I'd forgotten something important." I rubbed my hand over my bleary eyes.

"What time is it?" I asked my familiar.

"About an hour before dawn, Master," came the reply.

"Then there's still time to get things going. I want you to bear a message for me when it's light. Meanwhile, rouse What's-Her-Name to fix me some breakfast, if you please."

"Yes, Sir," the creature said, and scampered off.

"Who's What's-Her-Name?" the Lady asked.

So I told her, perhaps against my better judgment. "I have to do a reading for her to determine if her 'friend' has been true to her. I strongly suspect that he hasn't. She had to indenture herself to me for seven months to gain the service I'm providing."

"Why didn't you simply charge her a fee?" she asked. "Isn't that your normal practice?"

"Uh, I guess…uh…."

"Is she pretty?"

"Well, if you like dark-headed women, perhaps…."

"Is she charming?"

"She's a professional dancer," I said. "Niobë, why should you care _what_ she looks like? I agreed to provide her with a fore-seeing; actually, under the laws of Kórynthia, I could do nothing else once she'd insisted. I needed a cook, so I took advantage of the situation."

"It does sound very strange to me."

"No stranger, I suspect," I said, "than conducting a conversation with someone I've never met who lives halfway across the void."

"True. Try probing the book, Morpheús—with appropriate protections in place, of course. That might prove efficacious in determining some of the artifact's powers or potentialities. Do call again soon, please."

"I shall," I said, "and I apologize for my abruptness. I do not function well early in the morning."

And then I cut the connection. Dawn would soon be upon us, and despite the hour, I had much to do this day.

CHAPTER FORTY-TWO
"THE GOODS, THE BADS, AND THE UGLIES"

First thing that morning, I sent a message via Scooter to Sergeant Strook (or Hawk), asking him to meet me at the Bridge of Sighs in Julianople that afternoon. I wanted to stay as far away from Paltyrrha as possible, to avoid any potential assassins.

There was just a hint of fall in the cool breeze coming off the Sea of Marmara, but the great capital of the Byzantine Julian Empire was much as I remembered it from my days at University—and the Bridge was still a slice of sublime stateliness slithering over the St. Joseph Canal. I transited to town an hour early, just to enjoy a quiet interlude all by myself—a rare luxury these days.

"Have you fully recovered from your celebrations?" I asked Hawk, when he finally appeared.

"Yes, Sir," he said, "although I'm not as young as I used to be, and I'm still a bit foggy from last night."

"Aren't we all," I said. "Sergeant, I want to do something to commemorate Sparrow's passing. What was his real name? Did he have any family?"

"When I knew him in the service, Sir, he was called Stylian of Samothrace," he said. "He came from a small village there—Therma, I think. Last I knew, his old Ma was still livin', and he also had a sister or two, and some nieces and nephews."

"Any wife or children?"

"No, Sir. He was the kind of man who kept a girl in every port, if you know what I mean. If he had any kids, he never told me."

"Did he ever say what he wanted done after he was gone?" I asked.

"Well, Sir, we did talk about this a couple of times, and he told me once that if anythin' ever happened to him, he'd like to be buried back home. Of course, we all know that's sometimes not possible."

"I put the body in stasis, so it's easily retrievable for the funeral," I said. "Do you have the time right now to transit to Samothrace?"

"Yes, Sir, I do."

As we slowly made our way back towards the main transit station in Julianople, enjoying the fine sunny day, a street vendor blocked our way, trying to push his paltry cart of wares upon us, the circle of bells hanging off the back tinkling with every movement he made. I waved him off, several times, but he was a particularly persistent little pest, and he followed us all the way down Belissarios Boulevard.

"What *is* the matter with you?" I finally said, stopping in front of the Office of Æthernet Services and accosting him directly. "I've told you that we're not interested."

"With all respect, Sir, you ain't actually looked at my stuff, now, have you?" The man was dressed in a shoddy, dirty shirt that had once been crimson, and a pair of tattered pants of a pale emerald hue. He almost looked like a circus performer. "See here, Sir, I've got the goods, the bads, and the uglies"—he swept his right hand in a circle—"Only the discerning customer, the one who can foresee for one, can tell us the difference."

When the Sergeant made a motion as if to draw his short sword, I held up my hand. "I'll give you five minutes, no more," I said to the junkmonger. "So, seller...convince me that any of these trinkets are actually worth buying."

"What's 'bout this, then, Sir?" He held up a small glowlight, but the sun was shining too brightly for me to see anything emanating from the bug or bugs inside.

"I've seen a hundred of these before," I said. "It's just like all the others."

"No, 'tain't, Sir, 'tain't like any of 'em," he said. "This one lights yer way through the ætherspace."

"Poppycock!" the Sergeant said, "there's no such thing."

"Indeed," I said, "glowlights work on a set of standard principles, vendor. The luminosity is generated by the excitation of the critters contained within the specially-treated glass. That only works in real space and time."

"These aren't like that, Sir," the junkman said. "My lights *only* work in the æther."

"But you *can't* perceive things there," I said. "You can feel presences sometimes, and you can find your way across ætherspace, if you're accomplished and/or lucky, but that's it. What good is this light, even if it works as you say it does, if you can't actually see it?"

"That ain't my problem, Sir," the poorly-dressed man said. "It does what it does. I dunno how it works. Howsomever...." He laid it aside. "What's 'bout *this* wee gem?"

It looked like a compass stuck in a small, clear sphere. I held my hand out, and then turned it over on my palm several times. As I shifted the artifact, its needle moved to remain fixed in the same direction, which was up and to the right. The thing wasn't fashioned of glass, of that I was certain—but what exactly it did and how it had been made, I truly had no idea.

"What is it?" I asked.

"I call it the Pathfinder, Sir," the seller said. "You say where 'tis you want to go, and it points in that direction till you get there. *Any*where."

Without thinking, I blurted out, "I want to go to Naprimér"—and the needle moved this way and that, shifting itself until it finally froze in a position that pointed down and to the right.

"But it doesn't tell you *how* to get there," I asked, "or even how far the distance is?"

"No, Sir, it don't."

"Then what good is it, really?"

"That's for you to say, Sir," the junkmonger said. He took the sphere back and replaced it in its hollow on the cart. "What's 'bout this, then?"

He handed me a small, dark, very heavy chunk of metal that had been cast in the shape of dog, somewhat long and narrow like a dachshund, but with different features.

"It looks like a miniature andiron," I said, hefting it in my hand. It weighed more than it should have for its size.

"'Tis a firedog, Sir," the vendor said, "a Canignis, as the Romans woulda had it. It can warm or illuminate or enflame just 'bout anything."

"Really?" I put the image on the edge of the cart and commanded, *"Fiat lux!"*

The firedog slowly began to glow, and then three lights emerged from its mouth and eyes, discernible even in the blaze of the sun.

Then I stated: *"Fiat flamma!"*—and the little beast started to heat up, to the point where, within a few minutes, the piece of wood on which it was resting began to smoke. I immediately ordered it to desist, and the reddish aura of the thing abruptly faded away.

"Now, *that* is very interesting," I said. "I've never seen one of these before. What do you want for it?"

"A service, if you please, Sir."

"Ah, yes," I murmured beneath my breath, "it's always something." And then to the seller: "Specifically what?"

"I want to know the exact time and place of my death."

"What!" I was wholly astonished. No one ever wanted to be told of the circumstances of their ultimate passing. "Are you certain? You understand that this knowledge, once given, cannot be wiped from your memory. It will taint you for the rest of your life."

"Nonetheless, Sir, this is what I want. And I will give you all three of the goods, the bads, and the uglies in return, for they seem to belong together."

"Come, Sir," Sergeant Strook said, grabbing my elbow, "let's not spend any more time on this junker's junk. It's not worth it."

"Wait," I said, shaking off his hand. I turned back again to the vendor: "*Why* do you want to know?"

"That's *my* business, Sir," the man said, "and that's my price. Nothing else will do."

For some reason, I really wanted that firedog. I'd heard of these things before, and they could prove very useful under certain circumstances. But the truth is, it just took my fancy.

Scooter and I used to play a game sometimes in years past, when we were walking through the big city streets. He would point to someone, and I'd say, *sotto voce*, "May 6, 1652" or "September 11, 1648" or "June 2, 1655," or whatever date applied. Because I could look at someone—I mean really *look*—and tell you when they were going to die. They had to be present in person, and close enough physically that I could see them as individuals. But it never failed, and I was able to validate several of my "guesses" at a later date. They were invariably correct. We quit this little charade when I inadvertently "pronounced" one of my friends, and it ceased being funny thereafter.

But the talent was always there. So I "looked" at the junk-monger's soul and said, "February 29, 2012"—and then realized what I'd uttered. "Who...?" I began.

"Where?" the seller said, cutting me off.

I reached out and grabbed his right hand. It was icy cold to the touch. "Colman Green," I blurted out without thinking.

"I see that you *do* have the talent, Sir," he said. "That corresponds with what I already know. I will die on February 29, 2012 at Colman Green on Zmaragdus, and you, Morpheús the Mage, will be the one to kill me."

Then he went back to his cart and picked up the three implements, one at a time. The firedog he turned on its back, so that its four legs stuck straight up in the air, and he somehow attached the Pathfinder to them. Then he put the glowlight into the creature's open mouth. I heard a "click" as the orb seated itself. And finally, he took a square stone etched with a round hollow at its center, and placed the other side of the compass into its base. He twisted it once, and I could hear it latch.

"There," he finally said, "all done. This is no longer my burden, Dream Weaver." He somehow began folding it back in upon itself from each corner, four times, and then handed me a light, thin wallet that I could carry in my pouch. "Use it wisely, Sir."

As he started pushing his cart back up Belissarios, I shouted to him, "Wait! You haven't told me your name."

"No, Sir, I haven't," I heard him say, just before he turned down a narrow alleyway. We ran after him, but when we reached the corner, there was just a trash-strewn passage to be seen, dead-ending at a blank brick wall. There was no place he could have gone or hidden, no doorways, no nothing.

"That's impossible, Sir," the Sergeant said.

Many things are impossible, but they happen anyway, and we poor mages are left to explain them to the *hoi polloi*. But all too often, we have no answers ourselves, or at least none that make any sense. We then have several choices. We could be honest and tell the people that we just don't know. Or we could make something up.

Usually, we just lie.

CHAPTER FORTY-THREE
"BE GLAD YOU
HAVE A FUR COAT"

Samothrace is easier to access by transit-mirror than by boat, since the island has no natural harbor. I twisted the leys and sent myself first to Julianople, where I'd arranged to meet Strook and his remaining men; and from there I moved us through æther-space to the town of Samothrace, the chief municipality on the rocky crag.

We stayed overnight at the Inn of the Seven Fables, a rustic place that offered rough comfort for weary travelers; and managed to catch a meal that evening at the Julian Opal, a tavern that offered heaping bowls full of a highly seasoned stew made from fish, mussels, clams, and sea urchins.

The next day, we piled out of our cots, and found ourselves facing a chill, windy, showery day in fall.

"Be glad you have a fur coat," I told Scooter, who was perched at its usual spot on my right shoulder. I pulled my cloak tighter over my back—and I was still cold.

We transited to the Church of St. Gorgo, not far from the village of Therma, and there I introduced myself to Statia, Sparrow's mother, and to his sisters, Merula and Elumba. The latter was married to a goatherd named Opus, whom she shyly introduced to me, along with her several small children.

It appeared that the entire community had turned out for the ceremony, along with many of their neighbors. The service was conducted by Father Pavlinos.

During the homily, he said: "Our brother Stylian went out into the world five years ago to seek his fortune, and now he has returned, bearing with him the gold he had promised his family, and the echoes of the grand deeds he accomplished.

"He was present at the Battle of Isteria, where he saved the Emperor's cousin, and again at the Battles of Kyklope, Metacarbomol, Epris, and Lorianburg. By all accounts, he served bravely and steadfastly, and was a credit to his units.

"After his discharge from the Royal Army, he hired himself out to others, and also became an instructor of the military arts under Sergeant Strook.

"We remember him as a bright, engaging lad who never complained or found fault, and who carried with him a dream of securing his family's future. This he accomplished, but at the cost of his own life. These men, his comrades-in-arms, have donated the money to create a plaque in his name to adorn the church walls, and to fashion a monument to preserve his memory.

"And now, if any of you wish to speak, please come forward one at a time."

I raised my hand, and then stepped to the front of the standing congregation.

"I knew Stylian just for a brief period," I said, "A matter of mere weeks; but in that time I came to respect and like him for the man he was. It was Stylian who ensured that our mission would be a success. No enemy bested him; he was struck down by a freak occurrence. His passing is a great loss to all who knew him. May he attain eternal rest in the eyes of the Lord."

And then, one by one, beginning with the Sergeant, the members of our small company joined me before the congregation, and made their own remarks to honor their late comrade's memory, with Strook, Eagle, Raven, Bird, Roc, and Warbler adding their poignant comments, and then bowing their heads in respect.

After them, members of the local community also spoke, many of them with sorrow in their voices, about a man who had obviously been popular while he lived on Samothrace, and who had, in their eyes, at least, done well by himself in the outside world.

I have never enjoyed funerals. They remind me overmuch of my own mortality; for although we wizards can spin out our lives through potions and trickery to a far greater degree than the average person, we still remain desperately susceptible—to accident, mayhem, or, ultimately, just plain old age. Everything and everyone wear out eventually.

That was why the idea of a magus who had perhaps lived more than a thousand years, as Mathurin was reputed to have done, greatly intrigued me. Who *was* this man, my purported ancestor? What had he discovered that the rest of us had yet to find? What had he accomplished so long ago?

I was determined to discover the truth, and to follow his footsteps through the æther.

CHAPTER FORTY-FOUR
"WHAT CAN I SAY? I
KNOW THESE THINGS"

Unfolding the future of Shah'rah the belly-dancer was not like the difficult conditional reading I'd done for Jécko the Mallet, nor did it bear much resemblance to the "flash" readings that I was accustomed to conducting for the gentry. This one required less energy, concentration, and supplies than the former, and more focus on my part than the latter. There were, of course, potential dangers to both the reader and the "readee" if that focus was disturbed during the course of the spell.

The colddust helped settle the æther around us. I took another drop of blood from the woman, and a small snippet of Sevastiano's locks from the black curl she provided me. Then I told her to be absolutely quiet while I peered through the veil.

I calmed my spirit, and gained strength from the wherret curled on my arm. It linked with me, and then touched its tongue to the ruby essence of the dancer, and abruptly I was drawn into a maelstrom of swirling possibilities. I had already lighted a small charcoal brazier, and I now laid the man's hair on the hot fire. It sizzled and twisted while it burned.

Suddenly I saw Shah'rah's visage as it was perhaps five years ago, when she would have been about twenty; someone hovered near her in that mental picture and spoke her name. I could see part of the room behind her: a rich, sumptuously decorated area filled with too-bright artwork and elaborate divans and ornately carved tables. Then I saw her again, dressed in beautifully-tailored clothing, her hair and face made up so intricately that it had to have been done by a maid. This was no peasant girl, that much was clear!

As the pages of her life turned before my eyes, the man Sevastiano—whom she called "Don Sebastián—gradually made his appearance. He was, I gathered, some kind of emissary from the east, although his role was never clear. I gradually came to believe that he was Greek in origin, his name actually being Sevastianos—although whether that was his original moniker was doubtful. She became so enamored of him that she'd followed him when he finally returned home, against the will of her father, secreting herself on the vessel that would take him to Italia, and then emerging when it became too late to turn back.

Again, it was unclear to me whether her sudden reappearance had actually pleased Sevastiano or not. Obviously, at some point this had become unclear to Shah'rah as well.

When they'd finally reached Julianople, Sevastiano had confessed that he already had a wife and family stashed somewhere else (but not there!), and that he could have her put aside and marry Shah'rah. But he was burdened with a great many debts and obligations, and these would have to be retired before he could move forward in his life again. They would both have to work until he was free of these financial…impediments.

She agreed, and he sent her to receive training at a high-class whorehouse in the Imperial capital. After she "graduated," he took her to Adrianople, and then to Paltyrrha a year later, and she had worked there for three years, trying to pay off the man's seemingly unending stream of debts. Of late she had become disillusioned with her lover, and wondered if he was using her.

I probed his background and foreground more closely, and discovered that he actually derived from the Russian Hegemony, his real name being Barós Sevastiánovich. He was a spy for the Lietish Grand-Prince Rushán II. He actually had several wives scattered around different capitals of Nova Europa, but he was faithful to none of them. He was paid very well indeed to gather information, but spent every last gold corona that he received.

This was a very old and well-worn story, I perceived—but I probed more deeply, looking past today into tomorrow.

In the end, I saw, he would either abandon her completely, or, if he felt that she knew too much about him (a much more likely prospect), he would murder her and dispose of the body in such a way that it would appear to others that she'd been killed by one of her clients. He would never marry her or love her in the way that she wanted.

Shah'rah was sitting in a chair off to one side, as I'd instructed her, keeping perfectly quiet while understanding nothing of what was occurring. I abruptly walked over to her, the wherret still attached to my arm, put my hands on either side of her head, and force-fed the dancer the knowledge that I'd acquired.

She squirmed and twisted trying to escape my grasp—and the import of the news I was giving her.

"Noooo!" she screamed out loud, when she realized what she had seen. And then she fainted dead away—I had to catch her to keep her from falling to the hard floor and injuring herself.

I carried her to her bed, and forced a sedative between her lips. It allowed her to sleep for fifteen hours, and deadened the memory of what I'd instilled in her mind. I stayed by her the entire time, because I knew that if she woke too early, she might try to harm herself. Scooter remained for a short time only.

"This is a bad business, Master. What is it about you humans that you so readily abuse the others of your kind?"

"I don't know," I said. "I really don't know some days. I hate this kind of reading. If I give them the truth, they despise me for it, but if I lie, I despise myself. That's why I have to try something new in my life."

The next morning, she gradually emerged from the drugged sleep that I'd put upon her, and when she opened her eyes, I could see the torment that welled there.

"You…told me," she finally said.

"That doesn't make it any easier. You must have had some inkling yourself, or you wouldn't have insisted on knowing. The question is, what will you do now?"

"I want…to kill…him!" she said.

"There are hundreds like him out there," I said. "You do him too much honor by giving him an easy death. He's the kind of man who will find a bad ending on his own."

And then I took one of her hands in mine, and I showed her the rest of what I'd seen concerning the future of Sevastiano the Spy. None of the outcomes were good.

"You're indentured to me now," I said. "You belong to me, according to the law. If he harms you in any way, he'll have to answer to me—and I'll tell him that in such a way that he'll never want to see you again. That's all you can really hope for.

"Can you ever return to your home?"

She was crying now, a steady stream of tears down both cheeks.

"I…I have disgrace…*mi familia…mi padre*, he never…talk me again."

"I'm very sorry for you. But you'll always have a place here, if you wish that. When your term with me is up, you can choose what you wish do with yourself."

"I…cannot say…."

"I understand. But give it time. Do you know where Sevastiano is now?"

She thought he was staying at The Fox with the Socks in Paltyrrha.

"He comes…he goes," she said.

"I'll find him," I said.

I watched over her for two days, to make certain that she could live with herself, and I then ordered Scooter to observe her closely, and do what was necessary to preserve her health.

"Oh, when's Martana coming?" I asked, because the place really needed a thorough cleaning. Somehow, Madame Weasely just didn't seem to catch the lint in the corners.

"She'll be here this afternoon," the creature said.

"Good. I'm going to the capital. Be back later."

I transited to the main receiving station in Paltyrrha, and

then zipped locally to the inn where Sevastiano made his home.

"Yes," said the proprietor. "He always sleeps in—entertains his company late, if you know what I mean."

I bribed the man for a room number and key.

"You won't hurt him?" he asked.

"No, I just need to tell him something," I said, smiling demurely.

I slipped quietly through the door upstairs, and eased a stiletto from its scabbard beneath my left arm. The spy opened his eyes when he felt the chill steel caressing his Adam's apple.

"Wha...?" he asked.

The girl next to him shifted in bed and started to raise her head. I spoke a word of power and she went back to sleep again.

By then he was fully awake.

"Who the fuck are you?" he growled at me.

"Why, my dear Barós Sevastiánovich," I said, "That's not a very nice thing to say to a friend."

"Friend? Why, I've never met you before in my life. And who's this Barrow chap?" He was squirming to ease the pressure of the blade on his throat.

"But I've heard all about *you* from Shah'rah, Sevastiano."

"That whiny bitch. She's no friend of mine," he said.

"Obviously. And she's never going to be one again."

"What do you mean?"

"Barós, Barós," I said, "you don't seem to understand very much for a supposedly smart man. First of all, Shah'rah's now indentured to me. That makes her mine under law. I have connections in very high places. If you harm or intimidate her, I *will* come after you to retrieve my lost monetary value.

"Secondly, your time here is limited in any case. You're going to pack your things and leave Kórynthia by the end of the month."

"Why should I do that?"

"Because, my old friend, I'm going to tell the authorities who and what you are at that time, and give them a detailed portrait of your remarkable features—and then if you make any future appearance in the kingdom, you'll be seized and condemned outright for the role you play as spy for the Lietish Grand-Prince. Our public executions are quite extraordinary events, prolonged for the entire day to make the obvious point to the onlookers."

I could feel him gulp beneath my knife's keen edge. I pressed down a little to draw some blood, and then touched my index finger to the oozing liquid, linking myself with him without his awareness of same.

"Why are you doing this to me? I've never hurt you."

"But you hurt Shah'rah, not to mention a great many others." I whispered a string of names in his ear. He looked appropriately shocked.

"How...?"

"I'm a mage. What can I say?: I know these things. I know all about you and your comings and goings and dealings and petty treacheries, etc., etc., etc. And I mean what I tell you: do *not* cross me, Barós. Do *not* return to Kórynthia, unless you want to die—in a very nasty way."

Then I surged into his mind and quite literally scared the poop out of him. I left him unconscious—but he'd remember every little moment of our brief time together when he awoke a few hours later and had to clean up the mess.

When I returned to Barstölný, Shah'rah was talking to Martana, and they seemed to be communicating just fine, in spite of the dancer's horrendous accent. Perhaps they'd become friends. I didn't want to disturb them, so I sneaked off to my lab again.

"She seems all right, Master," Scooter said from one corner. "Did you take care of your business?"

"I took care of business," I said. "Sevastiano won't bother her again."

"You seem to be devoting a great deal of time to her situation," the wherret said. "So what's happened with Niobë?"

"Yes, I always seem to be taking in lost sheep—just like when you arrived. Niobë's still out there, and I'm still planning to rescue her."

"Well, I hope you do better with her than you did with me."

But when I looked it in the eyes, the wherret was forced to turn away. The truth of the matter was, the beast had been lucky to survive in any form—and Scooter knew it!

CHAPTER FORTY-FIVE
"ON GNOMETTE-NETTING DUTY"

When I went to bed that night, I had a hard time getting to sleep. I kept thinking about what Scooter'd said, and wondering just what had actually happened way back when, during the time when the little wherret had first appeared. I hadn't consciously thought about that event for a great many years, but certain things that it'd said in the last month or two had me wondering.

I put myself into a trance, and turned back the clock in my mind to that winter's day in the Year of Our Lord 1611, more than a decade ago. I'd been visiting the mage Gullielmus Shaking-Spear in East Anglia, staying at his country home in Avonshire. He was a garrulous windbag who never used one word when a dozen would do, but for all that, he had a remarkable command of the language, and that mastery of words gave him an enormous potency in magic. He always knew exactly the right phrase to employ in a spell—always!

But he also liked his booze, and that's when he could get himself into serious trouble, because although he had all those words arrayed very neatly in his mind, sometimes when he got soused, he'd mix them up—with results that were often wholly unexpected. Usually the mix-ups were harmless and easily undone, but occasionally the Chief Mage of the Kingdom had to become involved. For that reason, Gullielmus had never risen very far in the magical hierarchy, despite his many talents.

We were trading dark ale one evening at The Triple Bore, when Willie, as he liked to be called, suddenly exclaimed in

Latin, "You know, I found something very interesting on the 'Net the other day."

"Really?" I said, hiccupping a couple of times. They brewed strong stuff in those cold, damp isles—and even that wasn't enough to cut the chill. No wonder they all died young, hacking their lungs out with their interminable coughs.

"Yes, yes, yes, I was out on gnomette-netting duty, and I felt a presence in the 'beyond beyond'."

"Beyond 'beyond beyond'?" I asked, laughing out loud.

"Now, don't repeat me, Morphy," he said. "Yes, yes, yes, I found…uh, Lord Jesus Christ and the Holy Mother of God, what was it that I found?"

"Something?"

"Well, look for yourself," he said, and then Shaking-Spear pulled a sky-orb from his belt-pouch, plopped it on the barstand, tapped it once on the top, and muttered a long phrase that seemed a bit, well, "off" to me.

"What was that you said?" I asked. I gulped another slug of the dark. Damn it was good!

All I heard was mumble, mumble, mumble in return. And then the orb flashed a brilliant orange, illuminating the entire room, and gnasty gnomettes began tumbling out onto the counter. As each one hit the wood, he (or she or it—I have no idea whether the critters are sexually oriented) sat up, looked around, and then hopped down to the floor. Sky-orbs are not really designed to be transit-devices, except for small bits of inert matter, so how the beasties were being pulled through the æther to our location, I had no idea.

"Oh, scones and shitters," Willíe said, and again rambled off a spell.

The orb turned green and the gnomettes suddenly vanished. Then the glass began to pulse in syncopation, lighter and darker, darker and lighter.

"I don't like this, Willíe," I said. "I don't like it one bit. Shut it down!"

Another harrumphed spell, and once again I thought I

detected a few mangled consonants mixed in there.

The pulses increased in frequency as a result.

"What's it doing?" I asked. I was starting to get scared now.

"I don't know," my friend replied. *"I'm trying! Really!"*

I spoke several words of power that should have shut the thing off immediately, but they had no effect.

"Willíe…," I said.

The pulsing had become so rapid by now that the orb was glowing a brilliant, almost incandescent emerald, and I couldn't bear to look directly into the light. I heard a whining noise in the background, and then everything just went dead, all of a sudden.

A foot poked its way through the near side of the glass, and then another, and then a head, and then the rest of the body, and Scooter pulled itself through the hole in the 'Net, and plopped down in front of us. It looked around the room, and at each of us in turn; and then it came over to me, and laid its head in my hands. This was the universal sign of magical subservience. All I had to do was accept its fealty, and its indentureship was sealed.

"So mote it be," I said, almost without thinking.

"Zo moht vee," the wherret replied, and looked up into my eyes.

Willíe tried to grab it, and when it scooted sideways out of his grasp, I laughed out loud and said, "That li'l Scooter got away from you, Willíe."

"Zkuter," the beast said.

"Yes, *Scooter*," I said. "That'll be your name from now on, little one."

"Nahame ez Zkuter," it said.

About then the barkeep told us that we had to leave the premises, since we were scaring away his customers, but the little creature that Shaking-Spear had somehow conjured from the void never went away, and had remained with me for the past eleven years. It quickly picked up the language, and now spoke the common tongue and many others like a native. The wherret never told me of its origins, but I had assumed from the beginning that it came from the Spiritworld.

Now I wondered.

"Scooter!" I said to the darkness.

"Yes, Master," came its voice from the alcove that it maintained underneath my bed.

"Where are you from?"

For a long time, the creature said nothing, but finally I felt it hop on the end of the bed, and gradually make its way towards my head.

It curled its body up next to my chest, and then said quietly: "The Otherworlds, Master. I come from the Otherworlds."

CHAPTER FORTY-SIX
"WELL, I'M DAMNED"

"The Otherworlds?" I said. "But how's that possible? I thought you had a spiritual component. That's what you told me."

"Unlike you, I have both," Scooter said.

"But I also have a soul."

"Yes, but I can actually *dwell* in both spheres—and you cannot."

"But where specifically are you from?" I asked.

"That place is so far removed from here that you have no name for it. You might label it as part of the Sixth Circle, if such a thing were possible, but even that is not wholly accurate. There are no words for whence I derive, or the kind of being I am."

"But if you possess such a marvelous, well, entity, how did you come to be stuck here?"

"Ah, as to that, Master," Scooter said. "The answer is, *well*, complicated. I was fleeing from an enemy who would have harmed or even killed me (yes, we can die). I had but an instant to decide, so I reached out through the æthernet, seeking a refuge anywhere I could find one. At the same time, I felt something alien latch onto me and pull me out of my world and into yours. That was your late friend's sky-orb. I think that perhaps even he didn't know what he'd done to retrieve me—and, in any case, he had no idea how to put me back again, even if I had wanted to go."

"Why did you choose me?"

"You looked harmless enough, particularly when compared to the other. He had a cynical streak in him. He would have used me in ways that I would have found, uh, uncomfortable. I didn't sense that in you, so I picked the lesser of two evils, you might say."

"If I released you from your servitude, could you find your way home again?" I asked, for, truth be told, I would not have held the creature against its will.

I felt it sigh where it was cuddling against me. "No, Master. I have absolutely no idea of how I can ever go back. There is nothing on this world that would provide me with the information that I need. It is possible, I suppose, that one of your transit-mirrors could be adapted for long-travel, but I don't know how to do that either, and neither does anyone else here. No, I am well and firmly trapped in this place."

"I'm sorry," I said, and I truly was.

"It is a matter of little consequence. The Great Being that governs the universe of words and the semblance of forms will ultimately determine the outcome of my story. I have, alas, very little say in the matter."

"That's a rather curious philosophy."

"But that is what I believe," the wherret said. "There are no accidents in the universe. And at this time and in this place, I choose to serve you, and you are *my* destiny as well."

"How can that help you?" I asked.

"Perhaps it won't," it said. "I can only wait and see."

"Then, I suppose, we must take the next step, and visit Doctor Scarabbaios. Perhaps *he'll* have some answers for us. But first I want to take a look again at *The Necropompeion*, more closely this time. There's something in that artifact that we're missing."

But Scooter was already snoring and snorting by my side. It didn't sleep very often (at least I rarely saw—or in this instance, heard—it do so), but this was one affectation that reminded me of the physical portion of the wherret's nature. I'd grown rather fond of the little bugger over the years. It was every bit as intelligent as any human I knew, and often more perceptive. I couldn't imagine life without it.

I reached over and touched the linked sky-orbs that I'd placed by my bed, and was immediately able to reach Niobë, one of the few occasions recently when the connection had come so readily.

"Greetings, dear friend," she said. "It is a pleasure, as always, to hear your voice. What's happened to you recently?"

I told her about the muted funeral of Sparrow on Samothrace, and mentioned the strange little junkmonger of Julianople, and what I'd purchased from him. I said nothing, however, about Shah'rah and the reading of Sevastiano.

"Another rare and unusual implement of power," she said. "Strange that you seem to be accumulating them, Morpheús, whether you wish to or not. First it was the statue of Matrin. Then came the book tied to the Netherworld. And now the firedog. I wonder…."

"You wonder what, my Lady?" I asked.

"You said that the firedog was linked to two other devices."

"Yes, a glowlight that shines only in the æther, and a universal compass of some kind."

"Of what is the firedog fashioned?" she asked.

I pulled it out of my pouch, and unfolded the artifact. I felt the canine sculpture, and then hefted it in my hand. "I don't know," I said. "It could be some kind of pewter or lead, but it has a curiously shiny surface for something so dark in hue. I don't think it's gold."

"Try asking it a question."

"What?"

"Just humor me, Morphy. Try asking it…um…if it can locate me."

Scooter woke up about this time, and I had the sense that it had been listening in its sleep to the entire conversation.

"Firedog!" I said, glaring down at its black face. I felt something shift slightly in my hand, but I didn't see anything. "Firedog! Can you find the Lady Niobë?"

Its eyes began to shine with a reddish interior glow, and then it really did move, its tail wagging slightly. It reached up with one paw, and removed the glowlight from its mouth. Then it said in a soft but quite audible voice, "Yes, Master."

"Where is she?"

Something within the mechanism of the globe which the creature straddled began to move, and I could hear this click-click-clicking sound as the needle shifted this way and that; the 'dog picked up the ætherlight again and reinserted it in its mouth-socket, and I felt a kind of buzz in the air as the glowlight began to warm. And then the beast pointed—I can employ no other term—at a spot off to one side, and said through the mumbling interference of the implement in its mouth, "On the world called Naprimér, in the Fifth Circle, Fourth Range, Sixty-First Inclination, between Delirant and Moucheron, not far from Zezament."

"Niobë, is that right?"

"So far as I know," she said. "I'm aware of the three worlds that it mentioned: they are, in fact, located within our region. As for the rest, well, who can know?"

"Firedog! Can you take me there?" I asked.

"I can, Master," came the hissed reply.

"Well, I'm damned," I muttered. Could it really be that easy?

Of course, nothing is ever *that* easy, as all of us soon discover; and even those tasks that seem easy at the time often require payments of blood, toil, and torment that make the ultimate accounting of the transaction rather dubious in the end. But avoiding that requires wisdom, something which the Morpheús of old always seemed to lack until it was too late.

For I *was* damned—by my own pride, by my own unwillingness to see the obvious, by my acceptance of myth over reality, and particularly by the myth of my own story.

But God—or the Devil—or something, obscures our vision and lets us continue traveling over the cliff until we've doomed ourselves with our own expectations.

"Be careful what you wish for." That's what my mother used

to say. The entity that governs the universe has a malicious or perhaps wry sense of humor, and I think he often grants our requests just to see what might happen.

CHAPTER FORTY-SEVEN
"THE HOLY GRAIL OF
ALL MAGICAL TOMES"

The next morning, Scooter and I tried to penetrate the mysteries of the magical volume, initially without much success. The cover and pages were impervious to flame, acid, ink, the knife, Kleen-All, citrus oil, and The Evacuator. In fact, I couldn't even determine the nature of the binding material.

"It's hard, shiny, and flexible, Sir," the wherret noted. "Water runs off the surface without permeating it."

The creature took a hot poker from the fireplace, and tried stabbing the book through its center. Nothing happened, except that it almost hit me with the thing when the point slipped off center.

"Hey, be careful!" I yelled. "You could have burned me!"

"Sorry, Master."

I looked very closely at the front cover of the thing—there wasn't even an indentation where the metal had touched it.

"Hellfire!" I said. "I don't know what else to try."

"What about a spell of merging?" my friend asked.

"That could be dangerous if there's a spirit already inhabiting this thing. However, I suppose that, with proper precautions, we could at least see if we get a response to a psychic probe, as Niobë suggested."

I started the brazier, and picked out several compounds from the shelf that would help induce the proper frame of mind: tranquillium, domarium, and laxus. These I sprinkled over the coals when they reached an appropriate glow, and sniffed in the smoke.

When I could feel my jowls loosening, I linked with Scooter and used its strength to center myself. Slowly, ever so slowly, I extended my consciousness towards *The Necropompeion*— only to find myself teetering on the abyss of the River Styx! I could see the shades crowded on the far shore, beckoning me to join them.

"Jesú!" I exclaimed, immediately drawing myself back to reality. "This thing is tied directly to the Netherworld. No wonder it can't be touched."

"That could, Sir, be an illusion generated by the maker of this artifact, to scare off potential experimenters. Perhaps a more pertinent question would be: can the book be employed in some other way to facilitate a journey to the Otherworlds?"

"I honestly don't see how," I said. "There's certainly immense power here, if it could be tapped. But the risk is enormous to anyone who resides in the land of the living. If either of us got lost on the other side of the Styx—if it's real, of course—then we'd never find our way out again."

"But part of my essence *is* spirit, Master," the wherret said. "Wouldn't that enable me to come and go as I please?"

"You're welcome to try, but I really wouldn't recommend it. Hades obviously exists in some form, despite the insistence of the philosophers that the afterlife consists only of Heaven and Hell, and possibly the Purgatory that the Holy Roman Cæsars continue to champion. What the place that I saw through the mirror of *The Necropompeion* really is, though, I have no idea. I don't think, however, that it's a shortcut to anywhere else that we want to visit."

"Then I don't know what else we can do, Master, other than give the book to Doctor Scarabbaios."

"I agree," I reluctantly said, and shut down the working with a word of command.

* * * * * * *

That afternoon, I contacted the good doctor once again.

He was about to cut me off when he realized who it was. *"Do you have it?"* he asked, energized in a way that he'd never displayed before.

"The Holy Grail of all magical tomes?" I said, "the only copy known to exist on Nova Europa?—oh yes, Doctor Scarabbaios, *I have it*!"

"Show it to me!" he said.

I held the volume up to the sky-orb.

"Mein Gott!" he said. "Is that really...?"

"Yes, it's *The Necropompeion*," I said, "and if you want it, Doctor Scarabbaios, you'll have to give me what I desire in return."

Damn, it was good to be on the other end of the stick for a change. Finally, I had something that someone *else* would give almost anything to possess.

There was a short burst of static over the orb.

"What do you want?" he finally asked.

"Everything you know about the Otherworlds, how to get there, how to get back, *everything*, Doctor S."

He sighed.

"You don't know what you're asking, boy. Still, if you're fool enough to inquire, you're fool enough to get an honest answer. I agree to your terms. By Hera's twin orbs, I swear that I shall faithfully and truthfully and completely respond to all of your questions regarding the Otherworlds, in exchange for which, and once you're satisfied that I have met your conditions, you will give me in perpetuity your copy of *The Necropompeion*. So mote it be!"

"So mote it be!" I said, sealing the bargain.

"Come to my home at noon tomorrow, and we'll share lunch together like two old gentlemen friends, and have our discussion afterwards." He then gave me the coordinates.

"We'll be there," I said.

Such is the way of life, balancing at times on the merest point of a rock, and then tipping one way or the other, almost in spite of ourselves. We rarely know the outcome of these decisions until much later. The only thing certain about the process is that we can never go home again.

CHAPTER FORTY-EIGHT
"IT'S DEFINITELY GETTING COLDER"

Doctor Scarabbaios was a native of Germania, that much was generally known, although precisely where he was born and when, or where he lived now, was the subject of much speculation in the magical community. His home was generally believed to be located somewhere in the Alps of Central Nova Europa. He hadn't told me the location of his residence in our brief conversation the previous day. All I had was the coordinates of the transit-mirror in his home or laboratory.

So when we exited the metal alcove on the other side, I had no idea what to expect—and being plunged into complete and utter darkness was certainly not what I'd imagined. Our presence caused a container of glowbugs on the ceiling to begin rustling, and as they started buzzing, they generated a pale green light that slowly allowed us to view our surroundings.

We were buried within a room cut out of the encircling rock, perhaps thirty feet to a side. The metallic indentation behind us had gone utterly dead, and I realized after a brief probe that it had been polarized to allow transit only in one direction. We could never return that way again.

On the opposite wall I saw a set of three alcoves, each containing another shiny metal surface. As we walked the short distance towards them, all three illuminated themselves.

"What do we have here?" I said to my little friend, who was riding again on my right shoulder.

"A test, Master," it said. "I suspect that two of these are trapped in some way, or lead to destinations that we would not find palatable."

"So the good Doctor likes to play games, eh? *Can you hear me, Scarabbaios*?" I yelled. My voice echoed back and forth through the room.

"He may just be exceedingly cautious," Scooter said.

"Well, let's try probing the three mirrors," I said.

I stepped forward, linked with the wherret, and gently extended my consciousness, briefly touching each of the devices in turn. However, I could feel nothing within.

"That's strange," I said. "I should at least be able to detect the power source of each, even get a whiff of the æthernet. There's not so much as a hint of static."

"That's not possible," Scooter said.

The wherret reached out a paw (it was really more like a small hand with opposable, retractable claws) to touch one of the mirrors, before I could stop it, and then yelped as it got stung.

"Well, we're not going to do it that way," I said.

We tried stepping back again, and the lights dimmed and then went out, except for the overhead "bugs."

"What's triggering the reaction?" I asked. "These don't work like anything I've ever encountered."

"Something is sensing our presence here," the creature said.

It jumped from my arm to the floor, and began sniffing around the edges of the wall where it met the cold, bare surface, while I started looking for additional devices that might be spying on us. We found nothing.

I shivered. The place hadn't seemed cold when we'd transited there earlier, but now I could see my breath.

"Is it just me…?" I asked.

"No, Master, it's definitely getting colder. I don't know how or why, but the temperature is dropping."

I held out my hand, and the creature jumped on it and ran up my shoulder. There it linked with me and gave me some of its warmth. Even so, the emerald cape I had draped over my back seemed to provide less and less cover as the minutes passed.

"If we don't find a way out, and soon, we're going to freeze to death in here."

"I think that's the general idea, Sir."

The illumination from the glowbugs was now beginning to dim.

"What do we do, Master?"

"This is a one-way transit site," I said. "We're not meant to leave the same way. That means that there must be a real door here somewhere. All we h-have to do is f-f-find it." I couldn't keep my teeth from chattering.

I went back to the place where we'd entered the stone cell, and crammed my bare hand, which was almost numb, into the cracks in the facing that held the great metal mirror in place. Suddenly I encountered a protrusion that shouldn't have been there. I pulled down on it, there was a faint click, and the entire structure swung slightly inward. I leveraged it towards me and opened the door.

We were standing in front of a bare stone platform on the side or top of a mountain (I couldn't tell which from my vantage point). A series of steps cut right into the rock ran off to the left somewhere. I stepped outside with the ferret firmly in place, and heard the door behind me swing back and latch shut.

The wind at this height was bone-chilling in its caress, so I followed the open stairway over a small stone ridge and down into a shallow valley covered with patches of half-melted snow. The great manse, almost a fortress, was partially set into a granite backdrop about two thousand feet along the pathway. Icicles dangled from the eaves. The long, narrow windows that pocked the walls reminded me of Niobë's prison cell, but they weren't there for defense, I suspected, but to reduce the loss of warmth from inside.

"Who would have thought…?" I muttered beneath my breath, as I trudged over the rock path, trying to keep from slipping on the ice.

The one massive door creaked open just before we arrived,

and I didn't even look ahead before plunging right through it. The air inside must have been fifty degrees warmer—it felt like a steam bath by comparison with the chill that we'd just experienced.

The old man was sitting in a worn chair in front of a huge open fireplace flanked by andirons fashioned like gargoyles. He motioned for us to join him in the open seat on the other side.

"Thank you, Sir, for seeing us…," I began, but he hissed us into silence.

"Some luncheon, first, if you please, gentlebeings," he said. His voice was more gravelly in person, deep and resonant and full of angst. He clapped his hands.

Servants brought several small tables that they set by each chair, and then placed thereupon two small bowls filled with steaming water, together with towels with which to wash our hands and face. The kiss of the warmth was utterly delicious. I gave one of the…attendants my cape and pack, and settled back into the upholstered seat, feeling relaxed for the first time since we'd embarked.

Scooter was given a kind of trellis-stand on which to perch, perfectly suited to a being of its size and shape, and a small cage hooked beneath that included live crickets, frogs, and mice—a typical wherret-style banquet!

The first course was turtle soup served *en carapace*, seasoned with onions, garlic, pepper, salt, and several other herbs and spices that I couldn't immediately place. Accompanying the appetizer were chunks of freshly-baked rye bread, with mulled ale as a chaser. Utterly delicious! I could have made a meal just of that.

The *entrée* consisted of small roasted fowl braised with a dark, sweet sauce, surrounded by some kind of purple tubers chopped into pieces and fried in grease, several short, cylindrical green things that had shiny skins, and a curious rod covered with small white, red, and brown nodes. I didn't recognize either the species of the birds or the names of the accompaniments.

"What are these?" I asked, as I picked the delicate bones loose from the tender game.

"A fowl common in New Greece," he said. "The vegetables are imported from there as well. The natives call the purple plants 'poh-tah-toh.' The other is...well, I don't remember its name. You have to gnaw on it like this to get the meat off."

He picked up the large cylinder and careful snipped some of the small protuberances from the underlying structure with his yellow teeth. I tried this myself, and was surprised at how sweet the kernels seemed.

"Very good," I said, in between bites. "And the greens?"

"They're also from the new world. I would be care...."—but he spoke too late. I'd already bitten one of the shiny vegetables in half.

I was savoring the pungent taste when my mouth suddenly began to burn. I drank the rest of my ale—it didn't help! "More!" I yelled, and a servant rushed over with a pitcher. I grabbed it out of its hands, and began chugging the brew straight down. It felt like my tongue was on fire.

"Help!" I gasped again. The thought occurred to me that I'd just been poisoned by a master mage.

Scarabbaios spoke a word of power, and my pain rapidly diminished. When I was breathing normally again, I asked: "What *was* that?"

"Some kind of very potent spice," he said. "You have to nip them very gingerly before eating, because you can't tell by looking at them which are hot—and which are not. I did try to warn you."

I recalled now that he had said something just as I was getting ready to eat the thing. Scooter just thought this was funny, but then it regarded all earthly gastronomical customs as inherently hilarious.

"How can you know that *anything* is fresh?" the wherret once asked me. "Everything you eat is dead. That's not good for the digestion. We wherrets are much more civilized—we *know* our meals are fresh!"

I'd seen what that beast would eat on occasion, and it wasn't pretty, let me tell you. And the mess afterwards...!

The final course of our bizarre lunch was a kind of whipped ice mixed with small red fruits, and covered with ground-up bits of some brown gunk. I'd never seen anything quite like it. The sweet nectar of the mix almost overwhelmed me, and the topping...my God, I could have died right then and been happy through all eternity.

"What...*is*...that?" I said, pointing to the rough dark chunks littering the icy stuff.

"It comes from Aphrikania," he said. "Or maybe it's the new world again. I don't honestly recall. But they call it, uh, let me see, 'choh-koh-lah-teh'."

"It's divine," I said, holding out my empty bowl to one of the Doctor's minions. "More, please!"

When we'd finally finished the last scrap of food, and I was stuffed to the gills with delicious eats and drinks, I looked over at the old man and saw that he was sound asleep, his head slumped back in his chair, his chest slowly rising and falling amidst soft snores. Although I was somewhat anxious to proceed, I decided that it would be indecorous indeed to disturb my elderly host's rest, and instead relaxed in my own place, enjoying the warmth and crackle of the fire. Our dishes were cleared away by unseen helping hands.

Scooter dismounted its perch, and hopped to the arm of my chair and into my lap, where it curled up, hiding its face in its chest. Soon it was snorting its little grunts as well, twitching and moaning in what passed for wherret dreams.

What the hell? I thought to myself. *When in Rome....*

CHAPTER FORTY-NINE
"THE COMMODE, THE LOO,
THE JOHN, THE CRAPPER"

When I awoke, the old mage and my companion were both gone, and it was obvious from the reduced light that several hours had passed. I got up and stretched, and asked one of the, uh, "servants" where the facilities were housed.

"Fah-cul-ties, Sir?"

I could barely understand the thing through its heavy, almost guttural accent. These were creatures of a kind that I'd never encountered before. About four feet in height, they had furry arms and legs and hunched backs, and shuffled slowly around as if walking upright was difficult, even painful, to them.

"Yes," I said. "You know: the commode, the loo, the john, the crapper."

"Sorry, Sir, but I do *not*, uh, know such words," came the reply.

Just then I heard Doctor Scarabbaios talking to Scooter, and I quickly strode towards them and explained my predicament to the old gentleman. He pointed to a doorway near the far corner.

Afterwards we settled in front of the fire again.

"You had some questions for me," the old magician finally said.

"It's said that you traveled to the distant Otherworlds," I said.

"Yes, that's true."

"Please tell me of your voyage there and back again."

"In the Year of Our Lord Fourteen Hundred and Fifty-Two,

I was serving as Second Mage at the court of the great Julian Emperor, Kônstantinos XI. That was the year that the Turks, who had rebelled against the Autokratôr a decade earlier, launched a series of military and magical attacks against Julianople. These culminated in May of the following year, when the great wall of the city was breached by sorcery, and we thought all was lost.

"But with the help of my friend and mentor, the Magus Mago-rum Melanchthon Malitiosus (who was killed by the making), I called a terrible creature out of the æther, a beast that defeated the Sultan-Magus Môâmeth II and ultimately sent him reeling back to eastern Asia Minor, where he lived out the rest of his short life in disgrace, the penultimate ruler of his dynasty.

"However, the bargain that I'd made with this wretched being in return for its aid, a contract that was unbreakable and unbeat-able and became almost unbearable to me in the end, required that I discover some way to return it to its homeworld in the æther—for it was an utterly lost soul, unable to find its own way back again. It had ventured forth into the void many decades earlier, and despite the fact that it had significant magical powers and knowledge, had become entangled in the web of transit-points that span the ætherweb.

"I thought I'd be able to accomplish my task in due course with a reasonable amount of application on my part—as I'd done throughout my life to that point. I took a leave from my position at court, with the permission of the Autokratôr (the only one who knew of my nefarious arrangement), and began to gather whatever facts I could find about traveling through the æther.

"I located and read all the known literature on the subject. I knew that men had traveled to worlds in the First or Second Circles and returned, sometimes after great lapses of time. But the accounts that I found were, well, fuzzy at best. I could never determine exactly how they came back—and it was clear to me that even they, in some cases, were uncertain of what precisely had happened to them.

"Prince Théodoric of Neustria, for example, had gone missing through a transit-mirror just a few years before. I traveled to the

Holy Roman Empire, and talked to those who'd known him—but no one there understood anything about what had happened—or where he'd gone. I examined the great mirror itself, but it told me nothing about his destination. I finally purchased it from the government and had it installed here, since such things were officially forbidden in the areas under the hegemony of the Holy Roman Cæsars. It's in the other room, along with some others that I'll show you later.

"Rampstistóblostuk (for so the creature named itself, although I called it Blosk) was becoming increasingly impatient with my efforts, and threatened to destroy the great city, unless I accelerated my studies. So finally I was forced into making certain experiments.

"These I conducted here, both to protect innocent civilians, and to keep the creature close at hand. For several years I'd scattered my agents, bankrolled by the Emperor, throughout the civilized and barbarian realms, seeking unusual transit-mirrors, and purchasing or borrowing or stealing them when-ever possible. All were brought to this place, and established in my laboratory."

The old man burped loudly, and motioned to one of his minions to bring us both some mulled ale to take the bite out of the chill air. It was starting to get dark inside, so he snapped his fingers and lit the light-tubes mounted on the walls.

"I began these experiments, as I said, transiting first to points on the opposite side of the world, and then trying different casts and mixtures of magical aurum to fashion great mirrors of my own. I also took Blosk with me on these ventures, to keep it under observation and out of mischief.

"I can still recall the first day that I successfully jumped to a world outside our own. The place was very similar to Nova Europa, with only minor variations from our history and expe-rience. In fact, I didn't remain there long enough to determine where the node had switched tracks.

"The problem, I soon discovered, was not in *getting* to these Otherworlds—that was merely a function of focus and power.

You see, every world has its own unique signature in the æther, its vibration level, if you will. Once you discover it, you can transit there, so long as you can find a sympathetic surface on which to generate a reciprocal energy signature, and create enough power to move an individual through that distance of space and time.

"I had mirrors that could easily reach both First and Second Circle worlds. But getting back to *our* world was often not that easy.

"For example, one of the places that I visited in the year 1456 was dominated by what we call the Holy Roman Cæsars—but there they were known as Popes. The Emperor whom I'd served so faithfully here had been killed in 1453 when the Turks had overwhelmed 'Constantinople,' which is what they called Julianople. Magic there was officially forbidden, although sometimes practiced in back alleys, but its development was primitive at best. Transit-mirrors were completely unknown in that place. And Blosk, well, it would have been regarded as a demon if it'd been seen by anyone.

"I couldn't return home without constructing a device myself. Fortunately, I always carried with me a money belt laced with gold bullion, a seemingly universal currency, and my magical powers were still intact. Even so, I couldn't get back until the following year.

"That trip made me realize the hazards of dimensional travel, and why it was so hard to move from circle to circle. I'd found transit-mirrors that appeared to have the ability to send me to the outer limits of the five great circles of the Otherworlds—but the power required to do so would have drained ten of our worlds of everything they had. The further that one tries to transit, the more energy is needed to breech the æther.

"How, then, had something like Blosk come to Nova Europa? It clearly derived from a Fifth Circle world.

"Well, even the creature didn't know for sure. It'd wandered and wandered from place to place, not paying that much attention, until one of its trips sent it much further than before —and it couldn't get back, no matter what it tried.

"I decided ultimately that sometimes a random or deliberate surge of energy in the æthernet caused someone or something to be shifted into a far-distant place against or outside his or its will or desire. I suspect that Scooter here is the result of one of those accidents. They're more common than most mages think. The individuals involved either die very quickly at the other end—and are thereby forgotten—or find some way to move on. But they rarely come back to their starting points from such distances.

"The other problem, of course, was finding Blosk's home-world. The creature knew its name, but had no notion of where specifically it was located.

"While searching the literature for any clues to its origin, I came across a reference to the 'Overworld.' Maximus Pomptinus had suggested in his work, *Vexatio Peregrinationis*, that there had to be a central place from which all other variants emanated, a prime world, if you wish, from which the Otherworlds had derived. He even postulated an infinite number of such primes. However, no one had proved that such a world existed, despite numerous experiments. Further, Pomptinus had said that logic would suggest that all routes through the æthernet would merge and link on the Overworld, making it a natural crossroads to all other points in our universe. Finally, he postulated that the creatures who inhabited such a world, being the oldest and most developed in the æther, would naturally have exploited their central advantage over all other races by making the Overworld the dominant player in the development of *every* world.

"If such a place actually existed, and I could somehow reach it, I could discover the location of Blosk's homeworld and even-tually travel there, fulfilling my bargain. It was worth a try.

"Thereafter I bent all my efforts towards finding a route to the Overworld.

He yawned very widely. "But, gentlebeings, I find myself weary now, and must take my rest. I'll tell you the remainder of the tale tomorrow. I've provided a room for you and your familiar. You'll find food and drink there, and have only to clap your hands twice to have one of my myrmidons report to you, if you need anything else."

I thanked him for his concern, and followed the little creatures into the bowels of the manse. The guest facility was really quite well apportioned, with a very comfortable bed, chairs, table, writing well, and garde-robe. They'd even provided a cushion for Scooter. The old man's slaves brought us a platter of steaming meat and vegetables, and plenty of red wine for me, plus a container of live beetles and small rodents for the wherret.

"What did you think of his tale?" I asked my companion after we'd dined again.

"He was being truthful, Master, so far as he went, but I sensed a certain reticence in telling us the entire story. There were things he didn't want us to know, for whatever reason. It may be that he simply was ashamed of his own actions at times."

"What about this Blosk creature?"

"According to your histories, Sir, the defeat of the Turks was a great mystery of the time, called a 'miracle' by some. By all accounts, the Julian Empire had been soundly defeated on both the military and magical fronts, and was doomed to failure. Its sudden resurgence was attributed to an act of your God. However, I recall nothing specific about the appearance of Blosk."

"Hmm," I said.

I remembered a rumor that I'd heard at University of a great mage calling forth a savior from the void that had vanquished the Turks and driven them back into the Sea of Marmara, killing every one.

"But if he transited to the Fifth Circle, how did he return?"

"How indeed?" Scooter posed. "How indeed?"

CHAPTER FIFTY
"THEY'RE COVERED WITH METAL OBJECTS"

The next day dawned clear and cold, and I took advantage of the fine weather to stroll through the mage's "garden," a level pathway winding in and amongst molded rocks and sculptures in front of his manse. Some of the pieces resembled Doctor Scarabbaios's servants. At the furthest edge of the development, a fence consisting of piled-up flat stones anchored together by Bind-All overlooked a great abyss falling away in slope after slope, punctuated by what must have been cliffs (I couldn't see them from this side). Way down below I spied a blanket of thick evergreens covering the lower flank of this huge mountain—and far in the distance a hint of smoke coming off the plain or plateau that sheltered in the great peak's lee.

"What do you think?" I asked the wherret, who was perched, as usual, on my right shoulder.

"There's a town or settlement somewhere in that direction, Master," it said. "I wonder if they have any contact with this place."

"I wonder myself," I said. "All food and goods would have to be transported here magically—unless there's a way through the mountain that I haven't observed."

"Even to maintain one old man and his minions would require a great deal of effort, Sir."

"Then there must be other transit-portals. The one we used ourselves just isn't viable for such purposes."

We ambled slowly back towards the main door—it was the only entrance that I'd seen, since the main structure was partially built into the face of the bare rock—thoroughly glad that we didn't live on top of this Godforsaken peak.

Back inside, we settled down once again to a hearty breakfast in front of the large fireplace.

"I spend much of my time here now," the ancient mage said (he was waiting for us when we arrived). "I've seen too much of the world as it is, and have no desire to travel again."

"How do you supply yourself?" I asked.

"I have regular shipments sent through a dead-end transit-mirror several times a week. I remit coin back the other direction. It works. But let's enjoy the food, please."

This time we were served slices of baked ham covered with some kind of sweet sauce, German rolls of dark bread, a bowl of curious white fruit (from the Land of the Yellow Men, he said), raisins, quail eggs, sausages, and, and—well, I think the myrmidons would have continued bringing us victuals until we died of overeating, if I hadn't demurred.

"Quite excellent, Sir," I muttered, and Scooter snorted from its perch. I looked over—the wherret's muzzle was covered with fresh blood. This didn't bother me as much as it once might have; the little creature was actually very fastidious about its cleanliness.

When the plates were cleared away, I said: "You were telling us yesterday about the Overworld, Sir."

"Ah, yes. Well, I had no idea of how to reach such a place, if it existed, but I thought about the problem at length, and finally decided that there was a commonality evident in all of the Otherworld signatures that I'd seen, an underlying base set, if you will. It occurred to me then that this one element that was repeated in all of the other æthernet energies had to be the frequency of the Overworld.

"So I tried it, taking Blosk with me. We found ourselves in a place that was more bizarre by far than any other world I'd ever experienced. It seemed to consist of one large city, so far as I could tell—at least, I never saw any parks or green spaces. Perhaps they existed somewhere else.

"We were immediately apprehended by the gendarmerie—they have detection devices everywhere—and taken to a jail, where we were processed like common criminals. They found someone who spoke our language, and we were told that we'd violated all kinds of immigration laws by coming there.

"After being detained for at least a week, we were led before a tribunal. These creatures look very similar to us physically, but are perhaps a foot shorter on the average, and they're covered with metal objects, some of them obviously implanted in their skin. Occasionally one of them would light up like a witch being burned—but without the smoke and flame.

"We were asked why we'd transited there, and we told them. They talked among themselves for a moment, and then their leader said, 'Perhaps we can come to an arrangement.'

"'What kind of arrangement?' I asked.

"'You want something, and we want something. We'll do something for you, if you'll do something for us. We can find Blosk's homeworld and send you both there, but you must retrieve something for us in return.'

"'You have that power?' I asked, amazed that *any* civilization could master such energies.

"'We do,' the man said. 'Do you agree to our terms?'

"We both nodded.

"'You must say so out loud.'

"We did.

"'Very well,' he said. 'This is what we want you to do.'

"I won't go into the details of the task that was put upon us, which took us the better part of three years to accomplish. Suffice it to say, we met the terms of our agreement, and when we returned to the Overworld (they never told us its real name), they put Blosk in a trance and extracted enough information from the creature to identify where its world was located in the Fifth Circle.

"We were taken immediately thereafter to a building that

served as a giant transit station, with people and other things coming and going at a constant rate. How they kept track of it all, I have no idea.

"An alcove off to one side contained a strangely shaped mirror, hexagonal in nature, colored almost a dark blue-green, unlike any I've seen before or since. We were forced to disrobe, and they hung a medallion around each of our necks. I could feel the cold metal burning into the skin just above my breast-bone. An operator sat before a console to one side, manipulating a series of colored lights on a panel.

"Slowly, ever so slowly, the transit-portal begun to pulse, building up an energy charge that caused it gradually to emit more and more light.

"'Get ready,' we were told.

"'How do I get back again?' I asked.

"'You don't!' came the reply, 'Not through here, at least. This transit will complete our contract.'

"By now the pulsing was so constant that it had become one blazing star of power.

"'Jump!' came the shouted command, and we were literally pushed forward into the face of the hexagonal mirror.

"I've never felt anything like that transit. For the very first time, the exchange did not occur instantaneously, but seemed to stretch almost an eternity. We finally emerged on a way-station manned by the Overseers, and had to rest there for some days before making the subsequent jump to another station in the chain—and so on through a series of a half-dozen transit leaps. Then we materialized on the other side of a wall mirror in Blosk's world, shattering the glass behind us.

"But the great tragedy of this story is that three centuries had elapsed there during the time that the creature had been absent. We discovered, alas and alack, that time can work differently, moving faster or slower on some of the Fifth Circle worlds. All of its family and the friends that it'd known had died many years earlier. Although it'd found its way back to the beginning, so to speak, it was as lonely as ever.

"As for me, I had no way to return to *my* homeworld, for the Overseers had made it clear to me that a reverse trip was simply not possible. I had to find another way back."

Then the old man levered himself up from his chair, having to visit the facilities, and when he returned, he said that he had other things to do, and would continue the third and final part of his tale on the morrow. He suggested that we explore his library, and pointed to a closed door, one of many, on the opposite side of the greatroom. (I tried one of the other exits, and found it locked.)

We took his advice, and spent a pleasant couple of hours roaming the series of connected rooms that housed his books, including both bound volumes and rolled manuscripts. I found a copy of Cavaliere's *Quien Hace por Común, Hace por Ningún*, Shingletown's *Furor Scribendi*, Chien's *Force Majeure*, Wickheizer's *Mährchen*, Stavroula's *Krítis aei Pseústai*, and many others besides.

Even Scooter found something of interest. "Look, Master!" it said, pointing to a small textbook. It was engraved with wood-block cuts depicting unusual animals. One of them was obviously a member of the wherret race, and was labeled "Grit." The author was Melanchthon Malitiosus, the Master Mage of Julianople, the man who'd perished in the war against the Turks in 1453. This particular edition had been published in Worms just thirty years earlier.

"How...?" the little creature asked.

"I honestly don't know," I said. "But I think we ought to try finding out before we embark on our own journey through the æther."

CHAPTER FIFTY-ONE
"I MADE ONE LAST DEAL WITH THE DEVIL, HA, HA!"

"I want to see the book," Doctor Scarabbaios said.

"What?" I said.

"I've now related much of my tale, and before I give you the last little bit, I want to see what you brought me."

The Necropompeion had been stored in our room these past few days, tucked away safely in a pocket of ætherspace. I activated the æthereal tie between me and the great tome, brought it into real space and time, unwrapped the volume, and handed to the old mage.

"Ahhh," he said, caressing it by moving his hand up and down and back and forth on the cover. Then he opened the volume and flipped through the pages.

"I don't even want to know how you got this," he added.

"It was a legitimate transaction between us and the previous owner," I said, "And it'll be yours once you finish telling us your story. Although I *was* curious, if you don't mind me asking, why you wanted this particular object. It doesn't appear to have any obvious value, other than its rarity."

"Sometimes," he said, "Sometimes things are just what they are. I collect unusual items of magicana. This was one that I could never seem to acquire on my own. I'm glad finally to have found it before I die."

"I'm sure you'll live many more years, Sir," I said. "But you were telling us yesterday about finding your way home from the

Otherworlds."

"Yes," the old man said, putting the book aside. "Well, I'd fulfilled my bargain to Blosk, and I'd done what the Overseers had wanted me to do. Now, I thought, it was time to have a little fun, to explore places that no man had ever had a chance to visit. So I roamed through part of the Fifth Circle, roamed for many years, in fact, until I realized the impossibility of what I was doing.

"If you can imagine in your mind a concentric layer of spheres, each larger and thicker than the one below it, you come to understand, eventually, that the last of these Circles—if it is the last, and I'm still not convinced of that—is enormous, beyond anything that any one individual can encompass. What I personally saw in my voyages through this region was no more than an infinitesimal fraction of what was there. I finally knew the futility of it all. I couldn't live long enough to experience everything, not even a small part of it.

"So then I seriously began thinking about returning home and relating my adventures to my colleagues. But like Blosk, I was hopelessly lost. I had employed the various forms of transit-devices available to me 'out there'—indeed, had fashioned some of my own when necessary—but none, not a one, could take me out of the Fifth Circle. The distances were unimaginably immense. I didn't know how to 'dial down,' so to speak, how to jump into one of the lower rings.

"I finally encountered a being named Weex—at least that's what *I* called him, since I couldn't pronounce his real name—who said that he could help. But—and this was always the kicker, Morpheús—I had to do something for *him* first. His people, who were formed like giant erect birds, wanted to increase their territory into the areas beyond their own worlds, to provide homes for their ever-increasing population. To do this, they needed more powerful transit-devices than what they'd bought from some of their neighbors. They had very few technicians of their own. But they did possess one copy of a very singular book, *Transiting*, a tome that would tell me how to reach the lower Circles.

"So I built them a long-range transit-machine, one that they could use to travel beyond their immediate vicinity, and showed them how to employ and repair it. And in exchange, I got the knowledge that I needed.

"The key was creating a device that could be linked to the energy of a star without destroying the transit-machine itself. It took me decades to perfect such an implement, and I couldn't have built it without the willing labor of all those bird-folk. When I finally bid them *adieu*, I'd spent almost a century of my life out there amongst the Otherworlds. The machine worked, but it only brought me to the Fourth Circle, and there I had to build a mirror (this time) to move me down ever further. And so on.

"When I reached the First Circle, I was able to rely on existing transit-mirrors to move through the worlds until I finally came home to Nova Europa. *In toto*, I'd spent more than 150 years away from here, and by the time I returned, I was exhausted both in spirit and flesh. My colleagues had forgotten me, and they mostly didn't believe what I told them informally. I penned an account, to be sure, but I found myself fudging many of the details. And in the end, I found myself asking: what was it all for? What purpose did my trip accomplish?"

"You did save Julianople, Sir," Scooter said.

"Yes, I did save Julianople, and I suppose that was a good thing, although I didn't recognize the place when I got back. I'd visited too many variations of it, you see. Or maybe you don't. When you've walked through 100 or more analogues of the original, they blur together in your mind, and you lose any perspective on which version is the 'best' or 'most authentic.' They're all authentic in some way."

He picked up the book again, the hard-to-find *Necropompeion*, and held it up in front of him. "You asked why I wanted this volume so badly. Did you feel the energy within?"

"It's linked to the Netherworld," I said.

"Yes. That link connects this thing to the fount of Hades

itself, something that may or may not provide enough energy to power a trans-Circle mirror. You see, I collect more than books or implements. I also have gathered dozens, even hundreds, of transit-mirrors here from around the globe. Some are...well, come see for yourself!"

Then he rose from his chair and beckoned us to follow him through a door on the left side of the room. We entered a surprisingly large, circular chamber lined with metal and glass mirrors of all kinds, great and small. I gazed in wonder upon a collection of transit-devices far beyond anything I'd ever seen or even imagined: old and new, creations from green-gold, white-gold, red-gold, purple-gold, yellow-gold, silver-gold, blue-gold, brown-gold, and alloys of the magical metal that I couldn't even place.

I went from one to the other in quick succession, touching them briefly to get a glimpse of their powers, until I finally had to sit down, I was so overwhelmed by the experience. Then I spotted something I'd never, ever thought to see: the myth-ical black-gold mirror, a small (perhaps three and one-half feet in diameter) and utterly round fashioning of *atraurum*, a composite thought to be impossible, with a shape also believed to be impossible.

"Is that what I think it is?" I asked the master magician, jumping to my feet and running over to it. Scooter was attached to my shoulder, as usual.

"Yes," he said. "*That's* the one that could take you anywhere, if only you had the energy to make it work. But I know of nothing in or out of this world that could do so, except possibly *The Necropompeion*. The Overseers have the power, but I know of no one else who does.

"Then we should try it!" I said.

"Ha!" Scarabbaios said. "You don't know what you're saying, boy. That book's as dangerous as the device itself. Linked together, you don't know what they could or would do. The black mirror is almost uncontrollable. Some say it has a mind of its own."

"But where did you get it, Sir?" Scooter asked.

"Ah, as to that…well, let's just say that I made one last deal with the Devil, ha, ha."

"What do you mean?"

But the Doctor was already touching the *atraurum* and muttering several words under his breath.

"Master, there's something wrong here!" the wherret whispered in my ear.

Then Scarabbaios stepped to one side.

"All will be revealed," he said, "When you reach the other side. I've enjoyed your company, Morpheús. Really."

Suddenly the black-gold mirror activated without warning, and before I could react, generated a psychic whirlpool that began drawing me and Scooter into its bowels. I tried shouting a few spells to break the link, but not knowing how the device worked, I couldn't readily find the right combination. I was beginning to reach for my pouch to grab the image of Mathurin when I and my familiar were abruptly yanked by the suction of the æther right into the depths.

It was like falling down a long shaft without ever hitting bottom. I know I screamed my lungs out as I tumbled, head over heel, the wherret desperately clinging to my shirt. We were transited—I knew not where.

And then we were there!

EPILOGUE
"BE CAREFUL
WHAT YOU WISH FOR"

And now we come to the *pièce de résistance*, so to speak, for in saying "fare thee well" to one world, I had perforce opened myself to the prospect of another. I had built myself a comfortable, well-apportioned situation in Kórynthia, a life that most persons, even among the magical folk, would have envied. And now I'd cast it all away, willy-nilly, to venture "to the stars, through difficulties." Why?

It is the answer to that seemingly simple question that I have pursued eternally within myself, probing and pushing and perambulating in and around the uncomfortable truths that define my soul. Why indeed?

Yes, there was a woman somewhere out there in the void of space and time who required my services—another dreamer of dreams, another hypatomancer. That was the lure, but it wasn't the solution to the problem.

Yes, I'd grown dissatisfied with the sameness of my existence in Nova Europa, to the point where I feared saying something publicly that would reveal my discontent to an individual or group who might use that knowledge against me—or against those whom I served, indeed, against the very state itself. Such a betrayal of all that I'd sworn to uphold would be a self-damnation and -condemnation of the worst kind, of the unforgivable kind. I couldn't let that happen.

But there was more to it than that.

Despite the hard work that I'd expended in gaining a thoroughly excellent education, both in the School of Magick and at University, in spite of my efforts in the years since to improve myself and my prospects in the world at large, I had never felt truly challenged by anything that I'd accomplished. It had all come just a little too easy for me.

And every so often, just for a moment, I felt my lack of... fulfillment. I knew that I had more potential in me than I'd realized to date, but a potential for what or why or how, I had no idea. If I left the comfortable shores of the eastern Mediterranean, if I exuded myself into the beckoning multitude of worlds that filled the great ætherspace that I knew existed, I would be forced to redefine my persona in a new setting. Maybe then I'd find the peace that I sought and still seek, and had somehow had never excavated from the soil where I first took root.

There's just one thing that I remember my mother telling me, on the day that I left home, one piece of advice or warning or whatever. As Brother Amandos started to lead me away, she yelled after me, "I love you, my son!"

"I love you too, Ma," I shouted back, but in my heart I was supremely happy to be on the verge of suddenly expanding my universe, of leaving my birthplace for good.

Somehow she knew this, or guessed where my soul truly ventured, because she added, quite clearly, this admonition: "Be careful, dearest 'Ridión. Be careful what you wish for."

I didn't understand her words back then. I just thought she was old and full of fear and trying to hold me back. All I could see was the beckoning horizon.

But I do understand them now.

AFTERWORD

"CRACKING THE ELEPHANT'S EGG"

According to my notes, I penned the first few pages of this novel on March 24, 2006. I was intrigued with the idea of a long-distance romance, of creating the story of an impossible liaison between two individuals separated by an enormous void that was nearly unbridgeable.

Now, there have been many such tales in the literature, stories of star-crossed love spanning the bounds of time and space, and I'd already read many of the classics, including such works as Richard Matheson's *Bid Time Return*. I knew all the conventions, and I wanted to do something different with them.

So I started with the words, "Help me!"—and went on from there. As I recall, I either wrote the entire first chapter or the first two pages thereof—and then set the story aside until I had more time to develop it.

That time didn't arrive for more than two years.

I wrote the actual book in three stints spread over another two years—two weeks in July, 2008, just over four months beginning January 1, 2009, and from December 18, 2009 through May 7, 2010. By then the text had accumulated almost 600 pages and just under 200,000 words—and, strangely enough, I found myself continuing the tale in a kind of sequel set back in Nova Europa, beginning right *after* Morpheús and crew have returned from the æther; and this went on for several more chapters before I realized (with some horror) what I was doing.

I was just having too much fun with the characters to want to abandon them.

I shut things down immediately, capped off the narrative with an appropriate ending, and sent off part of the first section of the manuscript to my then-agent. She said that she liked the beginning chapters, but the book was too long to market as is.

A month later, I retired permanently from Cal State SB, and moved into full-time editing and writing, something that I'd wanted to do all my life. But *The Fourth Elephant's Egg*, as I was calling it, just sat there gathering literary motes. What to do with it was the problem—but that problem applied generally to all of my creative writing.

Of course, this wasn't my first fantasy of Nova Europa. I'd previously published three other long novels set in roughly the same *milieu* (but at different times and in different places) through a small California house, Ariadne Press. They'd made very little impression, although several had garnered excellent reviews from Tom Easton at *Analog*.

It was my dear wife, Mary, who suggested that all of my long fictions needed to be divided into trilogies to make them more palatable and salable to present-day readers. We started the process with the science-fiction saga, *Invasion!* (it had actually been penned as three separate books, although it had only been issued in omnibus form), and then turned to the unpublished fantasy, *Elephant's Egg*, which just a few individuals had then seen.

This novel, it turned out, also had potential breaking points at roughly the one-third and two-third marks in the narrative, and so was relatively easy to fracture. I divided the manuscript into more-or-less equal sections, re-edited the text and added the appropriate Prologues and Epilogues, as well as some small pieces of additional copy, and then renamed the three parts *The Cracks in the Æther*, *The Pachyderms' Lament*, and *The Fourth Elephant's Egg*. And that's what I offer to you now.

* * * * * *

What had started as a traditional romance quickly evolved into something very different as I actually began developing the novel. The title came from a silly list of potential fictions that I'd jotted down on a piece of notepaper, assigning one each to every letter of the alphabet. "F" was *The Fourth Elephant's Egg.* I have no idea whence it derived. I just liked (and like) playing with possible titles, and this one sounded intriguing to me.

Morpheús the Mage was facing some of the same issues as his creator—major changes in his career and life, major disruptions of society and culture, major questions about what to do and where to go. You can be certain that when one of my protagonists poses such queries, to himself or to others, those same interrogatories have already been asked by the writer.

But I wanted this book to be a "fun" read, and not a chore, so I deliberately eschewed the chapter head quotes that had often decorated my early fictions, and tried to keep the narrative light and airy throughout—without avoiding the sometimes grim work that had to be done. My magician was one of those intelligent, capable individuals that people my novels. But that very intelligence and ambition have kept him separated from those around him, and his personal life is almost nil when the book begins.

Scooter was roughly patterned after the ferrets that my brother Mark had kept as pets in previous years. These creatures are naturally curious and inquisitive little critters; I thought that having such a non-human observer as a foil made a great deal of sense. Morpheús relates better to "it" (wherrets have no sexual orientation) in many ways than he does to his fellow human beings.

I also liked the idea of having each solution to a problem create even more potential issues for the mage. Seemingly, he can't win: he solves one conundrum only to find himself thrust into the midst of another. Yet, he remains willing to fight on, to keep his eyes closely affixed on the distant goal.

Finally, I leavened my tale with a great deal of humor. For me, this is what "makes the medicine go down"—both in real life and in my fiction. Morpheús takes himself and his quest very seriously—sometimes too seriously—and he and we have to be reminded on occasion that this is something that he chose to do with eyes wide open, and that not every thing or every person he encounters is a life-or-death situation. Some are just odd—or funny.

So, I hope you enjoy my little venture into Nova Europa, Pachyderms, and the Otherworlds. Two more books will follow in short order—and then the rest of the volumes, as I get to them. And then, perhaps, I'll return to the unfinished sequel to *Elephant's Egg*.

—Robert Reginald
San Bernardino, California
20 April 2011

ABOUT THE AUTHOR

ROBERT REGINALD was born in Japan, and lived in Turkey as a youth. He starting writing as a child, and penned his first book during his senior year in college. He settled in Southern California in 1969, where he served as an academic librarian for forty years. He currently edits the Borgo Press Imprint of Wildside Press, and has also penned more than 125 books and 13,000 short pieces. His recent works of fiction include twelve Nova Europa historical fantasies (2004-11); six science fiction novels: The War of Two Worlds Trilogy: *Invasion!*, *Operation: Crimson Storm*, and *The Martians Strike Back!* (2007/2011); two Human-Knacker War SF novels: *Knack' Attack* (2010) and *"A Glorious Death"* (2011); and *Academentia: A Future Dystopia* (2011); two Phantom Detective period mysteries: *The Phantom's Phantom* (2007) and *The Nasty Gnomes* (2008); a comic mystery, *The Paperback Show Murders* (2011); a horror novel, *Hell's Belles* (forthcoming); and four story collections: *Katydid & Other Critters: Tales of Fantasy and Mystery* (2001), *The Elder of Days: Tales of the Elders* (2010), *The Judgment of the Gods and Other Verdicts of History* (2011), *Dead Librarians and Other Shades from Academe* (2011). He has also edited the SF anthology, *Yondering* (2011) and the mystery anthology, *Whodunit?* (2011). You can find him at:

www.millefleurs.tv

And watch for the concluding
volumes in *The Hypatomancer's Tale Trilogy*:

THE PACHYDERMS' LAMENT (Book Two)

THE FOURTH ELEPHANT'S EGG (Book Three)